G h o s t s

~~wnstar~~

Winterhold

#saarik Head

Winterhold

The Pale

Lake Yorgrim

River Yorgrim

White River

Windhelm

Dunmeth Pass

MORROWIND

~~rrun~~

White River

Eastmarch

Darkwater River

Throat of the World

Shor's Stone

~~wood~~

Ivarstead

Lake Geir

The Rift

Helgen

Riften

Treva River

Pale Pass

J e r a l l   M o u n t a i n s

Lake Honrich

C Y R O D I I L

THE ELDER SCROLLS V: SKYRIM®
THE SKYRIM® LIBRARY, VOLUME I: THE HISTORIES

ISBN: 9781783293193

Published by Titan Books,
A division of Titan Publishing Group Ltd.,
144 Southwark St., London, SE1 0UP, United Kingdom

Special thanks to Todd Howard, Bruce Nesmith, Kurt Kuhlmann, Emil Pagliarulo, Brian Chapin, Jon Paul Duvall, Shane Liesegang, Alan Nanes, William Shen, Matt Daniels, Nate Ellis, Matthew Carofano, Ray Lederer, Adam Adamowicz, and Natalia Smirnova with Bethesda Game Studios. Special thanks to Steve Perkins, Paris Nourmohammadi, and Mike Wagner with Bethesda Softworks.

www.elderscrolls.com
www.bethsoft.com

A CIP catalogue record for this title is available from the British Library.
First edition: May 2015

20 19 18 17 16 15 14 13 12 11

Printed in China.

THE SKYRIM LIBRARY

VOLUME 1
THE HISTORIES

TITAN BOOKS

Contents

History

Skyrim

Morrowind

Dragons

A Brief History Of The Empire

by Stronach K'Thojj III

Imperial Historian

Part One

efore the rule of Tiber Septim, all Tamriel was in chaos. The poet Tracizis called that period of continuous unrest "days and nights of blood and venom." The kings were a petty lot of grasping tyrants, who fought Tiber's attempts to bring order to the land. But they were as disorganized as they were dissolute, and the strong hand of Septim brought peace forcibly to Tamriel. The year was 2E 896. The following year, the Emperor declared the beginning of a new Era–thus began the Third Era, Year Aught.

For thirty–eight years, the Emperor Tiber reigned supreme. It was a lawful, pious, and glorious age, when justice was known to one and all, from serf to sovereign. On Tiber's death, it rained for an entire fortnight as if the land of Tamriel itself was weeping.

The Emperor's grandson, Pelagius, came to the throne. Though his reign was short, he was as strong and resolute as his father had been, and Tamriel could have enjoyed a continuation of the Golden Age. Alas, an unknown enemy of the Septim Family hired that accursed organization of cutthroats, the Dark Brotherhood, to kill the Emperor Pelagius I as he knelt at prayer at the Temple of the One in the Imperial City. Pelagius I's reign lasted less than three years.

Pelagius had no living children, so the Crown Imperial passed to his first cousin, the daughter of Tiber's brother Agnorith. Kintyra, former Queen of Silvenar, assumed the throne as Kintyra I. Her reign was blessed with prosperity and good harvests, and she herself was an avid patroness of art, music, and dance.

Kintyra's son was crowned after her death, the first Emperor of Tamriel to use the imperial name Uriel. Uriel I was the great lawmaker of the Septim Dynasty, and a promoter of independent organizations and guilds. Under his kind but firm hand, the Fighters Guild and the Mages Guild increased in prominence throughout Tamriel. His son and successor Uriel II reigned for eighteen years, from the death of Uriel I in 3E64 to Pelagius II's accession in 3E82. Tragically, the rule of Uriel II was cursed with blights, plagues, and insurrections. The tenderness he inherited from his father did not serve Tamriel well, and little justice was done.

Pelagius II inherited not only the throne from his father, but the debt from the latter's poor financial and judicial management. Pelagius dismissed all of the Elder Council, and allowed only those willing to pay great sums to resume their seats. He encouraged similar acts among his vassals, the kings of Tamriel, and by the end of his seventeen year reign, Tamriel had returned to prosperity. His critics, however, have suggested that any advisor possessed of wisdom but not of gold had been summarily ousted by

Pelagius. This may have led to some of the troubles his son Antiochus faced when he in turn became Emperor.

Antiochus was certainly one of the more flamboyant members of the usually austere Septim Family. He had numerous mistresses and nearly as many wives, and was renowned for the grandeur of his dress and his high good humor. Unfortunately, his reign was rife with civil war, surpassing even that of his grandfather Uriel II. The War of the Isle in 3E110, twelve years after Antiochus assumed the throne, nearly took the province of Summurset Isle away from Tamriel. The united alliance of the kings of Summurset and Antiochus only managed to defeat King Orghum of the island-kingdom of Pyandonea due to a freak storm. Legend credits the Psijic Order of the Isle of Artaeum with the sorcery behind the tempest.

SKYRIM CALENDAR

There are 12 months in a year.
They are:

1. Morning Star
2. Sun's Dawn
3. First Seed
4. Rain's Hand
5. Second Seed
6. Mid Year
7. Sun's Height
8. Last Seed
9. Heartfire
10. Frostfall
11. Sun's Dusk
12. Evening Star

There are 7 days in a week.
They are as follows:

1. Morndas
2. Tirdas
3. Middas
4. Turdas
5. Fredas
6. Loredas
7. Sundas

The story of Kintyra II, heiress to her father Antiochus' throne, is certainly one of the saddest tales in imperial history. Her first cousin Uriel, son of Queen Potema of Solitude, accused Kintyra of being a bastard, alluding to the infamous decadence of the Imperial City during her father's reign. When this accusation failed to stop her coronation, Uriel bought the support of several disgruntled kings of High Rock, Skyrim, and Morrowind, and with Queen Potema's assistance, he coordinated three attacks on the Septim Empire.

The first attack occurred in the Iliac Bay region, which separates High Rock and Hammerfell. Kintyra's entourage was massacred and the Empress taken captive. For two years, Kintyra II languished in an Imperial prison believed to be somewhere in Glenpoint or Glenmoril before she was slain in her cell under mysterious circumstances. The second attack was on a series of Imperial garrisons along the coastal Morrowind islands. The Empress' consort Kontin Arynx fell defending the forts. The third and final attack was a siege of the Imperial City itself, occurring after the Elder Council had split up the army to attack western High Rock and eastern Morrowind. The weakened government had little defence against Uriel's determined aggression, and capitulated after only a fortnight of resistance. Uriel took the throne that same evening and proclaimed himself Uriel III, Emperor of Tamriel. The year was 3E 121. Thus began the War of the Red Diamond,

Part Two

Volume I of this series described in brief the lives of the first eight Emperors of the Septim Dynasty, beginning with the glorious Tiber Septim and ending with his great, great, great, great, grandniece Kintyra II. Kintyra's murder in Glenpoint while in captivity is considered by some to be the end of the pure strain of Septim blood in the imperial family. Certainly it marks the end of something significant.

Uriel III not only proclaimed himself Emperor of Tamriel, but also Uriel Septim III, taking the eminent surname as a title. In truth, his surname was Mantiarco from his father's line. In time, Uriel III was deposed and his crimes reviled, but the tradition of taking the name Septim as a title for the Emperor of Tamriel did not die with him.

For six years, the War of the Red Diamond (which takes its name from the Septim Family's famous badge) tore the Empire apart. The combatants were the three surviving children of Pelagius II–Potema, Cephorus, and Magnus–and their various offspring. Potema, of course, supported her son Uriel III, and had the combined support of all of Skyrim and northern Morrowind. With the efforts of Cephorus and Magnus, however, the province of High Rock turned coat. The provinces of Hammerfell, Summurset Isle, Valenwood, Elsweyr, and Black Marsh were divided in their loyalty, but most kings supported Cephorus and Magnus.

In 3E127, Uriel III was captured at the Battle of Ichidag in Hammerfell. En route to his trial in the Imperial City, a mob overtook his prisoner's carriage and burned him alive within it. His captor and uncle continued on to the Imperial City, and by common acclaim was proclaimed Cephorus I, Emperor of Tamriel.

Cephorus' reign was marked by nothing but war. By all accounts, he was a kind and intelligent man, but what Tamriel needed was a great warrior — and he, fortunately, was that. It took an additional ten years of constant warfare for him to defeat his sister Potema. The so-called Wolf Queen of Solitude who died in the siege of her city-state in the year 137. Cephorus survived his sister by only three years. He never had time during the war years to marry, so it was his brother, the fourth child of Pelagius II, who assumed the throne.

The Emperor Magnus was already elderly when he took up the imperial diadem, and the business of punishing the traitorous kings of the War of the Red Diamond drained much of his remaining strength. Legend accuses Magnus' son and heir Pelagius III of patricide, but that seems highly unlikely–for no other reason than that Pelagius was King of Solitude following the death of Potema, and seldom visited the Imperial City.

Pelagius III, sometimes called Pelagius the Mad, was proclaimed Emperor in the 145th year of the Third Era. Almost from the start, his eccentricities of behaviour were noted at court. He embarrassed dignitaries, offended his vassal kings, and on one occasion marked the end of an imperial grand ball by attempting to hang himself. His long-suffering wife was finally awarded the Regency of Tamriel, and Pelagius III was sent to a series of healing institutions and asylums until his death in 3E153 at the age of thirty-four.

The Empress Regent of Tamriel was proclaimed Empress Katariah I upon the death of her husband. Some who do not mark the end of the Septim bloodline with the death of Kintyra II consider the ascendancy of this Dark Elf woman the true mark of its decline. Her defenders, on the other hand, assert that though Katariah was not descended from Tiber, the son she had with Pelagius was, so the imperial chain did continue. Despite racist assertions to the contrary, Katariah's forty-six-year reign was one of the most celebrated in Tamriel's history. Uncomfortable in the Imperial City, Katariah travelled extensively throughout the Empire such as no Emperor ever had since Tiber's day. She repaired much of the damage that previous emperor's broken alliances and bungled diplomacy created. The people of Tamriel came to love their Empress far more than the nobility did. Katariah's death in a minor skirmish in Black Marsh is a favorite subject of conspiracy minded historians. The Sage Montalius' discovery, for instance, of a disenfranchised branch of the Septim Family and their involvement with the skirmish was a revelation indeed.

When Cassynder assumed the throne upon the death of his mother, he was already middle-aged. Only half Elven, he aged like a Breton. In fact, he had left the rule of Wayrest to his half-brother Uriel due to poor health. Nevertheless, as the only true blood relation of Pelagius and thus Tiber, he was pressed into accepting the throne. To no one's surprise, the Emperor Cassynder's reign did not last long. In two years he joined his predecessors in eternal slumber.

Uriel Lariat, Cassynder's half-brother, and the child of Katariah I and her Imperial consort Gallivere Lariat (after the death of Pelagius III), left the kingdom of Wayrest to reign as Uriel IV. Legally, Uriel IV was a Septim: Cassynder had adopted him into the royal family when he had become King of Wayrest. Nevertheless, to the Council and the people of Tamriel, he was a bastard child of Katariah. Uriel did not possess the dynamism of his mother, and his long forty-three-year reign was a hotbed of sedition.

Part Three

The first volume of this series told in brief the story of the succession of the first eight Emperors of the Septim Dynasty, from Tiber I to Kintyra II. The second volume described the War of the Red Diamond and the six Emperors that followed its aftermath, from Uriel III to Cassynder I. At the end of that volume, it was described how the Emperor Cassynder's half-brother Uriel IV assumed the throne of the Empire of Tamriel.

It will be recalled that Uriel IV was not a Septim by birth. His mother, though she reigned as Empress for many years, was a Dark Elf married to a true Septim Emperor, Pelagius III. Uriel's father was actually Katariah I's consort after Pelagius' death, a Breton nobleman named Gallivere Lariat. Before taking the throne of Empire, Cassynder I had ruled the kingdom of Wayrest, but poor health had forced him to retire. Cassynder had no children, so he legally adopted his half-brother

Uriel and abdicated the kingdom. Seven years later, Cassynder inherited the Empire at the death of his mother. Three years after that, Uriel once again found himself the recipient of Cassynder's inheritance.

Uriel IV's reign was a long and difficult one. Despite being a legally adopted member of the Septim Family, and despite the Lariat Family's high position — indeed, they were distant cousins of the Septims — few of the Elder Council could be persuaded to accept him fully as a blood descendant of Tiber. The Council had assumed much responsibility during Katariah I's long reign and Cassynder I's short one, and a strong-willed "alien" monarch like Uriel IV found it impossible to command their unswerving fealty. Time and again the Council and Emperor were at odds, and time and again the Council won the battles. Since the days of Pelagius II, the Elder Council had consisted of the wealthiest men and women in the Empire, and the power they wielded was conclusive.

The Council's last victory over Uriel IV was posthumous. Andorak, Uriel IV's son, was disinherited by vote of Council, and a cousin more closely related to the original Septim line was proclaimed Cephorus II in 3E247. For the first nine years of Cephorus II's reign, those loyal to Andorak battled the Imperial forces. In an act that the Sage Eraintine called "Tiber Septim's heart beating no more," the Council granted Andorak the High Rock kingdom of Shornhelm to end the war, and Andorak's descendants still rule there.

By and large, Cephorus II had foes that demanded more of his attention than Andorak. "From out of a cimmerian nightmare," in the words of Eraintine, a man who called himself the Camoran Usurper led an army of Daedra and undead warriors on a rampage through Valenwood, conquering kingdom after kingdom. Few could resist his onslaughts, and as month turned to bloody month in the year 3E249, even fewer tried. Cephorus II sent more and more mercenaries into Hammerfell to stop the Usurper's northward march, but they were bribed or slaughtered and raised as undead.

The story of the Camoran Usurper deserves a book of its own. (It is recommended that the reader find Palaux Illthre's The Fall of the Usurper for more detail.) In short, however, the destruction of the forces of the Usurper had little do with the efforts of the Emperor. The result was a great regional victory and an increase in hostility toward the seemingly inefficacious Empire.

Uriel V, Cephorus II's son and successor, swivelled opinion back toward the latent power of the Empire. Turning the attention of Tamriel away from internal strife, Uriel V embarked on a series of invasions beginning almost from the moment he took the throne in 3E268. Uriel V conquered Roscrea in 271, Cathnoquey in 276, Yneslea in 279, and Esroniet in 284. In 3E288, he embarked on his most ambitious enterprise, the invasion of the continent kingdom of Akavir. This ultimately proved a failure, for two years later Uriel V was killed in Akavir on the battlefield of Ionith. Nevertheless, Uriel V holds a reputation second only to Tiber as one of the two great Warrior Emperors of Tamriel.

The Red Ring Road

Imperial City

Lake Rumare

White Rose R.

The Nibenay Valley

The Upper Niben

Part Four

The first book of this series described, in brief, the first eight Emperors of the Septim Dynasty beginning with Tiber I. The second volume described the War of the Red Diamond and the six Emperors who followed. The third volume described the troubles of the next three Emperors–the frustrated Uriel IV, the ineffectual Cephorus II, and the heroic Uriel V.

On Uriel V's death across the sea in distant, hostile Akavir, Uriel VI was but five years old. In fact, Uriel VI was born only shortly before his father left for Akavir. Uriel V's only other progeny, by a morganatic alliance, were the twins Morihatha and Eloisa, who had been born a month after Uriel V left. Uriel VI was crowned in the 290th year of the Third Era. The Imperial Consort Thonica, as the boy's mother, was given a restricted Regency until Uriel VI reached his majority. The Elder Council retained the real power, as they had ever since the days of Katariah I.

The Council so enjoyed its unlimited and unrestricted freedom to promulgate laws (and generate profits) that Uriel VI was not given full license to rule until 307, when he was already 22 years old. He had been slowly assuming positions of responsibility for years, but both the Council and his mother, who enjoyed even her limited Regency, were loath to hand over the reins. By the time he came to the throne, the mechanisms of government gave him little power except for that of the imperial veto.

This power, however, he regularly and vigorously exercised. By 313, Uriel VI could boast with conviction that he truly did rule Tamriel. He utilized defunct spy networks and guard units to bully and coerce the difficult members of the Elder Council. His half-sister Morihatha was (not surprisingly) his staunchest ally, especially after her marriage to Baron Ulfe Gersen of Winterhold brought her considerable wealth and influence. As the Sage Ugaridge said, "Uriel V conquered Esroniet, but Uriel VI conquered the Elder Council."

When Uriel VI fell off a horse and could not be resuscitated by the finest Imperial healers, his beloved sister Morihatha took up the imperial tiara. At 25 years of age, she had been described by (admittedly self-serving) diplomats as the most beautiful creature in all of Tamriel. She was certainly well-learned, vivacious, athletic, and a well-practised politician. She brought the Archmagister of Skyrim to the Imperial City and created the second Imperial Battlemage since the days of Tiber Septim.

Morihatha finished the job her brother had begun, and made the Imperial Province a true government under the Empress (and later, the Emperor). Outside the Imperial Province, however, the Empire had been slowly disintegrating. Open revolutions and civil wars had raged unchallenged since the days of her grandfather Cephorus II. Carefully coordinating her counterattacks, Morihatha slowly claimed back her rebellious vassals, always avoiding overextending herself.

Though Morihatha's military campaigns were remarkably successful, her deliberate pace often frustrated the Council. One Councilman, an Argonian who took the Colovian name of Thoricles Romus, furious at her refusal to send troops to his troubled Black Marsh, is commonly believed to have hired the assassins who claimed her life in 3E 339. Romus was summarily tried and executed, though he protested his innocence to the last.

Morihatha had no surviving children, and Eloisa had died of a fever four years before. Eloisa's 25-year-old son Pelagius was thus crowned Pelagius IV. Pelagius IV continued his aunt's work, slowly bringing back under his wing the radical and refractory kingdoms, duchies, and baronies of the Empire. He exercised Morihatha's poise and circumspect pace in his endeavours–but alas, he did not attain her success. The kingdoms had been free of constraint for so long that even a benign Imperial presence was considered odious. Nevertheless, when Pelagius died after a notably stable and prosperous twenty-nine-year reign, Tamriel was closer to unity than it had been since the days of Uriel I.

Our current Emperor, His Awesome and Terrible Majesty, Uriel Septim VII, son of Pelagius IV, has the diligence of his great-aunt Morihatha, the political skill of his great-uncle Uriel VI, and the military prowess of his great grand-uncle Uriel V. For twenty-one years he reigned and brought justice and order to Tamriel. In the year 3E389, however, his Imperial Battlemage, Jagar Tharn, betrayed him.

Uriel VII was imprisoned in a dimension of Tharn's creation, and Tharn used his sorcery of illusion to assume the Emperor's aspect. For the next ten years, Tharn abused imperial privilege but did not continue Uriel VII's schedule of reconquest. It is not yet entirely known what Tharn's goals and personal accomplishments were during the ten years he masqueraded as his liege lord. In 3E399, an enigmatic Champion defeated the Battlemage in the dungeons of the Imperial Palace and freed Uriel VII from his other-dimensional jail.

Since his emancipation, Uriel Septim VII has worked diligently to renew the battles that would reunite Tamriel. Tharn's interference broke the momentum, it is true –– but the years since then have proven that there is hope of the Golden Age of Tiber Septim's rule glorifying Tamriel once again.

A Social History of Cyrodiil

University of Gwylim Press

Historians often portray the human settlement of Tamriel as a straightforward process of military expansion of the Nords of Skyrim. In fact, human settlers occupied nearly every corner of Tamriel before Skyrim was even founded. These so-called "Nedic peoples" include the proto-Cyrodilians, the ancestors of the Bretons, the aboriginals of Hammerfell, and perhaps a now-vanished Human population of Morrowind. Strictly speaking, the Nords are simply another of these Nedic peoples, the only one that failed to find a method of peaceful accommodation with the Elves who already occupied Tamriel.

Ysgramor was certainly not the first human settler in Tamriel. In fact, in "fleeing civil war in Atmora," as the 'Song of Return' states, Ysgramor was following a long tradition of migration from Atmora; Tamriel had served as a "safety valve" for Atmora for centuries before Ysgramor's arrival. Malcontents, dissidents, rebels, landless younger sons, all made the difficult crossing from Atmora to the "New World" of Tamriel. New archeological excavations date the earliest human settlements in Hammerfell, High Rock, and Cyrodiil at ME800–1000, centuries earlier than Ysgramor, even assuming that the twelve Nord "kings" prior to Harald were actual historical figures.

The Nedic peoples were a minority in a land of Elves, and had no choice but to live peacefully with the Elder Race. In High Rock, Hammerfell, Cyrodiil, and possibly Morrowind, they did just that, and the Nedic peoples flourished and expanded over the last centuries of the Merethic Era. Only in Skyrim did this accommodation break down, an event recorded in the Song of Return. Perhaps, being close to reinforcements from Atmora, the proto-Nords did not feel it necessary to submit to the authority of the Skyrim Elves. Indeed, the early Nord chronicles note that under King Harald, the first historical Nord ruler (1E 113–221), "the Atmoran mercenaries returned to their homeland" following the consolidation of Skyrim as a centralized kingdom. Whatever the case, the pattern was set — in Skyrim, expansion would proceed militarily, with human settlement following the frontier of conquest, and the line between Human territory and Elven territory was relatively clear.

But beyond this "zone of conflict," the other Nedic peoples continued to merge with their Elven neighbors. When the Nord armies of the First Empire finally entered High Rock and Cyrodiil, they found Bretons and proto-Cyrodiils already living there among the Elves. Indeed, the Nords found it difficult to distinguish between Elf and Breton, the two races had already intermingled to such a degree. The arrival of the Nord armies upset the balance of power between the Nedic peoples and the Elves. Although the Nords' expansion into High Rock and Cyrodiil was relatively brief (less than two centuries), the result was decisive; from then on, power in those regions shifted from the Elves to the Humans.

War of the First Council

by Agrippa Fundilius

This account by the Imperial scholar Agrippa Fundilius is based on various Imperial and Dunmer sources, and written for Western readers.

The War of the First Council was a First Age religious conflict between the secular Dunmer Houses Dwemer and Dagoth and the orthodox Dunmer Houses Indoril, Redoran, Dres, Hlaalu, and Telvanni. The First Council was the first pan–Dunmer governing body, which collapsed over disputes about sorceries and enchantments practiced by the Dwemer and declared profane by the other Houses.

The Secular Houses, less numerous, but politically and magically more advanced, and aided by Nord and Orc clans drawn by promise of land and booty, initially campaigned with great success in the north of Morrowind, and occupied much of the land now comprising Redoran, Vvardenfell, and Telvanni District. The Orthodox Houses, widely dispersed and poorly organized, suffered defeat after defeat until Nerevar was made general of all House troops and levies.

Nerevar secured the aid of nomad barbarian tribesmen, and contrived to force a major battle at the Secular stronghold of Red Mountain on Vvardenfell. The Secular forces were outmaneuvered and defeated with the help of Ashlander scouts, and the survivors forced to take refuge in the Dwemer stronghold at Red Mountain.

After a brief siege, treason permitted Nerevar and his troops to enter the stronghold, where the Secular leaders were slain, and Nerevar mortally wounded. General slaughter followed, and Houses Dwemer and Dagoth were exterminated. Nerevar died shortly thereafter of his wounds.

Three of Nerevar's associates among the Orthodox Houses, Vivec, Almalexia, and Sotha Sil, succeeded to control of the re–created First Council, re–named the Grand Council of Morrowind, and went on to be come the god–kings and immortal rulers of Morrowind known as the Tribunal, or Almsivi.

The Five Songs of King Wulfharth

SHOR'S TONGUE

The first song of King Wulfharth is ancient, circa 1E500. After the defeat of the Alessian army at Glenumbria Moors, where King Hoag Merkiller was slain, Wulfharth of Atmora was elected by the Pact of Chieftains. His thu'um was so powerful that he could not verbally swear into the office, and scribes were used to draw up his oaths. Immediately thereafter the scribes wrote down the first new law of his reign: a fiery reinstatement of the traditional Nordic pantheon. The Edicts were outlawed, their priests put to the stake, and their halls set ablaze. The shadow of King Borgas had ended for a span. For his zealotry, King Wulfharth was called Shor's Tongue, and Ysmir, Dragon of the North.

KYNE'S SON

The second song of King Wulfharth glorifies his deeds in the eyes of the Old Gods. He fights the eastern Orcs and shouts their chief into Hell. He rebuilds the 41st step of High Hrothgar, which had been damaged by a dragon. When he swallowed a thundercloud to keep his army from catching cold, the Nords called him the Breath of Kyne.

OLD KNOCKER

The third song of King Wulfharth tells of his death. Orkey, an enemy god, had always tried to ruin the Nords, even in Atmora where he stole their years away. Seeing the strength of King Wulfharth, Orkey summoned the ghost of Alduin Time-Eater again. Nearly every Nord was eaten down to six years old. Boy Wulfharth pleaded to Shor, the dead Chieftain of the Gods, to help his people. Shor's own ghost then fought the Time-Eater on the spirit plane, as he did at the beginning of time, and he won, and Orkey's folk, the Orcs, were ruined. As Boy Wulfharth watched the battle in the sky he learned a new thu'um, What Happens When You Shake the Dragon Just So. He used this new magic to change his people back to normal. In his haste to save so many, though, he shook too many years out on himself. He grew older than the Greybeards, and died. The flames of his pyre were said to have reached the hearth of Kyne itself.

THE ASH KING

The fourth song of King Wulfharth tells of his rebirth. The Dwarves and Devils of the eastern kingdoms had started to fight again, and the Nords hoped they might reclaim their ancient holdings there because of it. They planned an attack, but then gave up, knowing that they had no strong King to lead them. Then in walked the Devil of Dagoth, who swore he came in peace. Moreover, he told the Nords a wondrous thing: he knew where the Heart of Shor was! Long ago the Chief of the Gods had been killed by Elven giants, and they ripped out Shor's Heart and used it as a standard to strike fear into the Nords. This worked until Ysgramor Shouted Some Sense and the Nords fought back again. Knowing that they were going to lose eventually, the Elven giants hid the Heart of Shor so that the Nords might never have their God back. But here was the Devil of Dagoth with good news! The Dwarves and Devils of the eastern kingdom had his Heart, and this was the reason for their recent unrest. The Nords asked the Devil of Dagoth why he might betray his countrymer so, and he said that the Devils have betrayed each other since the beginning of time, and this was so, and so the Nords believed him. The Tongues sung Shor's ghost into the world again. Shor gathered an army as he did of old, and then he sucked in the long-strewn ashes of King Wulfharth and remade him, for he needed a good general. But the Devil of Dagoth petitioned to be that general, too, and he pointed out his role as the blessed harbinger of this holy war. So Shor had two generals, the Ash King and the Devil of Dagoth, and he marched on the eastern kingdoms with all the sons of Skyrim.

RED MOUNTAIN

The fifth song of King Wulfharth is sad. The survivors of the disaster came back under a red sky. That year is called Sun's Death. The Devil of Dagoth had tricked the Nords, for the Heart of Shor was not in the eastern kingdoms, and had never been there at all. As soon as Shor's army had got to Red Mountain, all the Devils and Dwarves fell upon them. Their sorcerers lifted the mountain and threw it onto Shor, trapping him underneath Red Mountain until the end of time. They slaughtered the sons of Skyrim, but not before King Wulfharth killed King Dumalacath the Dwarf-Orc, and doomed his people. Then Vehk the Devil blasted the Ash King into Hell and it was over. Later, Kyne lifted the ashes of the ashes of Ysmir into the sky, saving him from Hell and showing her sons the color of blood when it is brought by betrayal. And the Nords will never trust another Devil again.

The Secret Song of Wulfharth Ash-King

THE TRUTH AT RED MOUNTAIN

The Heart of Shor was in Resdayn, as Dagoth-Ur had promised. As Shor's army approached the westernmost bank of the Inner Sea, they stared across at Red Mountain, where the Dwemeri armies had gathered. News from the scouts reported that the Chimeri forces had just left Narsis, and that they were taking their time joining their cousins against the Nords. Dagoth-Ur said that the Tribunal had betrayed their King's trust, that they sent Dagoth-Ur to Lorkhan (for that is what they called Shor in Resdayn) so that the god might wreak vengeance on the Dwarves for their hubris; that Nerevar's peace with the Dwemer would be the ruin of the Velothi way. This was the reason for the slow muster, Dagoth-Ur said.

THE ARMIES GROW

And Lorkhan (for that is what they called Shor in Resdayn) said: "I do not wreak vengeance on the Dwarves for the reasons that the Tribunal might believe I do. Nevertheless, it is true that they will die by my hand, and any whoever should side with them. This Nerevar is the son of Boethiah, one of the strongest Padomaics. He is a hero to his people despite his Tribunal, and he shall muster enough that this battle will be harder going still. We will need more than what we have." And so Dagoth-Ur, who wanted the Dwarves as dead as the Tribunal did, went to Kogoran and summoned his House chap'thil, his nix-hounds, his wizards, archers, his stolen men of brass. And the Ash King, Wulfharth, hoary Ysmir, went and made peace with the Orcs in spite of his Nordic blood, and they brought many warriors but no wizards at all. Many Nords could not bring themselves to ally with their traditional enemies, even in the face of Red Mountain. They were close to desertion. Then Wulfharth said: "Don't you see where you really are? Don't you know who Shor really is? Don't you know what this war is?" And they looked from the King to the God to the Devils and Orcs, and some knew, really knew, and they are the ones that stayed.

THE DOOM DRUM

Nerevar carried Keening, a dagger made of the sound of the shadow of the moons. His champions were Dumac Dwarfking, who carried a hammer of divine mass, and Alandro

Sul, who was the immortal son of Azura and wore the Wraith Mail. They met Lorkhan at the last battle of Red Mountain. Lorkhan had his Heart again, but he had long been from it, and he needed time. Wulfharth met Sul but could not strike him, and he fell from grievous wounds, but not before shouting Sul blind. Dagoth-Ur met Dumac and slew him, but not before Sunder struck his lord's Heart. Nerevar turned away from Lorkhan and struck down Dagoth-Ur in rage, but he took a mortal wound from Lorkhan in turn. But Nerevar feigned the death that was coming early and so struck Lorkhan with surprise on his side. The Heart had been made solid by Sunder's tuning blow and Keening could now cut it out. And it was cut out and Lorkhan was defeated and the whole ordeal was thought over.

Remanada

Chapter 1

SANCRE TOR AND THE BIRTH OF REMAN

And in those days the empire of the Cyrodiils was dead, save in memory only, for through war and slug famine and iniquitous rulers, the west split from the east and Colovia's estrangment lasted some four hundreds of years. And the earth was sick with this sundering. Once-worthy western kings, of Anvil and Sarchal, of Falkreath and Delodiil, became through pride and habit as like thief-barons and forgot covenant. In the heartland things were no better, as arcanists and false moth-princes lay in drugged stupor or the studies of vileness and no one sat on the Throne in dusted generations. Snakes and the warnings of snakes went unheeded and the land bled with ghosts and deepset holes unto cold harbors. It is said that even the Chim-el Adabal, the amulet of the kings of glory, had been lost and its people saw no reason to find it.

And it was in this darkness that King Hrol set out from the lands beyond lost Twil with a sortie of questing knights numbered eighteen less one, all of them western sons and daughters. For Hrol had seen in his visions the snakes to come and sought to heal all the borders of his forebears. And to this host appeared at last a spirit who resembled none other than El-Estia, queen of ancienttimes, who bore in her left hand the dragonfire of the aka-tosh and in her right hand the jewels of the covenant and on her breast a wound that spilt void onto her mangled feet. And seeing El-Estia and Chim-el Adabal, Hrol and his knights wailed and set

to their knees and prayed for all things to become as right. Unto them the spirit said, I am the healer of all men and the mother of dragons, but as you have run so many times from me so shall I run until you learn my pain, which renders you and all this land dead.

And the spirit fled from them, and they split among hills and forests to find her, all grieving that they had become a villainous people. Hrol and his shieldthane were the only ones to find her, and the king spoke to her, saying, I love you sweet Aless, sweet wife of Shor and of Auri–el and the Sacred Bull, and would render this land alive again, not through pain but through a return to the dragon–fires of covenant, to join east and west and throw off all ruin. And the shieldthane bore witness to the spirit opening naked to his king, carving on a nearby rock the words AND HROL DID LOVE UNTO A HILLOCK before dying in the sight of their union.

When the fifteen other knights found King Hrol, they saw him dead after his labors against a mound of mud. And they parted each in their way, and some went mad, and the two that returned to their homeland beyond Twil would say nothing of Hrol, and acted ashamed for him.

But after nine months that mound of mud became as a small mountain, and there were whispers among the shepherds and bulls. A small community of believers gathered around that growing hill during the days of its first churning, and they were the first to name it the Golden Hill, Sancre Tor. And it was the shepherdess Sed–Yenna who dared climb the hill when she heard his first cry, and at its peak she saw what it had yielded, an infant she named Reman, which is "Light of Man."

And in the child's forehead was the Chim–el Adabal, alive with the dragon–fires of yore and divine promise, and none dared obstruct Sed–Yenna when she climbed the steps of White–Gold Tower to place the babe Reman on his Throne, where he spoke as an adult, saying I AM CYRODIIL COME.

Chapter 2

THE CHEVALIER RENALD

BLADE OF THE PIG

And in the days of interregnum, the Chim–el Adabal was lost again amid the petty wars of gone–heathen kings. West and east knew no union then and all the lands outside of them saw Cyrodiil as a nest of snakemen and snakes. And for four more hundreds of years did the seat of Reman stay sundered, with only the machinations of a group of loyal knights keeping all its borders from throwing wide.

These loyal knights did go by no name then, but were known by their eastern swords and painted eyes, and it was whispered that they were descended from the bodyguard of old Reman. One of their number, called the Chevalier Renald, discovered the prowess of Cuhlecain and then supported him towards the throne. Only later would it be revealed that Renald did this thing to come closer to Talos, anon Stormcrown, the glorious yet-emperor Tiber Septim; only later still, that he was under instruction by a pig.

Long glory was wife to the all the knights of the dragon-banner, who knew no other and were brothers before beyond many seas and now were brothers under the law named the blade-surrender of Pale Pass. And having vampire blood these brother-knights lived for ages through and past Reman and then kept guard over his ward, the coiled king, Versidue-Shaie. The snake-captain Vershu became Renald became the protector of the northern west when the black dart was hooked into Savirien-Chorak.

Editor's Note: The rest of this ancient book has been lost.

Third Era: An Abbreviated Timeline

The Last Year of the First Era

by Jaspus Ignateous

It has been said that "citizens of the Empire who make the same mistakes as their forebears deserve to suffer the same fate." And while this may be true, it's hard to deny that the Empire's history is so long, and our forebears have made so many mistakes, it's sometimes hard to keep track.

This work is meant to serve as a concise compilation of the Empire's most recent events, in this, our current age – what we refer to as the Third Era. It is a period of time that has as yet comprised less than five hundred years. But it should at least serve as a starting point for those who wish to study our Empire's vast and varied history. And maybe, just maybe, prevent the repeat of a previous disaster.

It is also worth noting that when viewed in such a succinct structure, one truly gets a sense of just how often our great Empire has changed leadership. Indeed, it can be argued that much of the Empire's history in these past five centuries is the changing rule of that very Empire itself.

FIRST CENTURY

3E 0 – Beginning of Third Era, when all province in Tamriel are unified

3E 38 – Death of Emperor Tiber Septim, and crowning of Emperor Pelagius

3E 41 – Assassination of Emperor Pelagius, and crowning of Empress Kintyra

3E 48 – Death of Empress Kintyra , and crowning of Emperor Uriel I

3E 64 – Death of Emperor Uriel I, and crowning of Emperor Uriel II

3E 82 – Death of Emperor Uriel II, and crowning of Emperor Pelagius II

3E 99 – Death of Emperor Pelagius II Dies, and crowning of Emperor Antiochus

SECOND CENTURY

3E 110 – War of the Isle

3E 111 – Knights of the Nine founded by Sir Amiel Lannus

3E 114 – Reported death of Empress Kintyra II

3E 119 – Birth of Pelagius III

3E 121 – Uriel III Proclaimed Emperor

E 121 – War of the Red Diamond

3E 123, 23 Frostfall – Actual death of Empress Kintyra II, in captivity, in secret

3E 127 – Death of Emperor Uriel III, and crowing of Emperor Cephorus I

3E 137 – Death of Potema, the Queen of Solitude

3E 140 – Death of Emperor Cephorus I, and crowning of Emperor Magnus

3E 145 – Death of Emperor Magnus, and crowning of Emperor Pelagius III

3E 153 – Death of Emperor Pelagius III

3E 153 – Katariah takes throne from husband Pelagius, becoming Empress

THIRD CENTURY

3E 200 – Death of Empress Katariah, and crowning of Emperor Cassynder

3E 202 – Death of Emperor Cassynder, and crowning of Emperor Uriel IV

3E 247 – Death of Emperor Uriel IV, and crowning of Emperor Cephorus II

3E 249 – Invasion of the Empire by the lich, Camoran Usurper

3E 253 – Camoran Usurper controls the Dwynnen Region with "Nightmare Host"

3E 267 – Defeat of Camoran Usurper Defeated

3E 268 – Crowing of Emperor Uriel V

3E 271–3E 284 – Various Conquests of Emperor Uriel Septim IV

3E 288 – Invasion of Akavir by the forces of Emperor Uriel Septim IV

3E 290 – Death of Emperor Uriel V, and crowning of Emperor Uriel VI

FOURTH CENTURY

3E 307 – Uriel VI gain full power as Emperor

3E 320 – Death of Uriel VI, and crowning of Empress Morihatha

3E 331 – Publication of the second edition of "A Pocket Guide to The Empire"

3E 339 – Assassination of Empress Morihatha, and crowning of Emperor Pelagius IV

3E 389 – Jagar Tharn betrays Emperor Uriel Septim VII

3E 396 – Regional Wars Throughout Tamriel

3E 396 – The Arnesian War

3E 399 – Defeat of Jagar Tharn

3E 399 – The founding of Orsinium

FIFTH CENTURY

3E 403 – Assassination of Lysandus, the King of Daggerfall

3E 414 – Vvardenfell Territory opened for settlement

3E 417 – The "Warp in the West" occurs

3E 421 – Greywyn founds the Crimson Scars.

3E 427 – Beginning of the Blight Curse in Vvardenfell, and arrival of the Nerevar

3E 427 – The Bloodmoon Prophecy comes to pass, on the isle of Solstheim

3E 432 – Publication of the third edition of "A Pocket Guide to The Empire"

3E 433 – Assassination of Emperor Uriel Septim VII

3E 433 – The "Oblivion Crisis"

3E 433 – The Knights of the Nine are reformed

A Short Life of Uriel Septim VII

by Rufus Hayn

3E 368–389: Strategist and Conciliator

he early decades of Emperor Uriel's life were marked by aggressive expansion and consolidation of Imperial influence throughout the empire, but especially in the East, in Morrowind and Black Marsh, where the Empire's power was limited, Imperial culture was weak, and native customs and traditions were strong and staunchly opposed to assimilation. During this period Uriel greatly benefitted from the arcane support and shrewd council of his close advisor, the Imperial Battlemage, Jagar Tharn.

The story of Uriel's marriage to the Princess Caula Voria is a less happy tale. Though she was a beautiful and charming woman, and greatly loved and admired by the people, the Empress was a deeply unpleasant, arrogant, ambitious, grasping woman. She snared Uriel Septim with her feminine wiles, but Uriel Septim thereafter soon regretted his mistake, and was repelled by her. They heartily detested one another, and went out of their ways to hurt one another. Their children were the victims of this unhappy marriage.

With his agile mind and vaunting ambition, Uriel soon outstripped his master in the balanced skills of threat and diplomacy. Uriel's success in co-opting House Hlaalu as an advance guard of Imperial culture and economic development in Morrowind is a noteworthy example. However, Uriel also grew in pride and self-assurance. Jagar Tharn fed Uriel's pride, and hiding behind the mask of an out-paced former master counselor, Tharn purchased the complete trust that led finally to Uriel's betrayal and imprisonment in Oblivion and Tharn's secret usurpation of the Imperial throne.

3E 389–399: Betrayed and Imprisoned

Little is known of Uriel's experience while trapped in Oblivion. He says he remembers nothing but an endless sequence of waking and sleeping nightmares. He says he believed himself to be dreaming, and had no notion of passage of time. Publicly, he long claimed to have no memory of the dreams and nightmares of his imprisonment, but from time to time, during the interviews with the Emperor that form the basis of this biography, he would relate details of nightmares he had, and would describe them as similar to the nightmares he had when he was imprisoned in Oblivion. He seemed not so much unwilling as incapable of describing the experience.

But it is clear that the experience changed him. In 3E 389 he was a young man, full of pride, energy, and ambition. During the Restoration, after his rescue and return to the throne, he was an old man, grave, patient, and cautious. He also became conservative and pessimistic, where the policies of his early life were markedly bold, even rash. Uriel accounts for this change as a reaction to and revulsion for the early teachings and counsel of Jagar Tharn. However, Uriel's exile in Oblivion also clearly drained and wasted him in body and spirit, though his mind retained the shrewd cunning and flexibility of his youth.

The story of Tharn's magical impersonation of the emperor, the unmasking of Tharn's imposture by Queen Barenziah, and the roles played by King Eadwyre, Ria Silmane, and her Champion in assembling the Staff of Chaos, defeating the renegade Imperial Battlemage Jagar Tharn, and restoring Uriel to the throne, is treated at length in Stern Gamboge's excellent three-Volume BIOGRAPHY OF BARENZIAH. There is no reason to recount that narrative here. Summarized briefly, Jagar Tharn's neglect and mismanagement of Imperial affairs resulted in a steady decline in the Empire's economic prosperity, allowed many petty lords and kings to challenge the authority of the Empire, and permitted strong local rulers in the East and the West to indulge in open warfare over lands and sovereign rights.

3E 399–415: Restoration, the Miracle of Peace, and Vvardenfell

During the Restoration, Uriel Septim turned from the aggressive campaign of military intimidation and diplomatic accommodation of his earlier years, and relied instead on clandestine manipulation of affairs behind the scenes, primarily through the agencies of the various branches of the Blades. A complete assessment of the methods and objectives of this period must wait until after the Emperor's death, when the voluminous diaries archived at his country estate may be opened to the public, and when the Blades no longer need to maintain secrecy to protect the identities of its agents.

Two signal achievements of this period point to the efficacy of Uriel's subtle policies: the 'Miracle of Peace' (also popularly known as 'The Warp in the West') that transformed the Iliac Bay region from an ruly assortment of warring petty kingdoms into the well-ordered and peaceful modern counties of Hammerfell, Sentinel, Wayrest, and Orsinium, and the colonization of Vvardenfell, presided over by the skillful machinations of King Helseth of Morrowind and Lady Barenziah, the Queen-Mother, which brought Morrowind more closely into the sphere of Imperial influence.

3E 415–430: The Golden Peace, King Helseth's Court, and the Nine in the East

Following the 'Miracle of Peace' (best described in Per Vetersen's DAGGERFALL: A MODERN HISTORY), the Empire entered a period of peace and prosperity comparable to the early years of Uriel's reign. With the Imperial Heartland and West solidly integrated into the Empire, Uriel was able to turn his full attention to the East — to Morrowind.

Exploiting conflicts at the heart of Morrowind's monolithic Tribunal religion and the long-established Great House system of government, and taking advantage of the terrible threat that the corrupted divine beings at the heart of the Tribunal religion presented to the growing colonies on Vvardenfell, Uriel worked through shadowy agents of the Blades and through the court of King Helseth in Mournhold to shift the center of political power in Morrowind from the Great House councils to Helseth's court, and took advantage of the collapse of the orthodox Tribunal cults to establish the Nine Divines as the dominant faiths in Hlaalu and Vvardenfell Districts.

Hasphat Anabolis's treatment of the establishment of the Nine in the East in his four-volume LIFE AND TIMES OF THE NEREVARINE is comprehensive; however, he fails to resolve the central mystery of this period — how much did Uriel know about the prophecies of the Nerevarine, and how did he learn of their significance? The definitive resolution of this and other mysteries must await the future release of the Emperor's private papers, or a relenting of the Blades' strict policies of secrecy concerning their agents.

Report of the Imperial Commission on the Disaster at Ionith

by Lord Pottreid, Chairman

Part I: Preparations

The Emperor's plans for the invasion of Akavir were laid in the 270s, when he began the conquest of the small island kingdoms that lie between Tamriel and Akavir. With the fall of Black Harbor in Esroniet in 282, Uriel V was already looking ahead to the ultimate prize. He immediately ordered extensive renovations to the port, which would serve as the marshalling point for the invasion force and as the main supply source throughout the campaign. At this time he also began the construction of the many large, ocean-going transports that would be needed for the final crossing to Akavir, in which the Navy was previously deficient. Thus it can be seen that the Emperor's preparations for the invasion were laid well in advance, before even the conquest of Esroniet was complete, and was not a sudden whim as some have charged.

When Prince Bashomon yielded Esroniet to Imperial authority in 284, the Emperor's full attention could be devoted to planning for the Akaviri campaign. Naval expeditions were dispatched in 285 and 286 to scout the sea lanes and coastlands of Akavir; and various Imperial intelligence agents, both magical and mundane, were employed to gather information. On the basis of all this information, the kingdom of the Tsaesci, in the southwest of Akavir, was selected as the initial target for the invasion.

Meanwhile the Emperor was gathering his Expeditionary Force. A new Far East Fleet was created for the campaign, which for a time dwarfed the rest of the Navy; it is said to be the most powerful fleet ever assembled in the history of Tamriel. The Fifth, Seventh, Tenth, and Fourteenth Legions were selected for the initial landing, with the Ninth and Seventeenth to follow as reinforcements once the beachhead was secured. While this may seem to the layman a relatively small fraction of the Army's total manpower, it must be remembered that this Expeditionary Force would have to be maintained at the end of a long and tenuous supply line; in addition, the Emperor and the Army command believed that the invasion would not be strongly opposed, at least at first. Perhaps most crucially, the Navy had only enough heavy transport capacity to move four legions at a time.

It should be noted here that the Commission does not find fault with the Emperor's preparations for the invasion. Based on the information available prior to the invasion, (which, while obviously deficient in hindsight, great effort had been made to accumulate), the Commission believes that the Emperor did not act recklessly or imprudently. Some have argued that the Expeditionary Force was too small. The Commission believes that on the contrary, even if shipping could have been found to transport and supply more legions (an impossibility without crippling the trade of the entire Empire), this would have merely added to the scale of the disaster; it would not have averted it. Neither could the rest of the Empire be denuded of legions; the memory of the Camoran Usurper was still fresh, and the Emperor believed (and this Commission agrees) that the security of the Empire precluded a larger concentration of military force outside of Tamriel. If anything, the Commission believes that the Expeditionary Force was too large. Despite the creation of two new legions during his reign (and the recreation of the Fifth), the loss of the Expeditionary Force left the Empire in a dangerously weak position relative to the provinces, as the current situation makes all too clear. This suggests that the invasion of Akavir was beyond the Empire's current strength; even if the Emperor could have fielded and maintained a larger force in Akavir, the Empire may have disintegrated behind him.

Part II: The Invasion of Akavir

The Expeditionary Force left Black Harbor on 23rd Rain's Hand, 2ss, and with fair weather landed in Akavir after six weeks at sea. The landing site was a small Tsaesci port at the mouth of a large river, chosen for its proximity to Tamriel as well as its location in a fertile river valley, giving easy access to the interior as well as good foraging for the army. All went well at first. The Tsaesci had abandoned the town when the Expeditionary Force approached, so they took possession of it and renamed it Septimia, the first colony of the new Imperial Province of Akavir. While the engineers fortified the town and expanded the port facilities to serve the Far East Fleet, the Emperor marched inland with two legions. The surrounding land was reported to be rich, well-watered fields, and meeting no resistance the army took the next city upriver, also abandoned. This was refounded as Ionith, and the Emperor established his headquarters there, being much larger than Septimia and better-located to dominate the surrounding countryside.

The Expeditionary Force had yet to meet any real resistance, although the legions were constantly shadowed by mounted enemy patrols which prevented any but large scouting parties from leaving the main body of the army. One thing the Emperor sorely lacked was cavalry, due to the limited space on the transport fleet, although for the time being the battlemages made up for this with magical reconnaissance.

The Emperor now sent out envoys to try to contact the Tsaesci king or whoever ruled this land, but his messengers never returned. In retrospect, the Commission believes that valuable time was wasted in this effort while the army was stalled at Ionith, which could have been better spent in advancing quickly while the enemy was still, apparently, surprised by the invasion. However, the Emperor believed at the time that the Tsaesci could be overawed by the Empire's power and he might win a province by negotiation with no need for serious fighting.

Meanwhile, the four legions were busy building a road between Septimia and Ionith, setting up fortified guard posts along the river, and fortifying both cities' defences, activities which would serve them well later. Due to their lack of cavalry, scouting was limited, and communication between the two cities constantly threatened by enemy raiders, with which the legions were still unable to come to grips.

The original plan had been to bring the two reinforcing legions across as soon as the initial landing had secured a port, but the fateful decision was now taken to delay their arrival and instead begin using the Fleet to transport colonists. The Emperor and the Council agreed that, due to the complete abandonment of the conquered area by its native population, colonists were needed to work the fields so that the Expeditionary Force would not have to rely entirely on the fleet for supplies. In addition, unrest had broken out in Yneslea, athwart the supply route to Akavir, and the Council believed the Ninth and Seventeenth legions would be better used in repacifying those territories and securing the Expeditionary Force's supply lines.

The civilian colonists and their supplies began arriving in Septimia in mid-Hearthfire, and they took over the preparation of the fields (which had been started by the legionnaires) for a spring crop. A number of cavalry mounts were also brought over at this time, and the raids on the two Imperial colonies subsequently fell off. Tsaesci emissaries also finally arrived in Ionith, purportedly to begin peace negotiations, and the Expeditionary Force settled in for what was expected to be a quiet winter.

At this time, the Council urged the Emperor to return to Tamriel with the Fleet, to deal with many pressing matters of the Empire while the army was in winter quarters, but the Emperor decided that it would be best to remain in Akavir. This turned out to be fortunate, because a large portion of the Fleet, including the Emperor's flagship, was destroyed by an early winter storm during the homeward voyage. The winter storm season of 288–289 was unusually prolonged and exceptionally severe, and prevented the Fleet from returning to Akavir as planned with additional supplies. This was reported to the Emperor via battlemage and it was agreed that the Expeditionary Force could survive on what supplies it had on hand until the spring.

Part III: The Destruction of the Expeditionary Force

The winter weather in Akavir was also much more severe than expected. Due to the supply problems and the addition of thousands of civilians, the Expeditionary Force was on tight rations. To make matters worse, the Tsaesci raiders returned in force and harried any foraging and scouting parties outside the walls of the two cities. Several watch forts on the road between Septimia and Ionith were captured during blizzards, and the rest had to be abandoned as untenable. As a result, communication between the two cities had to be conducted entirely by magical means, a continuing strain on the legions' battlemages.

On 5th Sun's Dawn, a large entourage of Tsaesci arrived at Ionith claiming to bring a peace offer from the Tsaesci king. That night, these treacherous envoys murdered the guards at one of the city gates and let in a strong party of their comrades who were waiting outside the city walls. Their clear intention was to assassinate the Emperor, foiled only by the vigilance and courage of troopers of the Tenth who were guarding his palace. Once the alarm was raised, the Tsaesci inside the city were hunted down and killed to the last man. Needless to say, this was the end of negotiations between the Emperor and the Tsaesci.

The arrival of spring only brought worse troubles. Instead of the expected spring rains, a hot dry wind began to blow from the east, continuing with varying strength through the entire summer. The crops failed, and even the river (which in the previous year had been navigable by small boats far upstream of Ionith) was completely dried up by Sun's Height. It is unknown if this was due to a previously unknown weather pattern unique to Akavir, or if the Tsaesci manipulated the weather through magical means. The Commission leans towards the former conclusion, as there is no direct evidence of

the Tsaesci possessing such fearsome arcane power, but the latter possibility cannot be entirely ruled out.

Due to prolonged bad weather, the supply fleet was late in setting out from Black Harbor. It finally left port in early Second Seed, but was again severely mauled by storms and limped into Septimia eight weeks later much reduced. Because of the increasingly desperate supply situation in Akavir, the Emperor dispatched most of his Battlemage Corps with the fleet to assist it in weathering the storms which seemed likely to continue all summer. At this time, the Council urged the Emperor to abandon the invasion and to return to Tamriel with the Expeditionary Force, but he again refused, noting that the fleet was no longer large enough to transport all four legions at once. The Commission agrees that leaving one or more legions behind in Akavir to await the return of the fleet would have damaged Army morale. But the Commission also notes that the loss of one legion would have been preferable to the loss of the entire Expeditionary Force. It is the unanimous opinion of the Commission that this was the last point at which complete disaster might have been averted. Once the decision was made to send the fleet back for reinforcements and supplies, events proceeded to their inevitable conclusion.

From this point on, much less is known about what transpired in Akavir. With most of the battlemages assisting the fleet, communication between the Expeditionary Force and Tamriel was limited, especially as the situation in Akavir worsened and the remaining battlemages had their powers stretched to the limit attending to all the needs of the legions. However, it appears that the Tsaesci may also have been actively interfering with the mages in some unknown manner. Some of the mages in Akavir reported their powers being abnormally weak, and the mages of the War College in Cyrodiil (who were handling communications for the Council) reported problems linking up with their compatriots in Akavir, even between master and pupil of long training. The Commission urges that the War College make a particular study of the arcane powers of the Tsaesci, should the Empire ever come into conflict with Akavir again.

What is known is that the Emperor marched out of Ionith in mid-Sun's Height, leaving only small garrisons to hold the cities. He had learned that the Tsaesci were massing their forces on the other side of a mountain range to the north, and he intended to smash their army before it could gather full strength and capture their supplies (of which he was in desperate need). This rapid advance seems to have taken the Tsaesci by surprise, and the Expeditionary Force crossed the mountains and fell on their camp, routing the Tsaesci army and capturing its leader (a noble of some kind). But the Emperor was soon forced to retreat, and the legions suffered heavily on their retreat to Ionith. The Emperor now found himself besieged in Ionith, cut off from the small garrison at Septimia which was also besieged. By this time, it seems that the efforts of the few remaining battlemages were devoted entirely to creating water to keep the army alive, a skill not normally emphasized at the War College. The fleet had arrived safely back to Black Harbor, thanks to the Battlemage Corps, but all attempts to return to Akavir were frustrated by a series of ever more savage storms that battered

Esroniet throughout the rest of 289.

The Council's last contact with the Emperor was in early Frostfall. By Evening Star, the Council was extremely worried about the situation in Akavir and ordered the fleet to sail regardless of the risk. Despite the continued storms, the fleet managed to press on to Akavir. Hope was raised when contact was made with the Emperor's battlemage, who reported that Ionith still held out. Plans were quickly laid for the Expeditionary Force to break out of Ionith and fall back on Septimia, where the fleet would meet them. This was the last direct contact with the Expeditionary Force. The fleet arrived in Septimia to find its garrison under savage assault from a large Tsaesci army. The battlemages with the fleet threw back the enemy long enough for the survivors to embark and the fleet to withdraw.

The few survivors of the Expeditionary Force who reached Septimia told how the Emperor had led the army out of Ionith by night two days earlier, successfully breaking through the enemy lines but then being surrounded by overwhelming forces on the road to Septimia. They told of a heroic last stand by the Emperor and the Tenth Legion, which allowed a remnant of the Fourteenth to reach Septimia. Two survivors of the Tenth arrived in Septimia that night, having slipped through the enemy lines during their undisciplined victory celebration. These men confirmed having seen the Emperor die, cut down by enemy arrows as he rallied the Tenth's shield wall.

Part IV: Conclusion

The Commission believes that the invasion of Akavir was doomed from the start for several reasons, none of which could have been foreseen beforehand, unfortunately.

Despite extensive intelligence-gathering, the Expeditionary Force was clearly unprepared for the situation in Akavir. The unexpected weather which plagued the army and navy was particularly disastrous. Without the loss of a majority of the Far East Fleet during the campaign, the Expeditionary Force could have been withdrawn in 289. The weather also forced the Emperor to assign most of his Battlemage Corps to the fleet, leaving him without their valuable assistance during the fighting which soon followed. And of course the unexpected drought which struck Ionith during 289 dashed the hopes of supplying the army locally, and left the Expeditionary Force in an untenable situation when besieged in Ionith.

The Tsaesci were also much stronger than intelligence reports had suggested. Information on the size of the army the Tsaesci were eventually able to field against the Expeditionary Force is vague, as the only serious fighting took place after regular communications were cut off between the Emperor and the Council. Nevertheless, it seems likely that the Tsaesci outnumbered the Emperor's forces by several times, as they were able to force four crack legions into retreat and then keep them under siege for several months.

As was stated previously, the Commission declines to criticize the initial decision to invade Akavir. Based on what was known at the time, the plan seemed sound. It is only with the benefit of hindsight does it become obvious that the invasion had very little chance of success. Nevertheless, the Commission believes several valuable lessons can be taken from this disaster.

First, the Tsaesci may have extremely powerful arcane forces at their command. The possibility that they may have manipulated the weather across such a vast region seems incredible (and it should be noted that three Commissioners strongly objected to this paragraph even being included in this Report), but the Commission believes that this matter deserves urgent investigation. The potential danger is such that even the slight possibility must be taken seriously.

Second, the Tsaesci appear to possess no navy to speak of. The Expeditionary Force was never threatened by sea, and the Far East Fleet fought nothing but the weather. Indeed, initial plans called for a portion of the Fleet to remain in Akavir for use in coastal operations, but in the event there were very few places where the large vessels of the Fleet could approach the land, due to the innumerable reefs, sandbars, islands, etc. that infested the coastal waters north and south from Septimia. Due to the utter lack of trees in the plain around Septimia and Ionith, the Expeditionary Force was unable to build smaller vessels which could have navigated the shallow coastal waters. Any future military expeditions against Akavir would do well to consider some way of bringing a means for inshore naval operations in order to exploit this clear advantage over the Tsaesci, an advantage that was sadly unexploited by the Expeditionary Force.

Third, much longer–term study needs to be made of Akavir before another invasion could even be contemplated. The information gathered over the four years prior to the invasion was extensive, but clearly inadequate. The weather conditions were completely unexpected; the Tsaesci much stronger than expected; and the attempted negotiations by the Emperor with the Tsaesci a disaster. Akavir proved alien beyond expectation, and the Commission believes any future attempt to invade Akavir should not be contemplated without much greater knowledge of the conditions, politics, and peoples of that continent than presently obtains.

Finally, the Commission unanimously concludes that given what we now know, any attempt to invade Akavir is folly, at least in the present state of the Empire. The Empire's legions are needed at home. One day, a peaceful, united Empire will return to Akavir and exact severe retribution for the disaster at Ionith and for our fallen Emperor. But that day is not now, nor in the foreseeable future.

The Dragon Break Reexamined

by Fal Droon

The late 3rd era was a period of remarkable religious ferment and creativity. The upheavals of the reign of Uriel VII were only the outward signs of the historical forces that would eventually lead to the fall of the Septim Dynasty. The so called "Dragon Break" was first proposed at this time, by a wide variety of cults and fringe sects across the Empire, connected only by a common obsession with the events surrounding Tiber Septim's rise to power — the "founding myth," if you will, of the Septim Dynasty.

The basis of the Dragon Break doctrine is now known to be a rather prosaic error in the timeline printed in the otherwise authoritative "Encyclopedia Tamrielica," first published in 3E 12, during the early years of Tiber Septim's reign. At that time, the archives of Alinor were still inaccessible to human scholars, and the extant records from the Alessian period were extremely fragmentary. The Alessians had systematically burned all the libraries they could find, and their own records were largely destroyed during the War of Righteousness.

The author of the Encyclopedia Tamrielica was apparently unfamiliar with the Alessian "year," which their priesthood used to record all dates. We now know this refers to the length of the long vision–trances undertaken by the High Priestess, which might last anywhere from a few weeks to several months. Based on analysis of the surviving trance scrolls, as well as murals and friezes from Alessian temples, I estimate that the Alessian Order actually lasted only about 150 years, rather than the famous "one thousand and eight years" given by the Encyclopedia Tamrielica. The "mystery" of the millennial–plus rule of the Alessians was accepted but unexplained until the spread of the Lorkhan cults in the late 3rd era, when the doctrine of the Dragon Break took hold. Because this dating (and explanation) was so widely held at the time, and then repeated by historians down through today, it has come to have the force of tradition. Recall, however, that the 3rd era historians were already separated from the Alessians by a gulf of more than 2,000 years. And history was still in its infancy, relying on the few archives from those early days.

Today, modern archaeology and paleonumerology have confirmed what my own research in Alessian dating first suggested: that the Dragon Break was invented in the late 3rd era, based on a scholarly error, fueled by obsession with eschatology and Numidiumism, and perpetuated by scholarly inertia.

Where Were You When the Dragon Broke?

by Various

A BRIEF DESCRIPTION AND MULTIPLE ACCOUNTS OF THE DRAGON BREAK

Corax, Cyrodiil, Elder Council:

"No one understands what happened when the Selectives danced on that tower. It would be easy to dismiss the whole matter as nonsense were it not for the Amulet of Kings. Even the Elder Scrolls do not mention it — let me correct myself, the Elder Scrolls cannot mention it. When the Moth priests attune the Scrolls to the timeless time their glyphs always disappear. The Amulet of Kings, however, with its oversoul of emperors, can speak of it at length. According to Hestra, Cyrodiil became an Empire across the stars. According to Shor-El, Cyrodiil became an egg. Most say something in a language they can only speak sideways. The Council has collected texts and accounts from all of its provinces, and they only offer stories that never coincide, save on one point: all the folk of Tamriel during the Middle Dawn, in whatever 'when' they were caught in, tracked the fall of the eight stars. And that is how they counted their days."

Mehra Nabisi, Dunmer, Triune Mistress of the New Temple:

"Accounts of the Middle Dawn are the province of the Empire of Men, and proof of the deceit that call themselves the Aedra. Eight stars fell on Tamriel, one for each iniquity that Lorkhan made clear to the world. Veloth read these signs, and he told Boethiah, who confirmed them, and he told Mephala, who made wards against them, and he told Azura, who sent ALMSIVI to steer the True Folk clear of harm. Even the Four Corners of the House of Troubles rose to protect the periphery of your madness. We watched our borders and saw them shift like snakes, and saw you run around in it like the spirits of old, devoid of math, without your if-thens, succumbing to the Ever Now like slaves of the slim folly, stasis. Do not ask us where we were when the Dragon Broke, for, of all the world, only we truly know, and we might just show you how to break it again."

R'leyt-harhr, Khajiit, Tender to the Mane:

"Do you mean, where were the Khajiit when the Dragon Broke? R'leyt tells you where: recording it. 'One thousand eight years,' you've heard it. You think the Cyro-Nordics came up with that all on their own. You humans are better thieves than even Rajhin! While you were fighting wars with phantoms and giving birth to your own fathers, it was the Mane that watched the ja-Kha'jay, because the moons were the only constant, and you didn't have the sugar to see it. We'll give you credit: you broke Alkosh something fierce, and that's not easy. Just don't think you solved what you accomplished by it, or can ever solve it. You did it again with Big Walker, not once, but twice! Once at Rimmen, which we'll never learn to live with. The second time it was in Daggerfall, or was it Sentinel, or was it Wayrest, or was it in all three places at once? Get me, Cyrodiil? When will you wake up and realize what really happened to the Dwarves?"

Mannimarco, God of Worms, the Necromancers:

"The Three Thieves of Morrowind could tell you where they were. So could the High King of Alinor, who was the one who broke it in the first place. There are others on this earth that could, too: Ysmir, Pelinal, Arnand the Fox or should I say Arctus? The Last Dwarf would talk, if they would let him. As for myself, I was here and there and here again, like the rest of the mortals during the Dragon Break. How do you think I learned my mystery? The Maruhkati Selectives showed us all the glories of the Dawn so that we might learn, simply: as above, so below."

The Madness of Pelagius

by Tsathenes

The man who would be Emperor of all Tamriel was born Thoriz Pelagius Septim, a prince of the royal family of Wayrest in 3E 119 at the end of the glorious reign of his uncle, Antiochus I. Wayrest had been showered by much preference during the years before Pelagius' birth, for King Magnus was Antiochus' favorite brother.

It is hard to say when Pelagius' madness first manifested itself, for, in truth, the first ten years of his life were marked by much insanity in the land itself. When Pelagius was just over a year old, Antiochus died and a daughter, Kintyra, assumed the throne to the acclaim of all. Kintyra II was Pelagius' cousin and an accomplished mystic and sorceress. If she had sufficient means to peer into the future, she would have surely fled the palace.

The story of the War of the Red Diamond has been told in many other scholarly journals, but as most historians agree, Kintyra II's reign was usurped by her and Pelagius' cousin Uriel, by the power of his mother, Potema — the so-called Wolf Queen of Solitude. The year after her coronation, Kintyra was trapped in Glenpoint and imprisoned in the Imperial dungeons there.

All of Tamriel exploded into warfare as Prince Uriel took the throne as Uriel III, and High Rock, because of the imprisoned Empress' presence there, was the location of some of the bloodiest battles. Pelagius' father, King Magnus, allied himself with his brother Cephorus against the usurper Emperor, and brought the wrath of Uriel III and Queen Potema down on Wayrest. Pelagius, his brothers and sisters, and his mother Utheilla fled to the Isle of Balfiera. Utheilla was of the line of Direnni, and her family manse is still located on that ancient isle even to this day.

There is thankfully much written record of Pelagius' childhood in Balfiera recorded by nurses and visitors. All who met him described him as a handsome, personable boy, interested in sport, magic, and music. Even assuming diplomats' lack of candor, Pelagius seemed, if anything, a blessing to the future of the Septim Dynasty.

When Pelagius was eight, Cephorus slew Uriel III at the Battle of Ichidag and proclaimed himself Emperor Cephorus I. For the next ten years of his reign, Cephorus battled Potema. Pelagius' first battle was the Siege of Solitude, which ended with Potema's death and the final end of the war. In gratitude, Cephorus placed Pelagius on the throne of Solitude.

As king of Solitude, Pelagius' eccentricities of behavior began to be noticeable. As a favorite nephew of the Emperor, few diplomats to Solitude made critical commentary about Pelagius. For the first two years of his reign, Pelagius was at the very least noted for his alarming shifts in weight. Four months after taking the throne, a diplomat from Ebonheart called Pelagius "a hale and hearty soul with a heart so big, it widens his waist"; five months after that, the visiting princess of Firsthold wrote to her brother that "the king's gripped my hand and it felt like I was being clutched by a skeleton. Pelagius is greatly emaciated, indeed."

Cephorus never married and died childless three years after the Siege of Solitude. As the only surviving sibling, Pelagius' father Magnus left the throne of Wayrest and took residence at the Imperial City as the Emperor Magnus I. Magnus was elderly and Pelagius was his oldest living child, so the attention of Tamriel focused on Sentinel. By this time, Pelagius' eccentricities were becoming infamous.

There are many legends about his acts as King of Sentinel, but few well-documented cases exist. It is known that Pelagius locked the young princes and princesses of Silvenar in his room with him, only releasing them when an unsigned Declaration of War was slipped under the door. When he tore off his clothes during a speech he was giving at a local festival, his advisors apparently decided to watch him more carefully. On the orders of Magnus, Pelagius was married to the beautiful heiress of an ancient Dark Elf noble family, Katariah Ra'athim.

Nordic kings who marry Dark Elves seldom improve their popularity. There are two reasons most scholars give for the union. Magnus was trying to cement relations with Ebonheart, where the Ra'athim clan hailed. Ebonheart's neighbor, Mournhold, had been a historical ally of the Empire since the very beginning, and the royal consort of Queen Barenziah had won many battles in the War of the Red Diamond. Ebonheart had a poorly-kept secret of aiding Uriel III and Potema.

The other reason for the marriage was more personal: Katariah was as shrewd a diplomat as she was beautiful. If any creature was capable of hiding Pelagius' madness, it was she.

On the 8th of Second Seed, 3E 145, Magnus I died quietly in his sleep. Jolethe, Pelagius' sister took over the throne of Solitude, and Pelagius and Katariah rode to the Imperial City to be crowned Emperor and Empress of Tamriel. It is said that Pelagius fainted when the crown was placed on his head, but Katariah held him up so only those closest to the thrones could see what had happened. Like so many Pelagius stories, this cannot be verified.

Pelagius III never truly ruled Tamriel. Katariah and the Elder Council made all the decisions and only tried to keep Pelagius from embarrassing all. Still, stories of Pelagius III's reign exist.

It was said that when the Argonian ambassador from Blackrose came to court, Pelagius insisted on speaking in all grunts and squeaks, as that was the Argonian's natural language.

It is known that Pelagius was obsessed with cleanliness, and many guests reported waking to the noise of an early-morning scrubdown of the Imperial Palace. The legend of Pelagius while inspecting the servants' work, suddenly defecating on the floor to give them something to do, is probably apocryphal.

When Pelagius began actually biting and attacking visitors to the Imperial Palace,

it was decided to send him to a private asylum. Katariah was proclaimed regent two years after Pelagius took the throne. For the next six years, the Emperor stayed in a series of institutions and asylums.

Traitors to the Empire have many lies to spread about this period. Whispered stories of hideous experiments and tortures performed on Pelagius have almost become accepted as fact. The noble lady Katariah became pregnant shortly after the Emperor was sent away, and rumors of infidelity and, even more absurd, conspiracies to keep the sane Emperor locked away, ran amok. As Katariah proved, her pregnancy came about after a visit to her husband's cell. With no other evidence, as loyal subjects, we are bound to accept the Empress' word on the matter. Her second child, who would reign for many years as Uriel IV, was the child of her union with her consort Lariate, and publicly acknowledged as such.

On a warm night in Suns Dawn, in his 34th year, Pelagius III died after a brief fever in his cell at the Temple of Kynareth in the Isle of Betony. Katariah I reigned for another forty six years before passing the scepter onto the only child she had with Pelagius, Cassynder.

Pelagius' wild behavior has made him perversely dear to the province of his birth and death. The 2nd of Suns Dawn, which may or may not be the anniversary of his death (records are not very clear) is celebrated as Mad Pelagius, the time when foolishness of all sorts is encouraged. And so, one of the least desirable Emperors in the history of the Septim Dynasty, has become one of the most famous ones.

A Dance in Fire

by Waughin Jarth

Book 1

Scene: The Imperial City, Cyrodiil
Date: 7 Frost Fall, 3E 397

It seemed as if the palace had always housed the Atrius Building Commission, the company of clerks and estate agents who authored and notarized nearly every construction of any note in the Empire. It had stood for two hundred and fifty years, since the reign of the Emperor Magnus, a plain-fronted and austere hall on a minor but respectable plaza in the Imperial City. Energetic and ambitious middle-class lads and ladies worked there, as well as complacent middle-aged ones like Decumus Scotti. No one could imagine a world without the Commission, least of all Scotti. To be accurate, he could not imagine a world without himself in the Commission.

"Lord Atrius is perfectly aware of your contributions," said the managing clerk, closing the shutter that demarcated Scotti's office behind him. "But you know that things have been difficult."

"Yes," said Scotti, stiffly.

"Lord Vanech's men have been giving us a lot of competition lately, and we must be more efficient if we are to survive. Unfortunately, that means releasing some of our historically best but presently underachieving senior clerks."

"I understand. Can't be helped."

"I'm glad that you understand," smiled the managing clerk, smiling thinly and withdrawing. "Please have your room cleared immediately."

Scotti began the task of organizing all his work to pass on to his successor. It would probably be young Imbrallius who would take most of it on, which was as it should be, he considered philosophically. The lad knew how to find business. Scotti wondered idly what the fellow would do with the contracts for the new statue of St Alessia for which the Temple of the One had applied. Probably invent a clerical error, blame it on his old predecessor Decumus Scotti, and require an additional cost to rectify.

"I have correspondence for Decumus Scotti of the Atrius Building Commission."

Scotti looked up. A fat-faced courier had entered his office and was thrusting forth a sealed scroll. He handed the boy a gold piece, and opened it up. By the poor penmanship, atrocious spelling and grammar, and overall unprofessional tone, it was manifestly evident who the writer was. Liodes Jurus, a fellow clerk some years before, who had left the Commission after being accused of unethical business practices.

"Dear Sckotti,

I emagine you alway wondered what happened to me, and the last plase you would have expected to find me is out in the woods. But thats exactly where I am. Ha ha. If your'e smart and want to make lot of extra gold for Lord Atrius (and yourself, ha ha), youll come down to Vallinwood too. If you have'nt or have been following the politics hear lately, you may or may not know that ther's bin a war between the Boshmer and there neighbors Elswere over the past two years. Things have only just calm down, and ther's a lot that needs to be rebuilt.

Now Ive got more business than I can handel, but I need somone with some clout, someone representing a respected agencie to get the quill in the ink. That somone is you, my fiend. Come & meat me at the M'ther Paskos Tavern in Falinnesti, Vallinwood. Ill be here 2 weeks and you wont be sorrie.

-- Jurus

P.S.: Bring a wagenload of timber if you can."

"What do you have there, Scotti?" asked a voice.

Scotti started. It was Imbrallius, his damnably handsome face peeking through the shutters, smiling in that way that melted the hearts of the stingiest of patrons and the roughest of stonemasons. Scotti shoved the letter in his jacket pocket.

"Personal correspondence," he sniffed. "I'll be cleared up here in a just a moment."

"I don't want to hurry you," said Imbrallius, grabbing a few sheets of blank contracts from Scotti's desk. "I've just gone through a stack, and the junior scribes hands are all cramping up, so I thought you wouldn't miss a few."

The lad vanished. Scotti retrieved the letter and read it again. He thought about his life, something he rarely did. It seemed a sea of gray with a black insurmountable wall looming. There was only one narrow passage he could see in that wall. Quickly, before he had a moment to reconsider it, he grabbed a dozen of the blank contracts with the shimmering gold leaf ATRIUS BUILDING COMMISSION BY APPOINTMENT OF HIS IMPERIAL MAJESTY and hid them in the satchel with his personal effects.

The next day he began his adventure with a giddy lack of hesitation. He arranged for a seat in a caravan bound for Valenwood, the single escorted conveyance to the southeast leaving the Imperial City that week. He had scarcely hours to pack, but he remembered to purchase a wagonload of timber.

"It will be extra gold to pay for a horse to pull that," frowned the convoy head.

"So I anticipated," smiled Scotti with his best Imbrallius grin.

Ten wagons in all set off that afternoon through the familiar Cyrodilic countryside. Past fields of wildflowers, gently rolling woodlands, friendly hamlets. The clop of the horses' hooves against the sound stone road reminded Scotti that the Atrius Building Commission constructed it. Five of the eighteen necessary contracts for its completion were drafted by his own hand.

"Very smart of you to bring that wood along," said a gray-whiskered Breton man next to him on his wagon. "You must be in Commerce."

"Of a sort," said Scotti, in a way he hoped was mysterious, before introducing himself: "Decumus Scotti."

"Gryf Mallon," said the man. "I'm a poet, actually a translator of old Bosmer literature. I was researching some newly discovered tracts of the Mnoriad Pley Bar two years ago when the war broke out and I had to leave. You are no doubt familiar with the Mnoriad, if you're aware of the Green Pact."

Scotti thought the man might be speaking perfect gibberish, but he nodded his head.

"Naturally, I don't pretend that the Mnoriad is as renowned as the Meh Ayleidion, or as ancient as the Dansir Gol, but I think it has a remarkable significance to understanding the nature of the merelithic Bosmer mind. The origin of the Wood Elf aversion to cutting their own wood or eating any plant material at all, yet paradoxically their willingness to import plantstuff from other cultures, I feel can be linked to a passage in the Mnoriad," Mallon shuffled through some of his papers, searching for the appropriate text.

To Scotti's vast relief, the carriage soon stopped to camp for the night. They were high on a bluff over a gray stream, and before them was the great valley of Valenwood. Only the cry of seabirds declared the presence of the ocean to the bay to the west: here the timber was so tall and wide, twisting around itself like an impossible knot begun eons ago, to be impenetrable. A few more modest trees, only fifty feet to the lowest branches, stood on the cliff at the edge of camp. The sight was so alien to Scotti and he found himself so anxious about the proposition of entering the wilderness that he could not imagine sleeping.

Fortunately, Mallon had supposed he had found another academic with a passion for the riddles of ancient cultures. Long into the night, he recited Bosmer verse in the original and in his own translation, sobbing and bellowing and whispering wherever appropriate. Gradually, Scotti began to feel drowsy, but a sudden crack of wood snapping made him sit straight up.

"What was that?"

Mallon smiled: "I like it too. 'Convocation in the malignity of the moonless speculum, a dance of fire —'"

"There are some enormous birds up in the trees moving around," whispered Scotti, pointing in the direction of the dark shapes above.

"I wouldn't worry about that," said Mallon, irritated with his audience. "Now listen to how the poet characterizes Herma-Mora's invocation in the eighteenth stanza of the fourth book."

The dark shapes in the trees were some of them perched like birds, others slithered like snakes, and still others stood up straight like men. As Mallon recited his verse, Scotti watched the figures softly leap from branch to branch, half–gliding across impossible distances for anything without wings. They gathered in groups and then reorganized until they had spread to every tree around the camp. Suddenly they plummeted from the heights.

"Mara!" cried Scotti. "They're falling like rain!"

"Probably seed pods," Mallon shrugged, not turning around. "Some of the trees have remarkable —"

The camp erupted into chaos. Fires burst out in the wagons, the horses wailed from mortal blows, casks of wine, fresh water, and liquor gushed their contents to the ground. A nimble shadow dashed past Scotti and Mallon, gathering sacks of grain and gold with impossible agility and grace. Scotti had only one glance at it, lit up by a sudden nearby burst of flame. It was a sleek creature with pointed ears, wide yellow eyes, mottled pied fur and a tail like a whip.

"Werewolf," he whimpered, shrinking back.

"Cathay-raht," groaned Mallon. "Much worse. Khajiti cousins or some such thing, come to plunder."

"Are you sure?"

As quickly as they struck, the creatures retreated, diving off the bluff before the battlemage and knight, the caravan's escorts, had fully opened their eyes. Mallon and Scotti ran to the precipice and saw a hundred feet below the tiny figures dash out of the water, shake themselves, and disappear into the wood.

"Werewolves aren't acrobats like that," said Mallon. "They were definitely Cathay-raht. Bastard thieves. Thank Stendarr they didn't realize the value of my notebooks. It wasn't a complete loss."

Book 2

It was a complete loss. The Cathay-Raht had stolen or destroyed almost every item of value in the caravan in just a few minutes' time. Decumus Scotti's wagonload of wood he had hoped to trade with the Bosmer had been set on fire and then toppled off the bluff. His clothing and contracts were tattered and ground into the mud of dirt mixed with spilt wine. All the pilgrims, merchants, and adventurers in the group moaned and wept as they gathered the remnants of their belongings by the rising sun of the dawn.

"I best not tell anyone that I managed to hold onto my notes for my translation of the Mnoriad Pley Bar," whispered the poet Gryf Mallon. "They'd probably turn on me."

Scotti politely declined the opportunity of telling Mallon just how little value he himself placed on the man's property. Instead, he counted the coins in his purse. Thirty-four gold pieces. Very little indeed for an entrepreneur beginning a new business.

"Hoy!" came a cry from the wood. A small party of Bosmer emerged from the thicket, clad in leather mail and bearing arms. "Friend or foe?"

"Neither," growled the convoy head.

"You must be the Cyrodiils," laughed the leader of the group, a tall skeleton-thin youth with a sharp vulpine face. "We heard you were en route. Evidently, so did our enemies."

"I thought the war was over," muttered one of the caravan's now ruined merchants.

The Bosmer laughed again: "No act of war. Just a little border enterprise. You are going on to Falinesti?"

"I'm not," the convoy head shook his head. "As far as I'm concerned, my duty is done. No more horses, no more caravan. Just a fat profit loss to me."

The men and women crowded around the man, protesting, threatening, begging, but he refused to step foot in Valenwood. If these were the new times of peace, he said, he'd rather come back for the next war.

Scotti tried a different route and approached the Bosmer. He spoke with an authoritative but friendly voice, the kind he used in negotiations with peevish carpenters: "I don't suppose you'd consider escorting me to Falinesti. I'm a representative for an important Imperial agency, the Atrius Building Commission, here to help repair and alleviate some of the problems the war with the Khajiit brought to your province. Patriotism —"

"Twenty gold pieces, and you must carry your own gear if you have any left," replied the Bosmer.

Scotti reflected that negotiations with peevish carpenters rarely went his way either.

Six eager people had enough gold on them for payment. Among those without funds was the poet, who appealed to Scotti for assistance.

"I'm sorry, Gryf, I only have fourteen gold left over. Not even enough for a decent room when I get to Falinesti. I really would help you if I could," said Scotti, persuading himself that it was true.

The band of six and their Bosmer escorts began the descent down a rocky path along the bluff. Within an hour's time, they were deep in the jungles of Valenwood. A never-ending canopy of hues of browns and greens obscured the sky. A millennia's worth of fallen leaves formed a deep, wormy sea of putrefaction beneath their feet. Several miles were crossed wading through the slime. For several more, they took a labyrinthian path across fallen branches and the low-hanging boughs of giant trees.

All the while, hour after hour, the inexhaustible Bosmer host moved so fast, the Cyrodiils struggled to keep from being left behind. A red-faced little merchant with short legs took a bad step on a rotten branch and nearly fell. His fellow provincials had to help him up. The Bosmer paused only a moment, their eyes continually darting to the shadows in the trees above before moving on at their usual expeditious pace.

"What are they so nervous about?" wheezed the merchant irritably. "More Cathay-Raht?"

"Don't be ridiculous," laughed the Bosmer unconvincingly. "Khajiit this far into Valenwood? In times of peace? They'd never dare."

When the group passed high enough above the swamp that the smell was somewhat dissipated, Scotti felt a sudden pang of hunger. He was used to four meals a day in the Cyrodilic custom. Hours of nonstop exertion without food was not part of his regimen as a comfortably paid clerk. He pondered, feeling somewhat delirious, how long they had been trotting through the jungle. Twelve hours? Twenty? A week? Time was meaningless. Sunlight was only sporadic through the vegetative ceiling. Phosphorescent molds on the trees and in the muck below provided the only regular illumination.

"Is it at all possible for us to rest and eat?" he hollered to his host up ahead.

"We're near to Falinesti," came the echoing reply. "Lots of food there."

The path continued upward for several hours more across a clot of fallen logs, rising up to the first and then the second boughs of the tree line. As they rounded a long corner, the travelers found themselves midway up a waterfall that fell a hundred feet or more. No one had the energy to complain as they began pulling up the stacks of rock, agonizing foot by foot. The Bosmer escorts disappeared into the mist, but Scotti kept climbing until there was no more rock left. He wiped the sweat and river water from his eyes.

Falinesti spread across the horizon before him. Sprawling across both banks of the river stood the mighty graht-oak city, with groves and orchards of lesser trees crowding it like supplicants before their king. At a lesser scale, the tree that formed the moving city would have been extraordinary: gnarled and twisted with a gorgeous crown of gold and green, dripping with vines and shining with sap. At a mile tall and half as wide, it was the most magnificent thing Scotti had ever seen. If he had not been a starving man with the soul of a clerk, he would have sung.

"There you are," said the leader of the escorts. "Not too far a walk. You should be glad it's wintertide. In summertide, the city's on the far south end of the province."

Scotti was lost as to how to proceed. The sight of the vertical metropolis where people moved about like ants disoriented all his sensibilities.

"You wouldn't know of an inn called," he paused for a moment, and then pulled Jurus's

letter from his pocket. "Something like 'Mother Paskos Tavern'?"

"Mother Pascost?" the lead Bosmer laughed his familiar contemptuous laugh. "You won't want to stay there? Visitors always prefer the Aysia Hall in the top boughs. It's expensive, but very nice."

"I'm meeting someone at Mother Pascost's Tavern."

"If you've made up your mind to go, take a lift to Havel Slump and ask for directions there. Just don't get lost and fall asleep in the western cross."

This apparently struck the youth's friends as a very witty jest, and so it was with their laughter echoing behind him that Scotti crossed the writhing root system to the base of Falinesti. The ground was littered with leaves and refuse, and from moment to moment a glass or a bone would plummet from far above, so he walked with his neck crooked to have warning. An intricate network of platforms anchored to thick vines slipped up and down the slick trunk of the city with perfect grace, manned by operators with arms as thick as an ox's belly. Scotti approaches the nearest fellow at one of the platforms, who was idly smoking from a glass pipe.

"I was wondering if you might take me to Havel Slump."

The mer nodded and within a few minutes time, Scotti was two hundred feet in the air at a crook between two mighty branches. Curled webs of moss stretched unevenly across the fork, forming a sharing roof for several dozen small buildings. There were only a few souls in the alley, but around the bend ahead, he could hear the sound of music and people. Scotti tipped the Falinesti Platform Ferryman a gold piece and asked for the location of Mother Pascost's Tavern.

"Straight ahead of you, sir, but you won't find anyone there," the Ferryman explained, pointing in the direction of the noise. "Morndas everyone in Havel Slump has revelry."

Scotti walked carefully along the narrow street. Though the ground felt as solid as the marble avenues of the Imperial City, there were slick cracks in the bark that exposed fatal drops into the river. He took a moment to sit down, to rest and get used to the view from the heights. It was a beautiful day for certain, but it took Scotti only a few minutes of contemplation to rise up in alarm. A jolly little raft anchored down stream below him had distinctly moved several inches while he watched it. But it hadn't moved at all. He had. Together with everything around him. It was no metaphor: the city of Falinesti walked. And, considering its size, it moved quickly.

Scotti rose to his feet and into a cloud of smoke that drifted out from around the bend. It was the most delicious roast he had ever smelled. The clerk forgot his fear and ran.

The "revelry" as the Ferryman had termed it took place on an enormous platform tied to the tree, wide enough to be a plaza in any other city. A fantastic assortment of the most amazing people Scotti had ever seen were jammed shoulder-to-shoulder together, many eating, many more drinking, and some dancing to a lutist and singer perched on an offshoot above the crowd. They were largely Bosmer, true natives clad in colorful leather and bones, with a close minority of orcs. Whirling through the throng, dancing and bellowing at one another were a hideous ape people. A few heads bobbing over the tops of the crowd belonged not, as Scotti first assumed, to very tall people, but to a family of centaurs.

"Care for some mutton?" queried a wizened old mer who roasted an enormous beast on some red-hot rocks.

Scotti quickly paid him a gold piece and devoured the leg he was given. And then another gold piece and another leg. The fellow chuckled when Scotti began choking on a piece of gristle, and handed him a mug of a frothing white drink. He drank it and felt a quiver run through his body as if he were being tickled.

"What is that?" Scotti asked.

"Jagga. Fermented pig's milk. I can let you have a flagon of it and a bit more mutton for another gold."

Scotti agreed, paid, gobbled down the meat, and took the flagon with him as he slipped into the crowd. His co-worker Liodes Jurus, the man who had told him to come to Valenwood, was nowhere to be seen. When the flagon was a quarter empty, Scotti stopped looking for Jurus. When it was half empty, he was dancing with the group, oblivious to the broken planks and gaps in the fencework. At three quarters empty, he was trading jokes with a group of creatures whose language was completely alien to him. By the time the flagon was completely drained, he was asleep, snoring, while the revelry continued on all around his supine body.

The next morning, still asleep, Scotti had the sensation of someone kissing him. He made a face to return the favor, but a pain like fire spread through his chest and forced him to open his eyes. There was an insect the size of a large calf sitting on him, crushing him, its spiky legs holding him down while a central spiral-bladed vortex of a mouth tore through his shirt. He screamed and thrashed but the beast was too strong. It had found its meal and it was going to finish it.

It's over, thought Scotti wildly, I should have never left home. I could have stayed in the City, and perhaps found work with Lord Vanech. I could have begun again as a junior clerk and worked my way back up.

Suddenly the mouth released itself. The creature shivered once, expelled a burst of yellow bile, and died.

"Got one!" cried a voice, not too distantly.

For a moment, Scotti lay still. His head throbbed and his chest burned. Out of the corner of his eye he saw movement. Another of the horrible monsters was scurried towards him. He scrambled, trying to push himself free, but before he could come out, there was a sound of a bow cracking and an arrow pierced the second insect.

"Good shot!" cried another voice. "Get the first one again! I just saw it move a little!"

This time, Scotti felt the impact of the bolt hit the carcass. He cried out, but he could hear how muffled his voice was by the beetle's body. Cautiously, he tried sliding a foot out and rolling under, but the movement apparently had the effect of convincing the archers that the creature still lived. A volley of arrows was launched forth. Now the beast was sufficiently perforated so pools of its blood, and likely the blood of its victims, began to seep out onto Scotti's body.

When Scotti was a lad, before he grew too sophisticated for such sports, he had often gone to the Imperial Arena for the competitions of war. He recalled a great veteran of the fights, when asked, telling him his secret, "Whenever I'm in doubt of what to do, and I have a shield, I stay behind it."

Scotti followed that advice. After an hour, when he no longer heard arrows being fired, he threw aside the remains of the bug and leapt as quickly as he could to a stand. It was not a moment too soon. A gang of eight archers had their bows pointing his direction, ready to fire. When they saw him, they laughed.

"Didn't anyone ever tell you not to sleep in the western cross? How're we going to exterminate all the hoarvors if you drunks keep feeding 'em?"

Scotti shook his head and walked back along the platform, round the bend, to Havel Slump. He was bloodied and torn and tired and he had far too much fermented pig's milk. All he wanted was a proper place to lie down. He stepped into Mother Pascost's Tavern, a dank place, wet with sap, smelling of mildew.

"My name is Decumus Scotti," he said. "I was hoping you have someone named Jurus staying here."

"Decumus Scotti?" pondered the fleshy proprietress, Mother Pascost herself. "I've heard that name. Oh, you must be the fellow he left the note for. Let me go see if I can find it."

Book 3

Mother Pascost disappeared into the sordid hole that was her tavern, and emerged a moment later with a scrap of paper with Liodes Jurus's familiar scrawl. Decumus Scotti held it up before a patch of sunlight that had found its way through the massive boughs of the tree city, and read.

Sckotti,

So you made it to Falinnesti, Vallinwood! Congradulatens! Im sure you had quit a adventure getting here. Unfortonitly, Im not here anymore as you probaby guess. Theres a town down rivver called Athie Im at. Git a bote and join me! Its ideal! I hope you brot a lot of contracks, cause these peple need a lot of building done. They wer close to the war, you see, but not so close they dont have any mony left to pay. Ha ha. Meat me down here as son as you can.

Jurus

So, Scotti pondered, Jurus had left Falinesti and gone to some place called Athie.

Given his poor penmanship and ghastly spelling, it could equally well be Athy, Aphy, Othry, Imthri, Urtha, or Krakamaka. The sensible thing to do, Scotti knew, was to call this adventure over and try to find some way to get back home to the Imperial City. He was no mercenary devoted to a life of thrills: he was, or at least had been, a senior clerk at a successful private building commission. Over the last few weeks, he had been robbed by the Cathay–Raht, taken on a death march through the jungle by a gang of giggling Bosmeri, half–starved to death, drugged with fermented pig's milk, nearly slain by some kind of giant tick, and attacked by archers. He was filthy, exhausted, and had, he counted, ten gold pieces to his name. Now the man whose proposal brought him to the depths of misery was not even there. It was both judicious and seemly to abandon the enterprise entirely.And yet, a small but distinct voice in his head told him: You have been chosen. You have no other choice but to see this through.

Scotti turned to the stout old woman, Mother Pascost, who had been watching him curiously: "I was wondering if you knew of a village that was at the edge of the recent conflict with Elsweyr. It's called something like Ath–ie?"

"You must mean Athay," she grinned. "My middle lad, Viglil, he manages a dairy down there. Beautiful country, right on the river. Is that where your friend went?"

"Yes," said Scotti. "Do you know the fastest way to get there?"

After a short conversation, an even shorter ride to Falinesti's roots by way of the platforms, and a jog to the river bank, Scotti was negotiating transport with a huge fair–haired Bosmer with a face like a pickled carp. He called himself Captain Balfix, but even Scotti with his sheltered life could recognize him for what he was. A retired pirate for hire, a smuggler for certain, and probably much worse. His ship, which had clearly been stolen in the distant past, was a bent old Imperial sloop.

"Fifty gold and we'll be in Athay in two days time," boomed Captain Balfix expansively.

"I have ten, no, sorry, nine gold pieces," replied Scotti, and feeling the need for explanation, added, "I had ten, but I gave one to the Platform Ferryman to get me down here."

"Nine is just as fine," said the captain agreeably. "Truth be told, I was going to Athay whether you paid me or not. Make yourself comfortable on the boat, we'll be leaving in just a few minutes."

Decumus Scotti boarded the vessel, which sat low in the water of the river, stacked high with crates and sacks that spilled out of the hold and galley and onto the deck. Each was marked with stamps advertising the most innocuous substances: copper scraps, lard, ink, High Rock meal (marked "For Cattle"), tar, fish jelly. Scotti's imagination reeled picturing what sorts of illicit imports were truly aboard.

It took more than those few minutes for Captain Balfix to haul in the rest of his cargo, but in an hour, the anchor was up and they were sailing downriver towards Athay. The green gray water barely rippled, only touched by the fingers of the breeze. Lush plant life crowded the banks, obscuring from sight all the animals that sang and roared at one another. Lulled by the serene surroundings, Scotti drifted to sleep.

At night, he awoke and gratefully accepted some clean clothes and food from Captain Balfix.

"Why are you going to Athay, if I may ask?" queried the Bosmer.

"I'm meeting a former colleague there. He asked me to come down from the Imperial City where I worked for the Atrius Building Commission to negotiate some contracts," Scotti took another bite of the dried sausages they were sharing for dinner. "We're going to try to repair and refurbish whatever bridges, roads, and other structures that got damaged in the recent war with the Khajiiti."

"It's been a hard two years," the captain nodded his head. "Though I suppose good for me and the likes of you and your friend. Trade routes cut off. Now they think there's going to be war with the Summurset Isles, you heard that?"

Scotti shook his head.

"I've done my share of smuggling skooma down the coast, even helping some revolutionary types escape the Mane's wrath, but now the wars've made me a legitimate trader, a business-man. The first casualties of war is always the corrupted."

Scotti said he was sorry to hear that, and they lapsed into silence, watching the stars and moons' reflection on the still water. The next day, Scotti awoke to find the captain wrapped up in his sail, torpid from alcohol, singing in a low, slurred voice. When he saw Scotti rise, he offered his flagon of jagga.

"I learned my lesson during revelry at western cross."

The captain laughed, and then burst into tears, "I don't want to be legitimate. Other pirates I used to know are still raping and stealing and smuggling and selling nice folk like you into slavery. I swear to you, I never thought the first time that I ran a real shipment of legal goods that my life would turn out like this. Oh, I know, I could go back to it, but Baan Dar knows not after all I've seen. I'm a ruined man."

Scotti helped the weeping mer out of the sail, murmuring words of reassurance. Then he added, "Forgive me for changing the subject, but where are we?"

"Oh," moaned Captain Balfix miserably. "We made good time. Athay's right around the bend in the river."

"Then it looks like Athay's on fire," said Scotti, pointing.

A great plume of smoke black as pitch was rising above the trees. As they drifted around the bend, they next saw the flames, and then the blackened skeletal remains of the village. Dying, blazing villagers leapt from rocks into the river. A cacophony of wailing met their ears, and they could see, roaming along the edges of the town, the figures of Khajiiti soldiers bearing torches.

"Baan Dar bless me!" slurred the captain. "The war's back on!"

"Oh, no," whimpered Scotti.

The sloop drifted with the current toward the opposite shore away from the fiery town. Scotti turned his attention there, and the sanctuary it offered. Just a peaceful arbor, away from the horror. There was a shudder of leaves in two of the trees and a dozen lithe Khajiit dropped to the ground, armed with bows.

"They see us," hissed Scotti. "And they've got bows!"

"Well, of course they have bows," snarled Captain Balfix. "We Bosmer may have invented the bloody things, but we didn't think to keep them secret, you bloody bureaucrat."

"Now, they're setting their arrows on fire!"

"Yes, they do that sometimes."

"Captain, they're shooting at us! They're shooting at us with flaming arrows!"

"Ah, so they are," the captain agreed. "The aim here is to avoid being hit."

But hit they were, and very shortly thereafter. Even worse, the second volley of arrows hit the supply of pitch, which ignited in a tremendous blue blaze. Scotti grabbed Captain Balfix and they leapt overboard just before the ship and all its cargo disintegrated. The shock of the cold water brought the Bosmer into temporary sobriety. He called to Scotti, who was already swimming as fast as he could toward the bend.

"Master Decumus, where do you think you're swimming to?"

"Back to Falinesti!" cried Scotti.

"It will take you days, and by the time you get there, everyone will know about the attack on Athay! They'll never let anyone they don't know in! The closest village downriver is Grenos, maybe they'll give us shelter!"

Scotti swam back to the captain and side-by-side they began paddling in the middle of the river, past the burning residuum of the village. He thanked Mara that he had learned to swim. Many a Cyrodiil did not, as largely land-locked as the Imperial Province was. Had he been raised in Mir Corrup or Artemon, he might have been doomed, but the Imperial City itself was encircled by water, and every lad and lass there knew how to cross without a boat. Even those who grew up to be clerks and not adventurers.

Captain Balfix's sobriety faded as he grew used to the water's temperature. Even in wintertide, the Xylo River was fairly temperate and after a fashion, even comfortable. The Bosmer's strokes were uneven, and he'd stray closer to Scotti and then further away, pushing ahead and then falling behind.

Scotti looked to the shore to his right: the flames had caught the trees like tinder. Behind them was an inferno, with which they were barely keeping pace. To the shore on their left, all looked fair, until he saw a tremble in the river-reeds, and then what caused it. A pride of the largest cats he had ever seen. They were auburn-haired, green-eyed beasts with jaws and teeth to match his wildest nightmares. And they were watching the two swimmers, and keeping pace.

"Captain Balfix, we can't go to either that shore or the other one, or we'll be parboiled or eaten," Scotti whispered. "Try to even your kicking and your strokes. Breath like you would normally. If you're feeling tired, tell me, and we'll float on our backs for a while."

Anyone who has had the experience of giving rational advice to a drunkard would understand the hopelessness. Scotti kept pace with the captain, slowing himself, quickening, drifting left and right, while the Bosmer moaned old ditties from his pirate days. When he wasn't watching his companion, he watched the cats on the shore. After a stretch, he turned to his right. Another village had caught fire. Undoubtedly, it was Grenos. Scotti stared at the blazing fury, awed by the sight of the destruction, and did not hear that the captain had ceased to sing.

When he turned back, Captain Balfix was gone.

Scotti dove into the murky depths of the river over and over again. There was nothing to be done. When he surfaced after his final search, he saw that the giant cats had moved on, perhaps assuming that he too had drowned. He continued his lonely swim downriver. A tributary, he noted, had formed a final barrier, keeping the flames from spreading further. But there were no more towns. After several hours, he began to ponder the wisdom of going ashore. Which shore was the question.

He was spared the decision. Ahead of him was a rocky island with a bonfire. He did not know if he were intruding on a party of Bosmeri or Khajiiti, only that he could swim no more. With straining, aching muscles, he pulled himself onto the rocks.

They were Bosmer refugees he gathered, even before they told him. Roasting over the fire was the remains of one of the giant cats that had been stalking him through the jungle on the opposite shore.

"Senche-Tiger," said one of the young warriors ravenously. "It's no animal — it's as smart as any Cathay-Raht or Ohmes or any other bleeding Khajiiti. Pity this one drowned. I would have gladly killed it. You'll like the meat, though. Sweet, from all the sugar these asses eat."

Scotti did not know if he was capable of eating a creature as intelligent as a man or mer, but he surprised himself, as he had done several times over the last days. It was rich, succulent, and sweet, like sugared pork, but no seasonings had been added. He surveyed the crowd as he ate. A sad lot, some still weeping for lost family members. They were the survivors of both the villages of Grenos and Athay, and war was on every person's lips. Why had the Khajiiti attacked again? Why — specifically directed at Scotti, as a Cyrodiil — why was the Emperor not enforcing peace in his provinces?

"I was to meet another Cyrodiil," he said to a Bosmer maiden who he understood to be from Athay. "His name was Liodes Jurus. I don't suppose you know what might have happened to him."

"I don't know your friend, but there were many Cyrodiils in Athay when the fire came," said the girl. "Some of them, I think, left quickly. They were going to Vindisi, inland, in the jungle. I am going there tomorrow, so are many of us. If you wish, you may come as well."

Decumus Scotti nodded solemnly. He made himself as comfortable as he could in the stony ground of the river island, and somehow, after much effort, he fell asleep. But he did not sleep well.

Book 4

Eighteen Bosmeri and one Cyrodilic former senior clerk for an Imperial building commission trudged through the jungle westward from the Xylo River to the ancient village of Vindisi. For Decumus Scotti, the jungle was hostile, unfamiliar ground. The enormous vermiculated trees filled the bright morning with darkness, and resembled

nothing so much as grasping claws, bent on impeding their progress. Even the fronds of the low plants quivered with malevolent energy. What was worse, he was not alone in his anxiety. His fellow travelers, the natives who had survived the Khajiit attacks on the villages of Grenos and Athay, wore faces of undisguised fear.

There was something sentient in the jungle, and not merely the mad but benevolent indigenous spirits. In his peripheral vision, Scotti could see the shadows of the Khajiiti following the refugees, leaping from tree to tree. When he turned to face them, the lithe forms vanished into the gloom as if they had never been there. But he knew he had seen them. And the Bosmeri saw them too, and quickened their pace.

After eighteen hours, bitten raw by insects, scratched by a thousand thorns, they emerged into a valley clearing. It was night, but a row of blazing torches greeted them, illuminating the leather-wrought tents and jumbled stones of the hamlet of Vindisi. At the end of the valley, the torches marked a sacred site, a gnarled bower of trees pressed closed together to form a temple. Wordlessly, the Bosmeri walked the torch arcade toward the trees. Scotti followed them. When they reached the solid mass of living wood with only one gaping portal, Scotti could see a dim blue light glowing within. A low sonorous moan from a hundred voices echoed within. The Bosmeri maiden he had been following held out her hand, stopping him.

"You do not understand, but no outsider, not even a friend may enter," she said. "This is a holy place."

Scotti nodded, and watched the refugees march into the temple, heads bowed. Their voices joined with the ones within. When the last wood elf had gone inside, Scotti turned his attention back to the village. There must be food to be had somewhere. A tendril of smoke and a faint whiff of roasting venison beyond the torchlight led him.

They were five Cyrodiils, two Bretons, and a Nord, the group gathered around a campfire of glowing white stones, pulling steaming strips of meat from the cadaver of a great stag. At Scotti's approach, they rose up, all but the Nord who was distracted by his hunk of animal flesh.

"Good evening, sorry to interrupt, but I was wondering if I might have a little something to eat. I'm afraid I'm rather hungry, after walking all day with some refugees from Grenos and Athay."

They bade him to sit down and eat, and introduced themselves.

"So the war's back on, it seems," said Scotti amiably.

"Best thing for these effete do-nothings," replied the Nord in between bites. "I've never seen such a lazy culture. Now they've got the Khajiiti striking them on land, and the high elves at sea. If there's any province that deserves a little distress, it's damnable Valenwood."

"I don't see how they're so offensive to you," laughed one of the Bretons.

"They're congenital thieves, even worse than the Khajiiti because they are so blessed meek in their aggression," the Nord spat out a gob of fat which sizzled on the hot stones of the fire. "They spread their forests into territory that doesn't belong to them, slowly infiltrating their neighbors, and they're puzzled when Elsweyr shoves back at them. They're all villains of the worst order."

"What are you doing here?" asked Scotti.

"I'm a diplomat from the court of Jehenna," muttered the Nord, returning to his food.

"What about you, what are you doing here?" asked one of the Cyrodiils.

"I work for Lord Atrius's building commission in the Imperial City," said Scotti. "One of my former colleagues suggested that I come down to Valenwood. He said the war was over, and I could contract a great deal of business for my firm rebuilding what was lost. One disaster after another, and I've lost all my money, I'm in the middle of a rekindling of war, and I cannot find my former colleague."

"Your former colleague," murmured another of the Cyrodiils, who had introduced himself as Reglius. "He wasn't by any chance named Liodes Jurus, was he?"

"You know him?"

"He lured me down to Valenwood in nearly the exact same circumstances," smiled Reglius, grimly. "I worked for your employer's competitor, Lord Vanech's men, where Liodes Jurus also formerly worked. He wrote to me, asking that I represent an Imperial building commission and contract some post-war construction. I had just been released from my employment, and I thought that if I brought some new business, I could have my job back. Jurus and I met in Athay, and he said he was going to arrange a very lucrative meeting with the Silvenar."

Scotti was stunned: "Where is he now?"

"I'm no theologian, so I couldn't say," Reglius shrugged. "He's dead. When the Khajiiti attacked Athay, they began by torching the harbor where Jurus was readying his boat. Or, I should say, my boat since it was purchased with the gold I brought. By the time we were even aware of what was happening enough to flee, everything by the water was ash. The Khajiiti may be animals, but they know how to arrange an attack."

"I think they followed us through the jungle to Vindisi," said Scotti nervously. "There was definitely a group of something jumping along the treetops."

"Probably one of the monkey folk," snorted the Nord. "Nothing to be concerned about."

"When we first came to Vindisi and the Bosmeri all entered that tree, they were furious, whispering something about unleashing an ancient terror on their enemies," the Breton shivered, remembering. "They've been there ever since, for over a day and a half now. If you want something to be afraid of, that's the direction to look."

The other Breton, who was a representative of the Daggerfall Mages Guild, was staring off into the darkness while his fellow provincial spoke. "Maybe. But there's something in the jungle too, right on the edge of the village, looking in."

"More refugees maybe?" asked Scotti, trying to keep the alarm out his voice.

"Not unless they're traveling through the trees now," whispered the wizard. The Nord and one of the Cyrodiils grabbed a long tarp of wet leather and pulled it across the fire, instantly extinguishing it without so much as a sizzle. Now Scotti could see the intruders, their elliptical yellow eyes and long cruel blades catching the torchlight. He froze with fear, praying that he too was not so visible to them.

He felt something bump against his back, and gasped.

Reglius's voice hissed from up above: "Be quiet for Mara's sake and climb up here."

Scotti grabbed hold of the knotted double-vine that hung down from a tall tree at the edge of the dead campfire. He scrambled up it as quickly as he could, holding his breath lest any grunt of exertion escape him. At the top of the vine, high above the village, was an abandoned nest from some great bird in a trident-shaped branch. As soon as Scotti had pulled himself into the soft, fragrant straw, Reglius pulled up the vine. No one else was there, and when Scotti looked down, he could see no one below. No one, that is except the Khajiiti, slowly moving toward the glow of the temple tree.

"Thank you," whispered Scotti, deeply touched that a competitor had helped him. He turned away from the village, and saw that the tree's upper branches brushed against the mossy rock walls that surrounded the valley below. "How are you at climbing?"

"You're mad," said Reglius under his breath. "We should stay here until they leave."

"If they burn Vindisi like they did Athay and Grenos, we'll be dead sure as if we were on the ground," Scotti began the slow careful climb up the tree, testing each branch. "Can you see what they're doing?"

"I can't really tell," Reglius stared down into the gloom. "They're at the front of the temple. I think they also have ... it looks like long ropes, trailing off behind them, off into the pass."

Scotti crawled onto the strongest branch that pointed toward the wet, rocky face of the cliff. It was not a far jump at all. So close, in fact, that he could smell the moisture and feel the coolness of the stone. But it was a jump nevertheless, and in his history as a clerk, he had never before leapt from a tree a hundred feet off the ground to a sheer rock. He pictured in his mind's eye the shadows that had pursued him through the jungle from the heights above. How their legs coiled to spring, how their arms snapped forward in an elegant fluid motion to grasp. He leapt.

His hands grappled for rock, but long thick cords of moss were more accessible. He held hard, but when he tried to plant his feet forward, they slipped up skyward. For a few seconds, he found himself upside down before he managed to pull himself into a more conventional position. There was a narrow outcropping jutting out of the cliff where he could stand and finally exhale.

"Reglius. Reglius. Reglius," Scotti did not dare to call out. In a minute, there was a shaking of branches, and Lord Vanech's man emerged. First his satchel, then his head, then the rest of him. Scotti started to whisper something, but Reglius shook his head violently and pointed downward. One of the Khajiiti was at the base of the tree, peering at the remains of the campfire.

Reglius awkwardly tried to balance himself on the branch, but as strong as it was it was exceedingly difficult with only one free hand. Scotti cupped his palms and then pointed at the satchel. It seemed to pain Reglius to let it out of his grasp, but he relented and tossed it to Scotti.

There was a small, almost invisible hole in the bag, and when Scotti caught it, a single gold coin dropped out. It rang as it bounced against the rock wall on the descent, a high soft sound that seemed like the loudest alarm Scotti had ever heard.

Then many things happened very quickly.

The Cathay-Raht at the base of the tree looked up and gave a loud wail. The other Khajiiti followed in chorus, as the cat below crouched down and then sprung up into the lower branches. Reglius saw it below him, climbing up with impossible dexterity, and panicked. Even before he jumped, Scotti could tell that he was going to fall. With a cry, Reglius the Clerk plunged to the ground, breaking his neck on impact.

A flash of white fire erupted from every crevice of the temple, and the moan of the Bosmeri prayer changed into something terrible and otherworldly. The climbing Cathay-Raht stopped and stared.

"Keirgo," it gasped. "The Wild Hunt."

It was as if a crack in reality had opened wide. A flood of horrific beasts, tentacled toads, insects of armor and spine, gelatinous serpents, vaporous beings with the face of gods, all poured forth from the great hollow tree, blind with fury. They tore the Khajiiti in front of the temple to pieces. All the other cats fled for the jungle, but as they did so, they began pulling on the ropes they carried. In a few seconds time, the entire village of Vindisi was boiling with the lunatic apparitions of the Wild Hunt.

Over the babbling, barking, howling horde, Scotti heard the Cyrodiils in hiding cry out as they were devoured. The Nord too was found and eaten, and both Bretons. The wizard had turned himself invisible, but the swarm did not rely on their sight. The tree the Cathay-Raht was in began to sway and rock from the impossible violence beneath it. Scotti looked at the Khajiiti's fear-struck eyes, and held out one of the cords of moss.

The cat's face showed its pitiful gratitude as it leapt for the vine. It didn't have time to entirely replace that expression when Scotti pulled back the cord, and watched it fall. The Hunt consumed it to the bone before it struck the ground.

Scotti's own jump up to the next outcropping of rock was immeasurably more successful. From there, he pulled himself to the top of the cliff and was able to look down into the chaos that had been the village of Vindisi. The Hunt's mass had grown and began to spill out through the pass out of the valley, pursuing the fleeing Khajiiti. It was then that the madness truly began.

In the moons' light, from Scotti's vantage, he could see where the Khajiiti had attached their ropes. With a thunderous boom, an avalanche of boulders poured over the pass. When the dust cleared, he saw that the valley had been sealed. The Wild Hunt had nowhere to turn but on itself.

Scotti turned his head, unable to bear to look at the cannibalistic orgy. The night jungle stood before him, a web of wood. He slung Reglius's satchel over his shoulder, and entered.

Book 5

"Soap! The forest will eat love! Straight ahead! Stupid and a stupid cow!"

The voice boomed out so suddenly that Decumus Scotti jumped. He stared off into the dim jungle glade from which he only heard animal and insect calls, and the low whistling of wind moments before. It was a queer, oddly accented voice of indiscriminate gender, tremulous in its modulations, but unmistakably human. Or, at very least, elven. An isolated Bosmer perhaps with a poor grasp of the Cyrodilic language. After countless hours of plodding through the dense knot of Valenwood jungle, any voice of slight familiarity sounded wondrous.

"Hello?" he cried.

"Beetles on any names? Certainly yesterday yes!" the voice called back. "Who, what, and when, and mice!"

"I'm afraid I don't understand," replied Scotti, turning toward the brambled tree, thick as a wagon, where the voice had issued. "But you needn't be afraid of me. My name is Decumus Scotti. I'm a Cyrodiil from the Imperial City. I came here to help rebuild Valenwood after the war, you see, and now I'm rather lost."

"Gemstones and grilled slaves ... The war," moaned the voice and broke down into sobs.

"You know about the war? I wasn't sure, I wasn't even sure how far away from the border I am now," Scotti began slowly walking toward the tree. He dropped Reglius's satchel to the ground, and held out his empty hands. "I'm unarmed. I only want to know the way to the closest town. I'm trying to meet my friend, Liodes Jurus, in Silvenar."

"Silvenar!" the voice laughed. It laughed even louder as Scotti circled the tree. "Worms and wine! Worms and wine! Silvenar sings for worms and wine!"

There was nothing to be found anywhere around the tree. "I don't see you. Why are you hiding?"

In frustration born of hunger and exhaustion, he struck the tree trunk. A sudden shiver of gold and red erupted from a hollow nook above, and Scotti was surrounded by six winged creatures scarcely more than a few inches long. Bright crimson eyes were set on either side of tunnel-like protuberances, the animals' always open mouths. They were legless, and their thin, rapidly beating, aureate wings seemed poorly constructed to transport their fat, swollen bellies. And yet, they darted through the air like sparks from a fire. Whirling about the poor clerk, they began chattering what he now understood to be perfect nonsense.

"Wines and worms, how far from the border am I! Academic garnishments, and alas, Liodes Jurus!"

"Hello, I'm afraid I'm unarmed? Smoken flames and the closest town is dear Oblivion."

"Swollen on bad meat, an indigo nimbus, but you needn't be afraid of me!"

"Why are you hiding? Why are you hiding? Before I begin to friend, love me, Lady Zuleika!"

Furious with the mimics, Scotti swung his arms, driving them up into the treetops. He stomped back to the clearing and opened up the satchel again, as he had done some hours before. There was still, unsurprisingly, nothing useful in the bag, and nothing to eat in any corner or pocket. A goodly amount of gold (he smiled grimly, as he had done before, at the irony of being financially solvent in the jungle), a stack of neat blank contracts from Lord Vanech's building commission, some thin cord, and an oiled leather cloak for bad weather. At least, Scotti considered, he had not suffered rain.

A rolling moan of thunder reminded Scotti of what he had suspected for some weeks now. He was cursed.

Within an hour's time, he was wearing the cloak and clawing his way through mud. The trees, which had earlier allowed no sunlight in, provided no shelter against the pounding storm and wind. The only sounds that pierced the pelting of the rain were the mocking calls of the flying creatures, flitting just above, babbling their nonsense. Scotti bellowed at them, threw rocks, but they seemed enamored of his company.

While he was reaching to grab a promising looking stone to hurl at his tormentors, Scotti felt something shift beneath his feet. Wet but solid ground suddenly liquefied and became a rolling tide, rushing him forward. Light as a leaf, he flew head over feet over head, until the mudflow dropped and he continued forward, plunging down into a river twenty-five feet below.

The storm passed quite as instantly as it had arrived. The sun melted the dark clouds and warmed Scotti as he swam for the shore. There, another sign of the Khajiiti incursion into Valenwood greeted him. A small fishing village had stood there once, so recently extinct that it smoldered like a still-warm corpse. Dirt cairns that had once housed fish by the smell of them had been ravaged, their bounty turned to ash. Rafts and skiffs lay broken, scuttled, half-submerged. All the villagers were no more, either dead or refugees far away. Or so he presumed. Something banged against the wall of one of the ruins. Scotti ran to investigate.

"My name is Decumus Scotti?" sang the first winged beast. "I'm a Cyrodiil from? The Imperial City? I came here to help rebuild Valenwood after the war, you see, and now I'm rather lost?"

"I swell to maculate, apeneck!" agreed one of its companions. "I don't see you. Why are you hiding?"

As they fell into chattering, Scotti began to search the rest of the village. Surely the cats had left something behind, a scrap of dried meat, a morsel of fish sausage, anything. But they had been immaculate in their complete annihilation. There was nothing to eat anywhere. Scotti did find one item of possible use under the tumbled remains of a stone hut. A bow and two arrows made of bone. The string had been lost, likely burned away in the heat of the fire, but he pulled the cord from Reglius's satchel and restrung it.

The creatures flew over and hovered nearby as he worked: "The convent of the sacred Liodes Jurus?"

"You know about the war! Worms and wine, circumscribe a golden host, apeneck!"

The moment the cord was taut, Scotti nocked an arrow and swung around, pulling the string tight against his chest. The winged beasts, having had experience with archers before, shot off in all directions in a blur. They needn't have bothered. Scotti's first arrow dove into the ground three feet in front of him. He swore and retrieved it. The mimics, having likewise had experience with poor archers before, returned at once to hovering nearby and mocking Scotti.

On his second shot, Scotti did much better, in purely technical terms. He remembered how the archers in Falinesti looked when he pulled himself out from under the hoarvor tick, and they were all taking aim at him. He extended his left hand, right hand, and right elbow in a symmetrical line, drawing the bow so his hand touched his jawline, and he could see the creature in his sight like the arrow was a finger he was pointing with. The bolt missed the target by only two feet, but it continued on its trajectory, snapping when it struck a rock wall.

Scotti walked to the river's edge. He had only one arrow left, and perhaps, he considered, it would be most practical to find a slow-moving fish and fire it on that. If he missed, at least there was less of a chance of breaking the shaft, and he could always retrieve it from the water. A rather torpid, whiskered fish rolled by, and he took aim at it.

"My name is Decumus Scotti!" one of the creatures howled, frightening the fish away. "Stupid and a stupid cow! Will you dance a dance in fire!"

Scotti turned and aimed the arrow as he had done before. This time, however, he remembered to plant his feet as the archers had done, seven inches apart, knees straight, left leg slightly forward to meet the angle of his right shoulder. He released the last arrow.

The arrow also proved a serviceable prong for roasting the creature against the smoking hot stones of one of the ruins. Its other companions had disappeared instantly after the beast was slain, and Scotti was able to dine in peace. The meat proved to be delicious, if scarcely more than a first course. He was picking the last of it from the bones, when a boat sailed into view from around the bend of the river. At the helm were Bosmer sailors. Scotti ran to the bank and waved his arms. They averted their eyes and continued past.

"You bloody, callous bastards!" Scotti howled. "Knaves! Hooligans! Apenecks! Scoundrels!"

A gray-whiskered form came out from a hatch, and Scotti immediately recognized him as Gryf Mallon, the poet translator he had met in the caravan from Cyrodiil.

He peered Scotti's direction, and his eyes lit up with delight, "Decumus Scotti! Precisely the man I hoped to see! I want to get your thoughts on a rather puzzling passage in the Mnoriad Pley Bar! It begins 'I went weeping into the world, searching for wonders,' perhaps you're familiar with it?"

"I'd like nothing better than to discuss the Mnoriad Pley Bar with you, Gryf!" Scotti called back. "Would you let me come aboard though first?"

Overjoyed at being on a ship bound for any port at all, Scotti was true to his word. For over an hour as the boat rolled down the river past the blackened remnants of Bosmeri villages, he asked no questions and spoke nothing of his life over the past weeks: he merely listened to Mallon's theories of merethic Aldmeri esoterica. The translator was undemanding of his guest's scholarship, accepting nods and shrugs as civilized conversation. He even produced some wine and fish jelly, which he shared with Scotti absent-mindedly, as he expounded on his various theses.

Finally, while Mallon was searching for a reference to some minor point in his notes, Scotti asked, "Rather off subject, but I was wondering where we're bound."

"The very heart of the province, Silvenar," Mallon said, not looking up from the passage he was reading. "It's somewhat bothersome, actually, as I wanted to go to Woodhearth first to talk to a Bosmer there who claims to have an original copy of Dirith Yalmillhiad, if you can believe it. But for the time being, that has to wait. Summurset Isle has surrounded the city, and is in the process of starving the citizenry until they surrender. It's a tiresome prospect, since the Bosmeri are happy to eat one another, so there's a risk that at the end, only one fat wood elf will remain to wave the flag."

"That is vexing," agreed Scotti, sympathetically. "To the east, the Khajiiti are burning everything, and to the west, the High Elves are waging war. I don't suppose the borders to the north are clear?"

"They're even worse," replied Mallon, finger on the page, still distracted. "The Cyrodiils and Redguards don't want Bosmer refugees streaming into their provinces. It only stands to reason. Imagine how much more criminally inclined they'd be now that they're homeless and hungry."

"So," murmured Scotti, feeling a shiver. "We're trapped in Valenwood."

"Not at all. I need to leave fairly shortly myself, as my publisher has set a very definite deadline for my new book of translations. From what I understand, one merely petitions to the Silvenar for special border protection and one can cross into Cyrodiil with impunity."

"Petition the Silvenar, or petition at Silvenar?"

"Petition the Silvenar at Silvenar. It's an odd nomenclature that is typical of this place, the sort of thing that makes my job as a translator that much more challenging. The Silvenar, he, or rather they are the closest the Bosmeri have to a great leader. The essential thing to remember about the Silvenar —" Mallon smiled, finding the passage he was looking for, "Here! 'A fortnight, inexplicable, the world burns into a dance.' There's that metaphor again."

"What were you saying about the Silvenar?" asked Scotti. "The essential thing to remember?"

"I don't remember what I was saying," replied Mallon, turning back to his oration.

In a week's time, the little boat bumped along the shallow, calmer waters of the foaming current the Xylo had become, and Decumus Scotti first saw the city of Silvenar. If Falinesti was a tree, then Silvenar was a flower. A magnificent pile of faded shades of green, red, blue, and white, shining with crystalline residue. Mallon had mentioned off-hand, when not otherwise explaining Aldmeri prosody, that Silvenar had once been a blossoming glade in the forest, but owing to some spell or natural cause, the trees' sap began flowing with translucent liqueur. The process of the sap flowing and hardening over the colorful trees had formed the web of the city. Mallon's description was intriguing, but it hardly prepared him for the city's beauty.

"What is the finest, most luxurious tavern here?" Scotti asked one of the Bosmer boatmen.

"Prithala Hall," Mallon answered. "But why don't you stay with me? I'm visiting an acquaintance of mine, a scholar I think you'll find fascinating. His hovel isn't much, but he has the most extraordinary ideas about the principles of a Merethic Aldmeri tribe the Sarmathi —"

"Under any other circumstances, I would happily accept," said Scotti graciously. "But after weeks of sleeping on the ground or on a raft, and eating whatever I could scrounge, I feel the need for some indulgent creature comforts. And then, after a day or two, I'll petition the Silvenar for safe passage to Cyrodiil."

The men bade each other goodbye. Gryf Mallon gave him the address of his publisher in the Imperial City, which Scotti accepted and quickly forgot. The clerk wandered the streets of Silvenar, crossing bridges of amber, admiring the petrified forest architecture. In front of a particularly estimable palace of silvery reflective crystal, he found Prithala Hall.

He took the finest room, and ordered a gluttonous meal of the finest quality. At a nearby table, he saw two very fat fellows, a man and a Bosmer, remarking how much finer the food was there than at the Silvenar's palace. They began to discuss the war and some issues of finances and rebuilding provincial bridges. The man noticed Scotti looking at them, and his eyes flashed recognition.

"Scotti, is that you? Kynareth, where have you been? I've had to make all the contacts here on my own!"

At the sound of his voice, Scotti recognized him. The fat man was Liodes Jurus, vastly engorged.

Book 6

Decumus Scotti sat down, listening to Liodes Jurus. The clerk could hardly believe how fat his former colleague at Lord Atrius's Building Commission had become. The piquant aroma of the roasted meat dish before Scotti melted away. All the other sounds and textures of Prithala Hall vanished all around him, as if nothing else existed but the vast form of Jurus. Scotti did not consider himself an emotional man, but he felt a tide flow over him at the sight and sound of the man whose badly written letters had been the guideposts that carried him from the Imperial City back in early Frost Fall.

"Where have you been?" Jurus demanded again. "I told you to meet me in Falinesti weeks ago."

"I was there weeks ago," Scotti stammered, too surprised to be indignant. "I got your note to meet you in Athay, and so I went there, but the Khajiiti had burned it to the ground. Somehow, I found my way with the refugees in another village, and someone there told me that you had been killed."

"And you believed that right away?" Jurus sneered.

"The fellow seemed very well-informed about you. He was a clerk from Lord Vanech's Building Commission named Reglius, and he said that you had also suggested that he come down to Valenwood to profit from the war."

"Oh, yes," said Jurus, after thinking a moment. "I recall the name now. Well, it's good for business to have two representatives from Imperial building commissions here. We just need to all coordinate our bids, and all should be well."

"Reglius is dead," said Scotti. "But I have his contracts from Lord Vanech's Commission."

"Even better," gasped Jurus, impressed. "I never knew you were such a ruthless competitor, Decumus Scotti. Yes, this could certainly improve our position with the Silvenar. Have I introduced you to Basth here?"

Scotti had only been dimly aware of the Bosmer's presence at the table with Jurus, which was surprising given that the mer's girth nearly equaled his dining companion. The clerk nodded to Basth coldly, still numb and confused. It had not left his mind that only any hour earlier, Scotti had intended to petition the Silvenar for safe passage through the border back to Cyrodiil. The thought of doing business with Jurus after all, of profiting from Valenwood war with Elsweyr, and now the second one with the Summurset Isle, seemed like something happening to another person.

"Your colleague and I were talking about the Silvenar," said Basth, putting down the leg of mutton he had been gnawing on. "I don't suppose you've heard about his nature?"

"A little, but nothing very specific. I got the impression that he's very important and very peculiar."

"He's the representative of the People, legally, physically, and emotionally," explained Jurus, a little annoyed at his new partner's lack of common knowledge. "When they're healthy, so is he. When they're mostly female, so is he. When they cry for food or trade or an absence of foreign interference, he feels it too, and makes laws accordingly. In a way, he's a despot, but he's the people's despot."

"That sounds," said Scotti, searching for the appropriate word. "Like ... bunk."

"Perhaps it is," shrugged Basth. "But he has many rights as the Voice of the People, including the granting of foreign building and trade contracts. It's not important whether you believe us. Just think of the Silvenar as being like one of your mad Emperors, like Pelagius. The problem facing us now is that since Valenwood is being attacked on all sides, the Silvenar's aspect is now one of distrust and fear of foreigners. The one hope of his people, and thus of the Silvenar himself, is that the Emperor will intervene and stop the war."

"Will he?" asked Scotti.

"You know as well as we do that the Emperor has not been himself lately," Jurus helped himself to Reglius's satchel and pulled out the blank contracts. "Who knows what he'll choose to do or not do? That reality is not our concern, but these blessings from the late good sir Reglius make our job much simpler."

They discussed how they would represent themselves to the Silvenar into the evening. Scotti ate continuously, but not nearly so much as Jurus and Basth. When the sun had begun to rise in the hills, its light reddening through the crystal walls of the tavern, Jurus and Basth left to their rooms at the palace, granted to them diplomatically in lieu of an actual immediate audience with the Silvenar. Scotti went to his room. He thought about staying up a little longer to ruminate over Jurus's plans and see what might be the flaw in them, but upon touching the cool, soft bed, he immediately fell asleep.

The next afternoon, Scotti awoke, feeling himself again. In other words, timid. For several weeks now, he had been a creature bent on mere survival. He had been driven to exhaustion, attacked by several jungle beasts, starved, nearly drowned, and forced into discussions of ancient Aldmeri poetical works. The discussion he had with Jurus and Basth about how to dupe the Silvenar into signing their contracts seemed perfectly reasonable then. Scotti dressed himself in his old battered clothes and went downstairs in search of food and a peaceful place to think.

"You're up," cried Basth upon seeing him. "We should go to the palace now."

"Now?" whined Scotti. "Look at me. I need new clothes. This isn't the way one should dress to pay a call on a prostitute, let alone the Voice of the People of Valenwood. I haven't even bathed."

"You must cease from this moment forward being a clerk, and become a student of mercantile trade," said Liodes Jurus grandly, taking Scotti by the arm and leading him into the sunlit boulevard outside. "The first rule is to recognize what you represent to the prospective client, and what angle best suits you. You cannot dazzle him with opulent fashion and professional bearing, my dear boy, and it would be fatal if you attempted to. Trust me on this. Several others besides Basth and I are guests at the palace, and they have made the error of appearing too eager, too formal, too ready for business. They will never be granted audience with the Silvenar, but we have remained aloof ever since the initial rejection. I've dallied about the court, spread my knowledge of life in the Imperial City, had my ears pierced, attended promenades, eaten and drunk of all that was given to me. I dare say I've put on a pound or two. The message we've sent is clear: it is in his, not our, best interest to meet."

"Our plan worked," added Basth. "When I told his minister that our Imperial representative had arrived, and that we were at last willing to meet with the Silvenar this morning, we were told to bring you there straightaway."

"Aren't we late then?" asked Scotti.

"Very," laughed Jurus. "But that's again part of the angle we're representing. Benevolent disinterest. Remember not to confuse the Silvenar with conventional nobility. His is the mind of the common people. When you grasp that, you'll understand how to manipulate him."

Jurus spent the last several minutes of the walk through the city expounding on his theories about what Valenwood needed, how much, and at what price. They were staggering figures, far more construction and far higher costs than anything Scotti had been used to dealing with. He listened carefully. All around them, the city of Silvenar revealed itself, glass and flower, roaring winds and beautiful inertia. When they reached the palace of the Silvenar, Decumus Scotti stopped, stunned. Jurus looked at him for a moment and then laughed.

"It's quite bizarre, isn't it?"

That it was. A frozen scarlet burst of twisted, uneven spires as if a rival sun rising. A blossom the size of a village, where courtiers and servants resembled nothing so much as insects walked about it sucking its ichor. Entering over a bent petal-like bridge, the three walked through the palace of unbalanced walls. Where the partitions bent close together and touched, there was a shaded hall or a small chamber. Where they warped away from one another, there was a courtyard. There were no doors anywhere, no any way to get to the Silvenar but by crossing through the entire spiral of the palace, through meetings and bedrooms and dining halls, past dignitaries, consorts, musicians, and many guards.

"It's an interesting place," said Basth. "But not very much privacy. Of course, that suits the Silvenar well."

When they reached the inner corridors, two hours after they first entered the palace, guards, brandishing blades and bows, stopped them.

"We have an audience with the Silvenar," said Jurus, patiently. "This is Lord Decumus Scotti, the Imperial representative."

One of the guards disappeared down the winding corridor, and returned moments later with a tall, proud Bosmer clad in a loose robe of patchwork leather. He was the Minister of Trade: "The Silvenar wishes to speak with Lord Decumus Scotti alone."

It was not the place to argue or show fear, so Scotti stepped forward, not even looking toward Jurus and Basth. He was certain they were showing their masks of benevolent indifference. Following the Minister into the audience chamber, Scotti recited to himself all the facts and figures Jurus had presented to him. He willed himself to remember the Angle and the Image he must project.

The audience chamber of the Silvenar was an enormous dome where the walls bent from bowl-shaped at the base inward to almost meet at the top. A thin ray of sunlight streamed through the fissure hundreds of feet above, and directly upon the Silvenar, who stood upon a puff of shimmering gray powder. For all the wonder of the city and the palace, the Silvenar himself looked perfectly ordinary. An average, blandly handsome, slightly tired-looking, extra-ordinary Wood Elf of the type one might see in any capitol in the Empire. It was only when he stepped from the dais that Scotti noticed an eccentricity in his appearance. He was very short.

"I had to speak with you alone," said the Silvenar in a voice common and unrefined.

"May I see your papers?"

Scotti handed him the blank contracts from Lord Vanech's Building Commission. The Silvenar studied them, running his finger over the embossed seal of the Emperor, before handing them back. He suddenly seemed shy, looking to the floor. "There are many charlatans at my court who wish to benefit from the wars. I thought you and your colleagues were among them, but those contracts are genuine."

"Yes, they are," said Scotti calmly. The Silvenar's conventional aspect made it easy for Scotti to speak, with no formal greetings, no deference, exactly as Jurus had instructed: "It seems most sensible to begin straightaway talking about the roads which need to be rebuilt, and then the harbors that the Altmeri have destroyed, and then I can give you my estimates on the cost of resupplying and renovating the trade routes."

"Why hasn't the Emperor seen fit to send a representative when the war with Elsweyr began, two years ago?" asked the Silvenar glumly.

Scotti thought a moment before replying of all the common Bosmeri he had met in Valenwood. The greedy, frightened mercenaries who had escorted him from the border. The hard-drinking revelers and expert pest exterminating archers in the Western Cross of Falinesti. Nosy old Mother Pascost in Havel Slump. Captain Balfix, the poor sadly reformed pirate. The terrified but hopeful refugees of Athay and Grenos. The mad, murderous, self-devouring Wild Hunt of Vindisi. The silent, dour boatmen hired by Gryf Mallon. The degenerate, grasping Basth. If one creature represented their total disposition, and that of many more throughout the province, what would be his personality? Scotti was a clerk by occupation and nature, instinctively comfortable cataloging and filing, making things fit in a system. If the soul of Valenwood were to be filed, where would it be put?

The answer came upon him almost before he posed himself the question. Denial.

"I'm afraid that question doesn't interest me," said Scotti. "Now, can we get back to the business at hand?"

All afternoon, Scotti and the Silvenar discussed the pressing needs of Valenwood. Every contract was filled and signed. So much was required and there were so many costs associated that addendums and codicils had to be scribbled into the margins of the papers, and those had to be resigned. Scotti maintained his benevolent indifference, but he found that dealing with the Silvenar was not quite the same as dealing with a simple, sullen child. The Voice of the People knew certain practical, everyday things very well: the yields of fish, the benefits of trade, the condition of every township and forest in his province.

"We will have a banquet tomorrow night to celebrate this commission," said the Silvenar at last.

"Best make it tonight," replied Scotti. "We should leave for Cyrodiil with the contracts tomorrow, so I'll need a safe passage to the border. We best not waste any more time."

"Agreed," said the Silvenar, and called for his Minister of Trade to put his seal on the contracts and arrange for the feast.

Scotti left the chamber, and was greeted by Basth and Jurus. Their faces showed the strain of maintaining the illusion of unconcern for too many hours. As soon as they were out of sight of the guards, they begged Scotti to tell them all. When he showed them the contract, Basth began weeping with delight.

"Anything about the Silvenar that surprised you?" asked Jurus.

"I hadn't expected him to be half my height."

"Was he?" Jurus looked mildly surprised. "He must have shrunk since I tried to have an audience with him earlier. Maybe there is something to all that nonsense about him being affected by the plight of his people."

Book 7

Scene: Silvenar, Valenwood
Date: 13 Sun's Dusk, 3E 397

The banquet at the palace of the Silvenar was well attended by every jealous bureaucrat and trader who had attempted to contract the rebuilding of Valenwood. They looked on Decumus Scotti, Liodes Jurus, and Basth with undisguised hatred. It made Scotti very uncomfortable, but Jurus delighted in it. As the servants brought in platter after platter of roasted meats, Jurus poured himself a cup of Jagga and toasted the clerk.

"I can confess it now," said Jurus. "I had grave doubts about inviting you to join me on this adventure. All the other clerks and agents of building commissions I contacted were more outwardly aggressive, but none of them made it through, let alone to the audience chamber of the Silvenar, let alone brokered the deals on their own like you did. Come, have a cup of Jagga with me."

"No thank you," said Scotti. "I had too much of that drug in Falinesti, and nearly got sucked dry by a giant tick because of it. I'll find something else to drink."

Scotti wandered about the hall until he saw some diplomats drinking mugs of a steaming brown liquid, poured from a large silver urn. He asked them if it was tea.

"Tea made from leaves?" scoffed the first diplomat. "Not in Valenwood. This is Rotmeth."

Scotti poured himself a mug and took a tentative sip. It was gamy, bitter and sugared, and very salty. At first it seemed very disagreeable to his palate, but a moment later he found he had drained the mug and was pouring another. His body tingled. All the sounds in the chamber seemed oddly disjointed, but not frighteningly so.

"So you're the fellow who got the Silvenar to sign all those contracts," said the second diplomat. "That must have required some deep negotiation."

"Not at all, not at all, just a little basic understand of mercantile trading," grimned Scotti, pouring himself a third mug of Rotmeth. "The Silvenar was very eager to involve the Imperial state with the affairs of Valenwood. I was very eager to take a percentage

of the commission. With all that blessed eagerness, it was merely a matter of putting quill to contract, bless you."

"You have been in the employ of his Imperial Majesty very long?" asked the first diplomat.

"It's a bite, or rather, a bit more complicated than that in the Imperial City. Between you and me, I don't really have a job. I used to work for Lord Atrius and his Building Commission, but I got sacked. And then, the contracts are from Lord Vanech and his Building Commission, 'cause I got em from this fellow Reglius who is a competitor but still a very fine fellow until he was made dead by those Khajiiti," Scotti drained his fifth mug. "When I go back to the Imperial City, then the real negotiations can begin, bless you. I can go to my old employer and to Lord Vanech, and say, look here you, which one of you wants these commissions? And they'll fall over each other to take them from me. It will be bidding war for my percentage the likes of which no one nowhere has never seen."

"So you're not a representative of his Imperial Majesty, the Emperor?" asked the first diplomat.

"Didn't you hear what I'm said? You stupid?" Scotti felt a surge of rage, which quickly subsided. He chuckled, and poured himself a seventh mug. "The Building Commissions are privately owned, but they're still representatives of the Emperor. So I'm a representative of the Emperor. Or I will be. When I get these contracts in. It's very complicated. I can understand why you're not following me. Bless you, it's all like the poet said, a dance in fire, if you follow the illusion, that is to say, allusion."

"And your colleagues? Are they representatives of the Emperor?" asked the second diplomat.

Scotti burst into laughter, shaking his head. The diplomats bade him their respects and went to talk to the Minister. Scotti stumbled out of the palace, and reeled through the strange, organic avenues and boulevards of the city. It took him several hours to find his way to Prithala Hall and his room. Once there, he slept, very nearly on his bed.

The next morning, he woke to Jurus and Basth in his room, shaking him. He felt half-asleep and unable to open his eyes fully, but otherwise fine. The conversation with the diplomats floated in his mind in a haze, like an obscure childhood memory.

"What in Mara's name is Rotmeth?" he asked quickly.

"Rancid, strongly fermented meat juices with lots of spices to kill the poisons," smiled Basth. "I should have warned you to stay with Jagga."

"You must understand the Meat Mandate by now," laughed Jurus. "These Bosmeri would rather eat each other than touch the fruit of the vine or the field."

"What did I say to those diplomats?" cried Scotti, panicking.

"Nothing bad apparently," said Jurus, pulling out some papers. "Your escorts are downstairs to bring you to the Imperial Province. Here are your papers of safe passage. The Silvenar seems very impatient about business proceeding forward rapidly. He promises to send you some sort of rare treasure when the contracts are fulfilled. See, he's already given me something."

Jurus showed off his new, bejeweled earring, a beautiful large faceted ruby. Basth showed that he had a similar one. The two fat fellows left the room so Scotti could dress and pack.

A full regiment of the Silvenar's guards was on the street in front of the tavern. They surrounded a carriage crested with the official arms of Valenwood. Still dazed, Scotti climbed in, and the captain of the guard gave the signal. They began a quick gallop. Scotti shook himself, and then peered behind. Basth and Jurus were waving him goodbye.

"Wait!" Scotti cried. "Aren't you coming back to the Imperial Province too?"

"The Silvenar asked that we stay behind as Imperial representatives!" yelled Liodes Jurus. "In case there's a need for more contracts and negotiations! He's appointed us Undrape, some sort of special honor for foreigners at court! Don't worry! Lots of banquets to attend! You can handle the negotiations with Vanech and Atrius yourself and we'll keep things settled here!"

Jurus continued to yell advice about business, but his voice became indistinct with distance. Soon it disappeared altogether as the convoy rounded the streets of Silvenar. The jungle loomed suddenly and then they were in it. Scotti had only gone through it by foot or along the rivers by slow-moving boats. Now it flashed all around him in profusions of greens. The horses seemed even faster moving through underbrush than on the smooth paths of the city. None of the weird sounds or dank smells of the jungle penetrated the escort. It felt to Scotti as if he were watching a play about the jungle with a background of a quickly moving scrim, which offered only the merest suggestion of the place.

So it went for two weeks. There was lots of food and water in the carriage with the clerk, so he merely ate and slept as the caravan pressed endlessly on. From time to time, he'd hear the sound of blades clashing, but when he looked around whatever had attacked the caravan had long since been left behind. At last, they reached the border, where an Imperial garrison was stationed.

Scotti presented the soldiers who met the carriage with the papers. They asked him a barrage of questions that he answered monosyllabically, and then let him pass. It took several more days to arrive at the gates of the Imperial City. The horses that had flown so fast through the jungle now slowed down in the unfamiliar territory of the wooded Colovian Estates. By contrast, the cries of his province's birds and smells of his province's plant life brought Decumus Scotti alive. It was if he had been dreaming all the past months.

At the gates of the City, Scotti's carriage door was opened for him and he stepped out on uncertain legs. Before he had a moment to say something to the escort, they had vanished, galloping back south through the forest. The first thing he did now that he was home was go to the closest tavern and have tea and fruit and bread. If he never ate meat again, he told himself, that would suit him very nicely.

Negotiations with Lord Atrius and Lord Vanech proceeded immediately thereafter.

It was most agreeable. Both commissions recognized how lucrative the rebuilding of Valenwood would be for their agency. Lord Vanech claimed, quite justifiably, that as the contracts had been written on forms notarized by his commission, he had the legal right to them. Lord Atrius claimed that Decumus Scotti was his agent and representative, and that he had never been released from employment. The Emperor was called to arbitrate, but he claimed to be unavailable. His advisor, the Imperial Battlemage Jagar Tharn, had disappeared long ago and could not be called on for his wisdom and impartial mediation.

Scotti lived very comfortably off the bribes from Lord Atrius and Lord Vanech. Every week, a letter would arrive from Jurus or Basth asking about the status of negotiations. Gradually, these letters ceased coming, and more urgent ones came from the Minister of Trade and the Silvenar himself. The War of the Blue Divide with Summurset Isle ended with the Altmeri winning several new coastal islands from the Wood Elves. The war with Elsweyr continued, ravaging the eastern borders of Valenwood. Still, Vanech and Atrius fought over who would help.

One fine morning in the early spring of the year 3E 398, a courier arrived at Decumus Scotti's door.

"Lord Vanech has won the Valenwood commission, and requests that you and the contracts come to his hall at your earliest convenience."

"Has Lord Atrius decided not to challenge further?" asked Scotti.

"He's been unable to, having died very suddenly, just now, from a terribly unfortunate accident," said the courier.

Scotti had wondered how long it would be before the Dark Brotherhood was brought in for final negotiations. As he walked toward Lord Vanech's Building Commission, a long, severe piece of architecture on a minor but respectable plaza, he wondered if he had played the game, as he ought to have. Could Vanech be so rapacious as to offer him a lower percentage of the commission now that his chief competitor was dead? Thankfully, he discovered, Lord Vanech had already decided to pay Scotti what he had proposed during the heat of the winter negotiations. His advisors had explained to him that other, lesser building commissions might come forward unless the matter were handled quickly and fairly.

"Glad we have all the legal issues done with," said Lord Vanech, fondly. "Now we can get to the business of helping the poor Bosmeri, and collecting the profits. It's a pity you weren't our representative for all the troubles with Bend'r-mahk and the Arnesian business. But there will be plenty more wars, I'm sure of that."

Scotti and Lord Vanech sent word to the Silvenar that at last they were prepared to honor the contracts. A few weeks later, they held a banquet in honor of the profitable enterprise. Decumus Scotti was the darling of the Imperial City, and no expense was spared to make it an unforgettable evening.

As Scotti met the nobles and wealthy merchants who would be benefiting from his business dealings, an exotic but somehow faintly familiar smell rose in the ballroom. He traced it to its source: a thick roasted slab of meat, so long and thick it covered several platters. The Cyrodilic revelers were eating it ravenously, unable to find the words to express their delight at its taste and texture.

"It's like nothing I've ever had before!"

"It's like pig-fed venison!"

"Do you see the marbling of fat and meat? It's a masterpiece!"

Scotti went to take a slice, but then he saw something imbedded deep in the dried and rendered roast. He nearly collided with his new employer Lord Vanech as he stumbled back.

"Where did this come from?" Scotti stammered.

"From our client, the Silvenar," beamed his lordship. "It's some kind of local delicacy they call Unthrappa."

Scotti vomited, and didn't stop for some time. It cast rather a temporary pall on the evening, but when Decumus Scotti was carried off to his manor house, the guests continued to dine. The Unthrappa was the delight of all. Even more so when Lord Vanech himself took a slice and found the first of two rubies buried within. How very clever of the Bosmer to invent such a dish, the Cyrodiils agreed.

The Argonian Account

by Waughin Jarth

Book One

n a minor but respectable plaza in the Imperial City sat, or perhaps lounged, Lord Vanech's Building Commission. It was an unimaginative, austere building not noted so much for its aesthetic or architectural design as for its prodigious length. If any critics wondered why such an unornamented, extended erection held such fascination for Lord Vanech, they kept it to themselves.

In the 39sth year of the 3rd Era, Decumus Scotti was a senior clerk at the Commission.

It had been a few months since the shy, middle-aged man had brought Lord Vanech the most lucrative of all contracts, granting the Commission the exclusive right to rebuild the roads of Valenwood which had been destroyed in the Five Year War. For this, he had become the darling of the managers and the clerks, spending his days recounting his adventures, more or less faithfully... although he did omit the ending of the tale, since many of them had partaken in the celebratory Unthrappa roast provided by the Silenstri. Informing one's listeners that they've gorged on human flesh improves very few stories of any good taste.

Scotti was neither particularly ambitious nor hard-working, so he did not mind that Lord Vanech had not given him anything to actually do.

Whenever the squat little gnomish man would happen upon Decumus Scotti in the offices, Lord Vanech would always say, "You're a credit to the Commission. Keep up the good work."

In the beginning, Scotti had worried that he was supposed to be doing something, but as the months went on, he merely replied, "Thank you. I will."

There was, on the other hand, the future to consider. He was not a young man, and though he was receiving a respectable salary for someone not doing actual work, Scotti considered that soon he might have to retire and not get paid for not doing work. It would be nice, he decided, if Lord Vanech, out of gratitude for the millions of gold the Valenwood contract was generating, might deign to make Scotti a partner. Or at least give him a small percentage of the bounty.

Decumus Scotti was no good at asking for things like that, which was one of the reasons why, previous to his signal successes in Valenwood as a senior clerk for Lord Atrius, he was a lousy agent. He had just about made up his mind to say something to Lord Vanech, when his lordship unexpectedly pushed things along.

"You're a credit to the Commission," the waddling little thing said, and then paused. "Do you have a moment free on your schedule?"

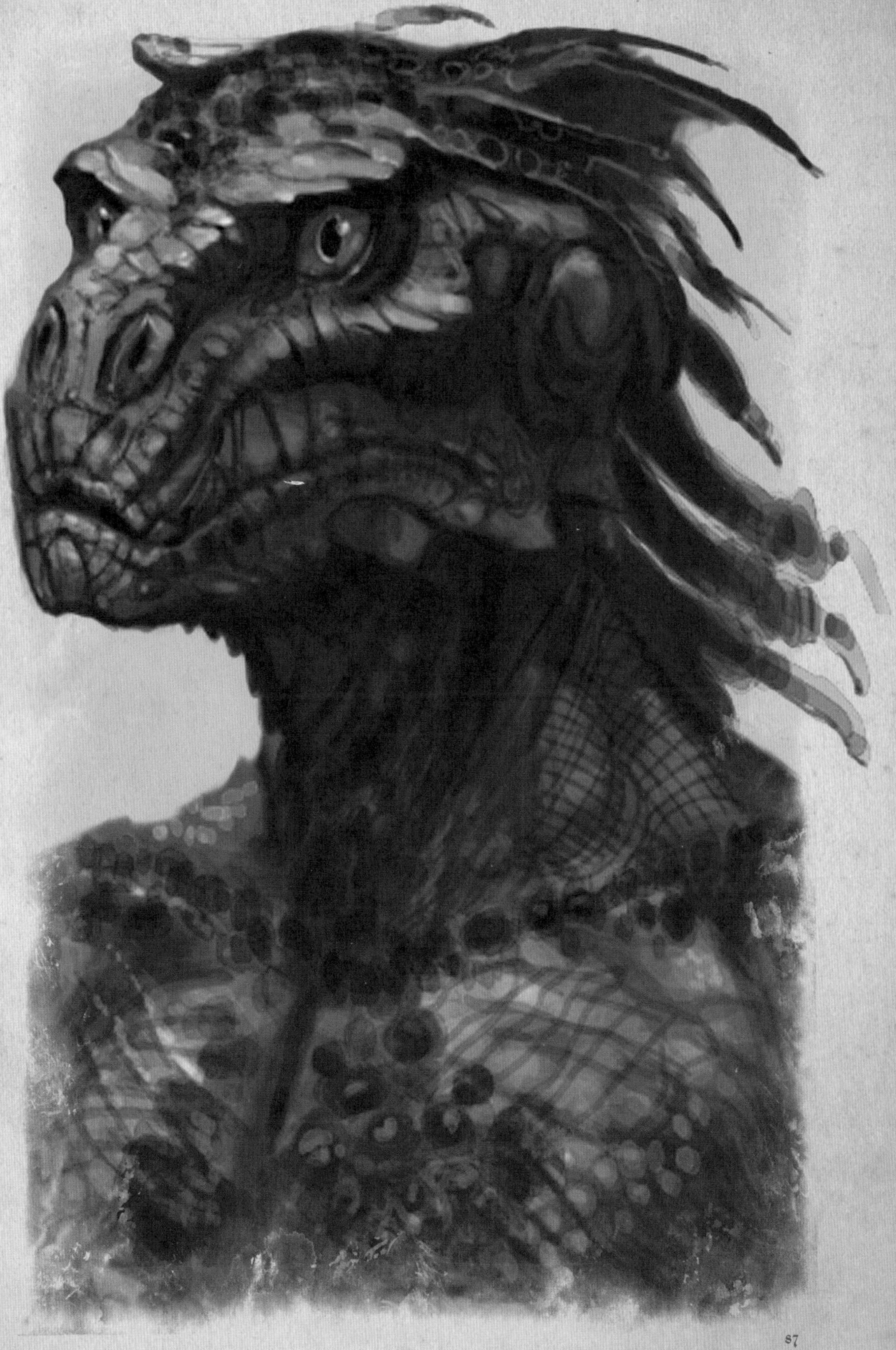

Scotti nodded eagerly, and followed his lordship to his hideously decorated and very enviable hectare of office space.

"Zenithar blesses us for your presence at the Commission," the little fellow squeaked grandly. "I don't know whether you know this, but we were having a bad time before you came along. We had impressive projects, for certain, but they were not successful. In Black Marsh, for example, for years we've been trying to improve the roads and other routes of travel for commerce. I put my best man, Flesus Tijjo, on it, but every year, despite staggering investments of time and money, the trade along those routes only gets slower and slower. Now, we have your very clean, very, very profitable Valenwood contract to boost the Commission's profits. I think it's time you were rewarded."

Scotti grinned a grin of great modesty and subtle avarice.

"I want you to take over the Black Marsh account from Flesus Tijjo."

Scotti shook as if awaking from a pleasant dream to hideous reality, "My Lord, I – I couldn't –"

"Nonsense," chirped Lord Vanech. "Don't worry about Tijjo. He will be happy to retire on the money I give him, particularly as soul–wrenchingly difficult as this Black Marsh business has been. Just your sort of a challenge, my dear Decumus."

Scotti couldn't utter a sound, though his mouth feebly formed the word "No" as Lord Vanech brought out the box of documentation on Black Marsh.

"You're a fast reader," Lord Vanech guessed. "You can read it all en route."

"En route to ..."

"Black Marsh, of course," the tiny fellow giggled. "You are a funny chap. Where else would you go to learn about the work that's being done, and how to improve it?"

The next morning, the stack of documentation hardly touched, Decumus Scotti began the journey south–east to Black Marsh. Lord Vanech had hired an able–bodied guard, a rather taciturn Redguard named Mailic, to protect his best agent. They rode south along the Niben, and then south–east along the Silverfish, continuing on into the wilds of Cyrodiil, where the river tributaries had no names and the very vegetation seemed to come from another world than the nice, civilized gardens of the northern Imperial Province.

Scotti's horse was tied to Mailic's, so the clerk was able to read. It made it difficult to pay attention to the path they were taking, but Scotti knew he needed at least a cursory familiarity with the Commission's business dealings in Black Marsh.

It was a huge box of paperwork going back forty years, when the Commission had first been given several million in gold by a wealthy trader, Lord Xellicles Pinos–Revina, to improve the condition of the road from Gideon to Cyrodiil. At that time, it took three weeks, a preposterously long time, for the rice and root he was importing to arrive, half–rotten, in the Imperial Province. Pinos–Revina was long dead, but many other investors over the decades, including Pelagius IV himself, had hired the Commission to build roads, drain swamps, construct bridges, devise anti–smuggling systems, hire mercenaries, and, in short, do everything that the greatest Empire in history knew would work to aid trade with Black Marsh. According to the latest figures, the result of this was that it took two and a half months for goods, now thoroughly rotten, to arrive.

Scotti found that when he looked up after concentrating on what he was reading, the landscape had always changed. Always dramatically. Always for the worse.

"This is Blackwood, sir," said Mailic to Scotti's unspoken question. It was dark and woodsy, so Decumus Scotti thought that a very appropriate name.

The question he longed to ask, which in due course he did ask, was, "What's that terrible smell?"

"Slough Point, sir," Mailic replied as they turned the next bend, where the umbrageous tunnel of tangled tree and vine opened to a clearing. There squatted a cluster of formal buildings in the dreary Imperial design favored by Lord Vanech's Commission and every Emperor since Tiber, together with a stench so eye-blindingly, stomach-wrenchingly awful that Scotti wondered, suddenly, if it were deadly poisonous. The swarms of blood-colored, sand-grain-sized insects obscuring the air did not improve the view.

Scotti and Mailic batted at the buzzing clouds as they rode their horses towards the largest of the buildings, which on approach revealed itself to be perched at the edge of a thick, black river. From its size and serious aspect, Scotti guessed it to be the census and excise office for the wide, white bridge that stretched across the burbling dark water to the reeds on the other side. It was a very nice, bright, sturdy-looking bridge, built, Scotti knew, by his Commission.

A poxy, irritable official opened the door quickly on Scotti's first knock. "Come in, come in, quickly! Don't let the fleshflies in!"

"Fleshflies?" Decumus Scotti trembled. "You mean, they eat human flesh?"

"If you're fool enough to stand around and let them," the soldier said, rolling his eyes. He had half an ear, and Scotti, looking around at the other soldiers in the fort noted that they all were well-chewed. One of them had no nose at all to speak of. "Now, what's your business?"

Scotti told them, and added that if they stood outside the fortress instead of inside, they might catch more smugglers.

"You better be more concerned with getting across that bridge," the soldier sneered. "Tide's coming up, and if you don't get a move on, you won't get to Black Marsh for four days."

That was absurd. A bridge swamped by a rising tide on a river? Only the look in the soldier's eyes told Scotti he wasn't joking.

Upon stepping out of the fort, he saw that the horses, evidently tired of being tortured by the fleshflies, had ripped free of their restraints and were bounding off into the woods. The oily water of the river was already lapping on the planks, oozing between the crevices. Scotti reflected that perhaps he would be more than willing to endure a wait of four days before going to Black Marsh, but Mailic was already running across.

Scotti followed him, wheezing. He was not in excellent shape, and never had been. The box of Commission materials was heavy. Halfway across, he paused to catch his breath, and then discovered he could not move. His feet were stuck.

The black mud that ran through the river was a thick gluey paste, and having washed over the plank Scotti was on, it held his feet fast. Panic seized him. Scotti looked up from his trap and saw Mailic leaping from plank to plank ahead of him, closing fast on the reeds on the other side.

"Help!" Scotti cried. "I'm stuck!"

Mailic did not even turn around, but kept jumping. "I know, sir. You need to lose weight."

Decumus Scotti knew he was a few pounds over, and had meant to start eating less and exercising more, but embarking on a diet hardly seemed to promise timely aid in his current predicament. No diet on Nirn would have helped him just then. However, on reflection, Scotti realized that the Redguard intended that he drop the box of documents, for Mailic was no longer carrying any of the essential supplies he had had with him previously.

With a sigh, Scotti threw the box of Commission notes into the glop, and felt the plank under him rise a quarter of an inch, just enough to free him from the mud's clutches. With an agility born of extreme fear, Scotti began leaping after Mailic, dropping onto every third plank, and springing up before the river gripped him.

In forty-six leaps, Decumus Scotti crashed through the reeds onto the solid ground behind Mailic, and found himself in Black Marsh. He could hear behind him a slurping sound as the bridge, and his container of important and official records of Commission affairs, was consumed by the rising flood of dark filth, never to be seen again.

Book Two

Decumus Scotti emerged from the dirt and reeds, exhausted from running, his face and arms sheathed in red fleshflies. Looking back towards Cyrodiil, he saw the bridge disappear beneath the thick black river, and he knew he was not getting back until the tide went down in a few days' time. The river also held in its adhesive depths his files on the Black Marsh account. He would have to rely on his memory for his contacts in Gideon.

Mailic was purposefully striding through the reeds ahead. Flailing ineffectually at the fleshflies, Scotti hurried after him.

"We're lucky, sir," said the Redguard, which struck Scotti as an extraordinarily odd thing to say, until his eyes followed where the man's finger was pointing. "The caravan is here."

Twenty-one rusted, mud-spattered wagons with rotting wood and wobbly wheels sat half-sunk in the soft earth ahead. A crowd of Argonians, gray-scaled and gray-eyed, the sort of sullen manual laborers that were common in Cyrodiil, pulled at one of the wagons which had been detached from the others. As Scotti and Mailic came closer, they saw it was filled with a cargo of black berries so decayed that they had become hardly recognizable... more a festering jelly than a wagonload of fruit.

Yes, they were going to the city of Gideon, and, yes, they said, Scotti could get a ride with them after they were finished unloading this shipment of lumberries.

"How long ago were they picked?" Scotti asked, looking at the wagon's rotten produce.

"The harvest was in Last Seed, of course," said the Argonian who seemed to be in charge of the wagon. It was now Sun's Dusk, so they had been en route from the fields for a little over two months.

Clearly, Scotti thought, there were problems with transportation. But fixing that, after all, was what he was doing here as a representative of Lord Vanech's Building Commission.

It took close to an hour of the berries rotting even more in the sun for the wagon to be pushed to the side, the wagons in front of it and behind it to be attached to one another, and one of the eight horses from the front of the caravan to be brought around to the now independent wagon. The laborers moved with dispirited lethargy, and Scotti took the opportunity to inspect the rest of the caravan and talk to his fellow travellers.

Four of the wagons had benches in them, fit for uncomfortable riders. All the rest were filled with grain, meat, and vegetation in various stages of corruption.

The travellers consisted of the six Argonian laborers, three Imperial merchants so bug-bitten that their skin looked as scaly as the Argonians themselves, and three cloaked fellows who were evidently Dunmer, judging by the red eyes that gleamed in the shadows under their hoods. All were transporting their goods along this, the Imperial Commerce Road.

"This is a road?" Scotti exclaimed, looking at the endless field of reeds that reached up to his chin or higher.

"It's solid ground, of a sort," one of the hooded Dunmer shrugged. "The horses eat some of the reed, and sometimes we set fire to it, but it just grows right back up."

Finally, the wagonmaster signalled that the caravan was ready to go, and Scotti took a seat in the third wagon with the other Imperials. He looked around, but Mailic was not on board.

"I agreed to get to you to Black Marsh and take you back out," said the Redguard, who had plumped down a rock in the sea of reeds and was munching on a hairy carrot. "I'll be here when you get back."

Scotti frowned, and not only because Mailic had dropped the deferential title "sir" while addressing him. Now he truly knew no one in Black Marsh, but the caravan slowly grinded and bumped forward, so there was no time to argue.

A noxious wind blew across the Commerce Road, casting patterns in the endless featureless expanse of reeds. In the distance, there seemed to be mountains, but they constantly shifted, and Scotti realized they were banks of mist and fog. Shadows flitted across the landscape, and when Scotti looked up, he saw they were being cast by giant birds with long, saw-like beaks nearly the size of the rest of their bodies.

"Hackwings," Chaero Gemullus, an Imperial on Scotti's left, who might have been young but looked old and beaten, muttered. "Like everything else in this damnable place, they'll eat you if you don't keep moving. Beggars pounce down and give you a nasty chop, and then fly off and come back when you're mostly dead from blood loss."

Scotti shivered. He hoped they'd be in Gideon before nightfall. It was then it occurred to him that the sun was on the wrong side of the caravan.

"Excuse me, sir," Scotti called to the wagonmaster. "I thought you said we were going to Gideon?"

The wagonmaster nodded.

"Why are we going north then, when we should be going south?"

There was no reply but a sigh.

Scotti confirmed with his fellow travellers that they too were going to Gideon, and none of them seemed very concerned about the circuitous route to getting there. The seats were hard on his middle-aged back and buttocks, but the bumping rhythm of the caravan, and the hypnotic waving reeds gradually had an effect on him, and Scotti drifted off to sleep.

He awoke in the dark some hours later, not sure where he was. The caravan was no longer moving, and he was on the floor, under the bench, next to some small boxes. There were voices, speaking a hissing, clicking language Scotti didn't understand, and he peeked out between someone's legs to see what was happening.

The moons barely pierced the thick mist surrounding the caravan, and Scotti did not have the best angle to see who was talking. For a moment, it looked like the gray wagonmaster was talking to himself, but the darkness had movement and moisture, in fact, glistening scales. It was hard to tell how many of these things there were, but they were big, black, and the more Scotti looked at them, the more details he could see.

When one particular detail emerged, huge mouths filled with dripping needle-like fangs, Scotti slipped back under the bench. Their black little eyes had not fallen on him yet.

The legs in front of Scotti moved and then began to thrash, as their owner was grabbed and pulled out of the wagon. Scotti crouched further back, getting behind the little boxes. He didn't know much about concealment, but had some experience with shields. He knew that having something, anything, in between you and bad things was always good.

A few seconds after the legs had disappeared from sight, there was a horrible scream. And then a second and a third. Different timbres, different accents, but the same inarticulate message... terror, and pain, horrible pain. Scotti remembered a long forgotten prayer to the god Stendarr and whispered it to himself.

Then there was silence... ghastly silence that lasted only a few minutes, but which seemed like hours... years.

And then the carriage started rolling forward again.

Scotti cautiously crawled out from under the carriage. Chaero Gemullus gave him a bemused grin.

"There you are," he said. "I thought the Nagas took you."

"Nagas?"

"Nasty characters," Gemullus said, frowning. "Puff adders with legs and arms, seven feet tall, eight when they're mad. Come from the inner swamp, and they don't like it here much so they're particularly peevish. You're the kind of posh Imperial they're looking for."

Scotti had never in his life thought of himself as posh. His mud and fleshfly-bespeckled clothing seemed eminently middle-class, at best, to him. "What would they want me for?"

"To rob, of course," the Imperial smiled. "And to kill. You didn't notice what happened to the others?" The Imperial frowned, as if struck by a thought. "You didn't sample from those boxes down below, did you? Like the sugar, do you?"

"Gods, no," Scotti grimaced.

The Imperial nodded, relieved. "You just seem a little slow. First time to Black Marsh, I gather? Oh! Heigh ho, Hist piss!"

Scotti was just about to ask Gemullus what that vulgar term meant when the rain began. It was an inferno of foul-smelling, yellow-brown rain that washed over the caravan, accompanied by the growl of thunder in the distance. Gemullus worked to pull the roof up over the wagon, glaring at Scotti until he helped with the laborious process.

He shuddered, not only from the cold damp, but from contemplation of the disgusting precipitation pouring down on the already nasty produce in the uncovered wagon.

"We'll be dry soon enough," Gemullus smiled, pointing out into the fog.

Scotti had never been to Gideon, but he knew what to expect. A large settlement more or less laid out like a Imperial city, with more or less Imperial style architecture, and all the Imperial comforts and traditions, more or less.

The jumble of huts half-sunk in mud was decidedly less.

"Where are we?" asked Scotti, bewildered.

"Hixinoag," replied Gemullus, pronouncing the queer name with confidence. "You were right. We were going north when we should have been going south."

Book Three

Decumus Scotti was supposed to be in Gideon, a thoroughly Imperialized city in southern Black Marsh, arranging business dealings to improve commerce in the province on behalf of Lord Vanech's Building Commission and its clients. Instead, he was in a half-submerged, rotten little village called Hixinoag, where he knew no one. Except for a drug smuggler named Chaero Gemullus

Gemullus was not at all perturbed that the merchant caravan had gone north instead of south. He even let Scotti share his bucket of trodh, tiny little crunchy fish, he had bought from the villagers. Scotti would have preferred them cooked, or at any rate, dead, but Gemullus blithely explained that dead, cooked trodh are deadly poison.

"If I were where I was supposed to be," Scotti pouted, putting one of the wriggling little creatures in his mouth. "I could be having a roast, and some cheese, and a glass of wine."

"I sell moon sugar in the north, and buy it in the south," he shrugged. "You have to be more flexible, my friend."

"My only business is in Gideon," Scotti frowned.

"Well, you have a couple choices," replied the smuggler. "You could just stay here. Most villages in Argonia don't stay put for very long, and there's a good chance Hixinoag will drift right down to the gates of Gideon. Might take you a month or two. Probably the easiest way."

"That'd put me far behind schedule."

"Next option, you could join up with the caravan again," said Gemullus. "They might be going in the right direction this time, and they might not get stuck in the mud, and they might not be all murdered by Naga highwaymen."

"Not tempting," Scotti frowned. "Any other ideas?"

"Ride the roots. The underground express," Gemullus grinned. "Follow me."

Scotti followed Gemullus out of the village and into a copse of trees shrouded by veils of wispy moss. The smuggler kept his eye on the ground, poking at the viscous mud intermittently. Finally he found a spot which triggered a mass of big oily bubbles to rise to the surface.

"Perfect," he said. "Now, the important thing is not to panic. The express will take you due south, that's the wintertide migration, and you'll know you're near Gideon when you see a lot of red clay. Just don't panic, and when you see a mass of bubbles, that's a breathing hole you can use to get out."

Scotti looked at Gemullus blankly. The man was talking perfect gibberish. "What?"

Gemullus took Scotti by the shoulder and positioning him on top of the mass of bubbles. "You stand right here..."

Scotti sank quickly into the mud, staring at the smuggler, horror-struck.

"And remember to wait 'til you see the red clay, and then the next time you see bubbles, push up..."

The more Scotti wriggled to get free, the faster he sank. The mud enveloped Scotti to his neck, and he continued staring, unable to articulate anything but a noise like "Oog."

"And don't panic at the idea that you're being digested. You could live in a rootworm's belly for months."

Scotti took one last panicked gasp of air and closed his eyes before he disappeared into the mud.

The clerk felt a warmth he hadn't expected all around him. When he opened his eyes, he found that he was entirely surrounded by a translucent goo, and was traveling rapidly forward, southward, gliding through the mud as if it were air, skipping along an intricate network of roots. Scotti felt confusion and euphoria in equal measures, madly rushing forward through an alien environment of darkness, spinning around and over the thick fibrous tentacles of the trees. It was if he were high in the sky at midnight, not deep beneath the swamp in the Underground Express.

Looking up slightly at the massive root structure above, Scotti saw something wriggle past. A eight-foot-long, armless, legless, colorless, boneless, eyeless, nearly shapeless creature, riding the roots. Something dark was inside of it, and as it came closer, Scotti could see it was an Argonian man. He waved, and the disgusting creature the Argonian was in flattened slightly and rushed onward.

Gemullus's words began to reappear in Scotti's mind at this sight. "The wintertide migration," "air hole," "you're being digested," — these were the phrases that danced around as if trying to find some place to live in a brain which was highly resistant to them coming in. But there was no other way to look at the situation. Scotti had gone from eating living fish to being eaten alive as a way of transport. He was in one of those worms.

Scotti made an executive decision to faint.

He awoke in stages, having a beautiful dream of being held in a woman's warm embrace. Smiling and opening his eyes, the reality of where he really was rushed over him.

The creature was still rushing madly, blindly forward, gliding over roots, but it was no longer like a flight through the night sky. Now it was like the sky at sunrise, in pinks and reds. Scotti remembered Gemullus telling him to look for the red clay, and he would be near Gideon. The next thing he had to find was the bubbles.

There were no bubbles anywhere. Though the inside of the worm was still warm and comfortable, Scotti felt the weight of the earth all around him. "Just don't panic"

Gemullus had said, but it was one thing to hear that advice, and quite another to take it. He began to squirm, and the creature began to move faster at the increased pressure from within.

Suddenly, Scotti saw it ahead of him, a slim spire of bubbles rising up through the mud from some underground stream, straight up, through the roots to the surface above him. The moment the rootworm went through it, Scotti pushed with all of his might upward, bursting through the creature's thin skin. The bubbles pushed Scotti up quickly, and before he could blink, he was popping out of the red slushy mud.

Two gray Argonians were standing under a tree nearby, holding a net. They looked in Scotti's direction with polite curiosity. In their net, Scotti noticed, were several squirming furry rat-like creatures. While he addressed them, another fell out of the tree. Though Scotti had not been educated in this practice, he recognized fishing when he saw it.

"Excuse me, lads," Scotti said jovially. "I was wondering if you'd point me in the direction of Gideon?"

The Argonians introduced themselves as Drawing-Flame and Furl-Of-Fresh-Leaves, and looked at one another, puzzling over the question.

"Who you seek?" asked Furl-of-Fresh-Leaves.

"I believe his name is," said Scotti, trying to remember the contents of his long gone file of Black Marsh contacts in Gideon. "Archein Right-Foot ...Rock?"

Drawing-Flame nodded, "For five gold, show you way. Just east. Is plantation east of Gideon. Very nice."

Scotti thought that the best business he had heard of in two days, and handed Drawing-Flames the five septims.

The Argonians led Scotti onto a muddy ribbon of road that passed through the reeds, and soon revealed the bright blue expanse of Topal Bay far to the west. Scotti looked around at the magnificent walled estates, where bright crimson blossoms sprang forth from the very dirt of the walls, and surprised himself by thinking, "This is very pretty."

The road ran parallel to a fast-moving stream, running eastward from Topal Bay. It was called the Onkobra River, he was told. It ran deep into Black Marsh, to the very dark heart of the province.

Peeking past the gates to the plantations east of Gideon, Scotti saw that few of the fields were tended. Most had rotten crops from harvests past still clinging to wilted vines, orchards of desolate, leafless trees. The Argonian serfs who worked the fields were thin, weak, near death, more like haunting spirits than creatures of life and reason.

Two hours later, as the three continued their trudge east, the estates were still impressive at least from a distance, the road was still solid if weedy, but Scotti was irritated, horrified by the field workers and the agricultural state, and no longer charitable towards the area. "How much further?"

Furl-of-Fresh-Leaves and Drawing-Flame looked at one another, as if that question was something that hadn't occurred to them.

"Archein is east?" Furl-of-Fresh-Leaves pondered. "Near or far?"

Drawing-Flame shrugged noncommittally, and said to Scotti, "For five gold, show you way. Just east. Is plantation. Very nice."

"You don't have any idea, do you?" Scotti cried. "Why couldn't you tell me that in the first place when I might have asked someone else?"

Around the bend up ahead, there was the sound of hoofbeats. A horse coming closer.

Scotti began to walk towards the sound to hail the rider, and didn't see Drawing-Flame's taloned claws flash out and cast the spell at him. He felt it though. A kiss of ice along his spine, the muscles along his arms and legs suddenly immobile as if wrapped in rigid steel. He was paralyzed.

The great curse of paralysis, as the reader may be unfortunate enough to know, is that you continue to see and think even though your body does not respond. The thought that went through Scotti's mind was, "Damn."

For Drawing-Flame and Furl-of-Fresh-Leaves were, of course, like most simple day laborers in Black Marsh, accomplished Illusionists. And no friend of the Imperial.

The Argonians shoved Decumus Scotti to the side of the road, just as the horse and rider came around the corner. He was an impressive figure, a nobleman in a flashing dark green cloak the exact same color as his scaled skin, and a frilled hood that was part of his flesh and sat upon his head like a horned crown.

"Greetings, brothers!" the rider said to the two.

"Greetings, Archein Right-Foot-Rock," they responded, and then Furl-of-Fresh-Leaves added. "What is milord's business on this fine day?"

"No rest, no rest," the Archein sighed regally. "One of my she-workers gave birth to twins. Twins! Fortunately, there's a good trader in town for those, and she didn't put up too much of a fuss. And then there's a fool of an Imperial from Lord Vanech's Building Commission I am supposed to meet with in Gideon. I'm sure he'll want the grand tour before he opens up the treasury for me. Such a lot of fuss."

Drawing-Flame and Furl-of-Fresh-Leaves sympathized, and then, as Archein Right-Foot-Rock rode off, they went to look for their hostage.

Unfortunately for them, gravity being the same in Black Marsh as elsewhere in Tamriel, their hostage, Decumus Scotti, had continued to roll down from where they left him, and was, at that moment, in the Onkobra River, drowning.

Book Four

Decumus Scotti was drowning, and he didn't think much of it. He couldn't move his arms or his legs to swim because of the paralysis spell the Argonian peasant had lobbed at him, but he wasn't quite sinking. The Onkobra River was a crashing force of white water and currents that could carry along large rocks with ease, so Scotti tumbled head over heels, spinning, bumping, bouncing along.

He figured that soon enough he would be dead, and that would be better than being in Black Marsh. He wasn't too panicked about it all when he felt his lungs fill with water and cold blackness fell upon him.

For a while, for the first time in some time, Decumus Scotti felt peace. Blessed darkness. And then pain came to him, and he felt himself coughing, spewing water up from his belly and his lungs.

A voice said, "Oh bother, he's alive, ain't he, now?"

Scotti wasn't quite sure if that were true, even when he opened his eyes and looked at the face above him. It was an Argonian, but unlike any he had seen anywhere. The face was thin and long like a thick lance; the scales were ruby-red, brilliant in the sunlight. It blinked at him, its eyelids opening and closing in vertical slits.

"I don't suppose we should eat you, should we now?" the creature smiled, and Scotti could tell from its teeth that it was no idle suggestion.

"Thank you," said Scotti weakly. He craned his head slightly to find out who the "we" were, and discovered he was on the muddy bank of the still, sludgy river, surrounded by a group of Argonians with similarly needle-like faces and a whole rainbow of scales. Bright greens and gem-like purples, blues, and oranges.

"Can you tell me, am I near – well, anywhere?"

The ruby-colored Argonian laughed. "No. You're in the middle of everywhere, and near nowhere."

"Oh," said Scotti, who grasped the idea that space did not mean much in Black Marsh. "And what are you?"

"We are Agacephs," the ruby-colored Argonian replied. "My name is Nomu."

Scotti introduced himself. "I'm a senior clerk in Lord Vanech's Building Commission in the Imperial City. My job was to come here to try to fix the problems with commerce, but I've lost my agenda, haven't met with any of my contacts, the Archeins of Gideon..."

"Pompous, assimiliated, slaver kleptocrats," a small lemon-colored Agaceph murmured with some feeling.

"...And now I just want to go home."

Nomu smiled, his long mouth arching up like a host happy to see an unwanted guest leave a party. "Shehs will guide you."

Shehs, it seemed, was the bitter little yellow creature, and he was not at all pleased at the assignment. With surprising strength, he hoisted Scotti up, and for a moment, the clerk was reminded of Gemullus dropping him into the bubbling muck that led to the Underground Express. Instead, Shehs shoved Scotti toward a tiny little raft, razor-thin, that bobbed on the surface of the water.

"This is how you travel?"

"We don't have the broken wagons and dying horses of our brothers on the outside," Shehs replied, rolling his tiny eyes. "We don't know better."

The Argonian sat at the back of the craft and used his whip-like tail to propel and navigate the craft. They traveled quickly around swirling pools of slime that stank of centuries of putrefaction, past pinnacled mountains that seemed sturdy but suddenly

fell apart at the slightest ripple in the still water, under bridges that might have once been metal but were now purely rust.

"Everything in Tamriel flows down to Black Marsh," Shehs said.

As they slid through the water, Shehs explained to Scotti that the Agacephs were one of the many Argonian tribes that lived in the interior of the province, near the Hist, finding little in the outside world worth seeing. He was fortunate to have been found by them. The Nagas, the toad-like Paatru, and the winged Sarpa would have killed him on the spot.

There were other creatures too to be avoided. Though there were few natural predators in inner Black Marsh, the scavengers that rooted in the garbage seldom shied away from a living meal. Hackwings circled overhead, like the ones Scotti had seen in the west.

Shehs fell silent and stopped the raft completely, waiting for something

Scotti looked in the direction Shehs was watching, and saw nothing unusual in the filthy water. Then, he realized that the pool of green slime in front of them was actually moving, and fairly quickly, from one bank to the other. It deposited small bones behind it as it oozed up into the reeds, and disappeared.

"Voriplasm," Shehs explained, moving the boat forward again. "Big word. It'll strip you to the bone by the second syllable."

Scotti, desirous to distract himself from the sights and smells that surrounded him, thought it a good time to compliment his pilot on his excellent vocabulary. It was particularly impressive, given how far from civilization they were. The Argonians in the east did, in fact, speak so well.

"They tried to erect a Temple of Mara near here, in Umpholo, twenty years ago," Shehs explained, and Scotti nodded, remembering reading about it in the files before they were lost. "They all perished quite dreadfully of swamp rot in the first month, but they left behind some excellent books."

Scotti was going to inquire further when he saw something so huge, so horrifying, it made him stop, frozen.

Half submerged in the water ahead was a mountain of spines, lying on nine-foot-long claws. White eyes stared blindly forward, and then suddenly the whole creature spasmed and lurched, the jaw of its mouth jutting out, exposing tusks clotted with gore.

"Swamp Leviathan," Shehs whistled, impressed. "Very, very dangerous."

Scotti gasped, wondering why the Agaceph was so calm, and more, why he was continuing to steer the raft forward towards the beast..

"Of all the creatures in the world, the rats are sometimes the worst," said Shehs, and Scotti noticed that the huge creature was only a husk. Its movement was from the hundreds of rats that had burrowed into it, rapidly eating their way from the inside out, bursting from the skin in spots.

"They are indeed," Scotti said, and his mind went to the Black Marsh files, buried deep in the mud, and four decades of Imperial work in Black Marsh.

The two continued westward through the heart of Black Marsh.

Shehs showed Scotti the vast complicated ruins of the Kothringi capitals, fields of ferns and flowered grasses, quiet streams under canopies of blue moss, and the most astonishing sight of Scotti's life — the great forest of full-grown Hist trees. They never saw a living soul until they arrived at the edge of the Imperial Commerce Road just east of Slough Point, where Mailic, Scotti's Redguard guide, was waiting patiently.

"I was going to give you two more minutes," the Redguard scowled, dropping the last of his food onto the pile at his feet. "No more, sir."

The sun was shining bright when Decumus Scotti rode into the Imperial City, and as it caught the morning dew, it lent a glisten to every building as if they had been newly polished for his arrival. It astonished him how clean the city was. And how few beggars there were.

The protracted edifice of Lord Vanech's Building Commission was the same as it had always been, but still the very sight of it seemed exotic and strange. It was not covered in mud. The people within actually, generally, worked.

Lord Vanech himself, though singularly squat and squinty, seemed immaculate, not only relatively clean of dirt and scabs, but also relatively uncorrupt. Scotti couldn't help but stare at him when he first caught sight of his boss. Vanech stared right back.

"You are a sight," the little fellow frowned. "Did your horse drag you to Black Marsh and back? I would say go home and fix yourself, but there are a dozen people here to see you. I hope you have solutions for them."

It was no exaggeration. Nearly twenty of Cyrodiil's most powerful and wealthiest people were waiting for him. Scotti was given an office even larger than Lord Vanech's, and he met with each.

First among the Commission's clients were five independent traders, blustering and loaded with gold, demanding to know what Scotti intended to do about improving the trade routes. Scotti summarized for them the conditions of the main roads, the state of the merchants' caravans, the sunken bridges, and all the other impediments between the frontier and the marketplace. They told him to have everything replaced and repaired, and gave him the gold necessary to do it.

Within three months, the bridge at Slough Point had disappeared into the muck; the great caravan had collapsed into decrepitude; and the main road from Gideon had been utterly swallowed up by swamp water. The Argonians began once again to use the old ways, their personal rafts and sometimes the Underground Express to transport the grain in small quantities. It took a third of the time, two weeks, to arrive in Cyrodiil, none of it rotten.

The Archbishop of Mara was the next client Scotti met with. A kindhearted man, horrified by the tales of Argonian mothers selling their children into slavery, he pointedly asked Scotti if it were true.

"Sadly, yes," Scotti replied, and the Archbishop showered him with septims, telling the clerk that food must be brought to the province to ease their suffering, and the schools must be improved so they could learn to help themselves.

Within five months, the last book had been stolen from the deserted Maran monastery in Umphollo. As the Archeins went bankrupt, their slaves returned to his parents' tiny farms. The backwater Argonians found that they could grow enough to feed their families provided they had enough hard workers in their enclave, and the buyers market for slaves sharply declined.

Ambassador Tsleeixth, concerned about the rising crime in northern Black Marsh, brought with him the contributions of many other expatriate Argonians like himself. They wanted more Imperial guards on the border at Slough Point, more magically lit lanterns posted along the main roads at regular intervals, more patrol stations, and more schools built to allow young Argonians to better themselves and not turn to crime.

Within six months, there were no more Nagas roaming the roads, as there were no merchants traveling them to rob. The thugs returned to the fetid inner swamp, where they felt much happier, their constitutions enriched by the rot and pestilence that they loved. Tsleeixth and his constituency were so pleased by the crime rate dropping, they brought even more gold to Decumus Scotti, telling him to keep up the good work.

Black Marsh simply was, is, and always shall be unable to sustain a large-scale, cash-crop plantation economy. The Argonians, and anyone else, the whole of Tamriel, could live in Black Marsh on subsistence farming, just raising what they needed. That was not sad, Scotti thought; that was hopeful.

Scotti's solution to each of their dilemmas had been the same. Ten percent of the gold they gave him went to Lord Vanech's Building Commission. The rest Scotti kept for himself, and did exactly nothing about the requests.

Within a year, Decumus Scotti had embezzled enough to retire very comfortably, and Black Marsh was better off than it had been in forty years.

The Lusty Argonian Maid

By Crassius Curio

ACT IV, SCENE III, CONTINUED

Lifts–Her–Tail	Certainly not, kind sir! I am here but to clean your chambers.
Crantius Colto	Is that all you have come here for, little one? My chambers?
Lifts–Her–Tail	I have no idea what it is you imply, master. I am but a poor Argonian maid.
Crantius Colto	So you are, my dumpling. And a good one at that. Such strong legs and shapely tail.
Lifts–Her–Tail	You embarrass me, sir!
Crantius Colto	Fear not. You are safe here with me.
Lifts–Her–Tail	I must finish my cleaning, sir. The mistress will have my head if I do not!
Crantius Colto	Cleaning, eh? I have something for you. Here, polish my spear.
Lifts–Her–Tail	But it is huge! It could take me all night!
Crantius Colto	Plenty of time, my sweet. Plenty of time.

END OF ACT IV, SCENE III

ACT VII, SCENE II, CONTINUED

Lifts–Her–Tail	My goodness, that's quite a loaf! But how ever shall it fit my oven?
Crantius Colto	This loaf isn't ready for baking, my sweet. It has yet to rise.
Lifts–Her–Tail	If only we could hurry that along. How would I accomplish such a task?
Crantius Colto	Oh, my foolish little Argonian maid, you must use your hands.
Lifts–Her–Tail	You wish me to kneed the loaf? Here?
Crantius Colto	Of course.
Lifts–Her–Tail	But what if the mistress catches me? Your loaf was meant to satisfy her appetite.
Crantius Colto	Don't fret, my delicate flower. I'll satisfy the mistress's cravings later.
Lifts–Her–Tail	Very well, but I'm afraid my oven isn't hot enough. It could take hours!
Crantius Colto	Plenty of time, my sweet. Plenty of time.

END OF ACT VII, SCENE II

The Sultry Argonian Bard

By Ellya Erdain

ACT VI, SCENE II, CONTINUED

Croon–Tail   My lady, I could never perform your request!

Ellya Erdain   Oh? Is it too fast for you?

Croon–Tail   I fear that it might damage my instrument.

Ellya Erdain   Ah. But you seem to handle your instrument so well, my darling.

Croon–Tail   You flatter me, my lady.

Ellya Erdain   Yes, well it is such a large and magnificent piece. May I hold it?

Croon–Tail   Goodness no! The innkeeper would never approve of such a public display.

Ellya Erdain   Then may I suggest a private performance? Perhaps, away from the noise of the inn where we both may enjoy your tremendous talent.

Croon–Tail   Surely you don't mean for me to accompany you to your room?

Ellya Erdain   Indeed I do, my sweet. Indeed I do.

END OF ACT VI, SCENE II

THE WOLF QUEEN

Book One
by Waughin Jarth

From the pen of the first century third era sage Montocai:

3E 63:

In the autumntide of the year, Prince Pelagius, son of Prince Uriel, who is son of the Empress Kintyra, who is niece of the great Emperor Tiber Septim, came to the High Rock city-state of Camlorn to pay court to the daughter of King Vulstaed. Her name was Quintilla, the most beauteous princess in Tamriel, skilled at all the maidenly skills and an accomplished sorceress.

Eleven years a widower with a young son named Antiochus, Pelagius arrived at court to find that the city-state was being terrorized by a great demon werewolf. Instead of wooing, Pelagius and Quintilla together went out to save the kingdom. With his sword and her sorcery, the beast was slain and by the powers of mysticism, Quintilla chained the beast's soul to a gem. Pelagius had the gem made into a ring and married her.

But it was said that the soul of the wolf stayed with the couple until the birth of their first child.

3E 80:

"The ambassador from Solitude has arrived, your majesty," whispered the steward Balvus.

"Right in the middle of dinner?" muttered the Emperor weakly. "Tell him to wait."

"No, father, it's important that you see him," said Pelagius, rising. "You can't make him wait and then give him bad news. It's undiplomatic."

"Don't go then, you're much better at diplomacy than I am. We should have all the family here," Emperor Uriel II added, suddenly aware how few people were present at his dinner table. "Where's your mother?"

"Sleeping with the archpriest of Kynareth," Pelagius would have said, but he was, as his father said, diplomatic. Instead he said, "At prayer."

"And your brother and sister?"

"Amiel is in Firsthold, meeting with the Archmagister of the Mages Guild. And Galana, though we won't be telling this to the ambassador, of course, is preparing for her wedding to the Duke of Narsis. Since the ambassador expects her to be marrying his patron the King of Solitude instead, we'll tell him that she's at the spa, having a cluster of pestilent boils removed. Tell him that, and he won't press too hard for the marriage, politically expedient though it may be," Pelagius smiled. "You know how queasy Nords are about warty women."

"But dash it, I feel like I should have some family around, so I don't look like some old fool despised by his nearest and dearest," growled the Emperor, correctly suspecting this to be the case. "What about your wife? Where's she and the grandchildren?"

"Quintilla's in the nursery with Cephorus and Magnus. Antiochus is probably whoring around the City. I don't know where Potema is, probably at her studies. I thought you didn't like children around."

"I do during meetings with ambassadors in damp staterooms," sighed the Emperor. "They lend an air of, I don't know, innocence and civility. Ah, show the blasted ambassador in," he said to Balvus.

Potema was bored. It was the rainy season in the Imperial Province, wintertide, and the streets and the gardens of the City were all flooded. She could not remember a time when it was not raining. Had it been only days, or had it been weeks or months since the sun shone? There was no judging of time any more in the constant flickering torch-light of the palace, and as Potema walked through marble and stone hallways, listening to the pelting of the rain, she could think nothing but that she was bored.

Asthephe, her tutor, would be looking for her now. Ordinarily, she did not mind studying. Rote memorization came easily to her. She quizzed herself as she walked down through the empty ballroom. When did Orsinium fall? 1E 980. Who wrote Tamrilean Tractates? Khosey. When was Tiber Septim born? 2E 288. Who is the current King of Daggerfall? Mortyn, son of Gothlyr. Who is the current Silvenar? Varbarenth, son of Varbaril. Who is the Warlord of Lilmoth? Trick question: it's a lady, Ioa.

What will I get if I'm a good girl, and don't get into any trouble, and my tutor says I'm an excellent student? Mother and father will renege on their promise to buy me a daedric katana of my own, saying they never remembered that promise, and it's far too expensive and dangerous for a girl my age.

There were voices coming from the Emperor's stateroom. Her father, her grandfather, and a man with a strange accent, a Nord. Potema moved a stone she had loosened behind a tapestry and listened in.

"Let us be frank, your imperial majesty," came the Nord's voice. "My sire, the King of Solitude, doesn't care if Princess Galana looked like an orc. He wants an alliance with the Imperial family, and you agreed to give him Galana or give back the millions of gold he gave to you to quell the Khajiiti rebellion in Torval. This was the agreement you swore to honor."

"I remember no such agreement," came her father's voice, "Can you, my liege?"

There was a mumbling noise that Potema took to be her grandfather, the ancient Emperor.

"Perhaps we should take a walk to the Hall of Records, my mind may be going," the Nord's voice sounded sarcastic. "I distinctly remember your seal being placed on the agreement before it was locked away. Of course, I may verily be mistaken."

"We will send a page to the Hall to get the document you refer to," replied her father's voice, with the cruel, soothing quality he used whenever he was about to break a promise. Potema knew it well. She replaced the loose stone and hurried out of the ballroom. She knew well how slowly the pages walked, used to running errands for a doddering emperor. She could make it to the Hall of Records in no time at all.

The massive ebony door was locked, of course, but she knew what to do. A year ago, she caught her mother's Bosmer maid pilfering some jewelry, and in exchange for her silence, forced the young woman to teach her how to pick locks. Potema pulled two pins off her red diamond broach and slid the first into the first lock, holding her hand steady, and memorizing the pattern of tumblers and grooves within the mechanism.

Each lock had a geography of its own.

The lock to the kitchen larder: six free tumblers, a frozen seventh, and a counter bolt. She had broken into that just for fun, but if she had been a poisoner, the whole Imperial household would be dead by now, she thought, smiling.

The lock to her brother Antiochus' secret stash of Khajiiti pornography: just two free tumblers and a pathetic poisoned quill trap easily dismantled with pressure on the counterweight. That had been a profitable score. It was strange that Antiochus, who seemed to have no shame, proved so easy to blackmail. She was, after all, only twelve, and the differences between the perversions of the cat people and the perversions of the Cyrodiils seemed pretty academic. Still, Antiochus had to give her the diamond broach, which she treasured.

She had never been caught. Not when she broke into the archmage's study and stole his oldest spellbook. Not when she broke into the guest room of the King of Gilane, and stole his crown the morning before Magnus's official Welcoming ceremony. It had become too easy to torment her family with these little crimes. But here was a document the Emperor wanted, for a very important meeting. She would get it first.

But this, this was the hardest lock she ever opened. Over and over, she massaged the tumblers, gently pushing aside the forked clamp that snatched at her pins, drumming the counterweights. It nearly took her a half a minute to break through the door to the Hall of Records, where the Elder Scrolls were housed.

The documents were well organized by year, province, and kingdom, and it took Potema only a short while to find the Promise of Marriage between Uriel Septim II, by the Grace of the Gods, Emperor of the Holy Cyrodiilic Empire of Tamriel and his daughter the Princess Galana, and His Majesty King Mantiarco of Solitude. She grabbed her prize and was out of the Hall with the door well-locked before the page was even in sight.

Back in the ball room, she loosened the stone and listened eagerly to the conversation within. For a few minutes, the three men, the Nord, the Emperor, and her father just spoke of the weather and some boring diplomatic details. Then there was the sound of footsteps and a young voice, the page.

"Your Imperial Majesty, I have searched the Hall of Records and cannot find the document you asked for."

"There, you see," came Potema's father's voice. "I told you it didn't exist."

"But I saw it!" The Nord's voice was furious. "I was there when my liege and the

emperor signed it! I was there!"

"I hope you aren't doubting the word of my father, the sovereign Emperor of all Tamriel, not when there's now proof that you must have been ... mistaken," Pelagius's voice was low, dangerous.

"Of course not," said the Nord, conceding quickly. "But what will I tell my king? He is to have no connection with the Imperial family, and no gold returned to him, as the agreement — as he and I believed the agreement to be?"

"We don't want any bad feelings between the kingdom of Solitude and us," came the Emperor's voice, rather feeble, but clear enough. "What if we offered King Mantiarco our granddaughter instead?"

Potema felt the chill of the room descend on her.

"The Princess Potema? Is she not too young?" asked the Nord.

"She is thirteen years old," said her father. "That's old enough to wed."

"She would an ideal mate for your king," said the Emperor. "She is, admittedly, from what I see of her, very shy and innocent, but I'm certain she would quickly grasp the ways of court — she is, after all, a Septim. I think she would be an excellent Queen of Solitude. Not too exciting, but noble."

"The granddaughter of the Emperor is not as close as his daughter," said the Nord, rather miserably. "But I don't see how we can refuse the offer. I will send word to my king."

"You have our leave," said the Emperor, and Potema heard the sound of the Nord leaving the stateroom.

Tears streamed down Potema's eyes. She knew who the King of Solitude was from her studies. Mantiarco. Sixty-two years old, and quite fat. And she knew how far Solitude was, and how cold, in the northernmost clime. Her father and grandfather were abandoning her to the barbaric Nords. The voices in the room continued talking.

"Well-acted, my boy. Now, make sure you burn that document," said her father.

"My Prince?" asked the page's querulous voice.

"The agreement between the Emperor and the King of Solitude, you fool. We don't want its existence known."

"My Prince, I told the truth. I couldn't find the document in the Hall of Records. It seems to be missing."

"By Lorkhan!" roared her father. "Why is everything in this palace always misplaced? Go back to the Hall and keep searching until you find it!"

Potema looked at the document. Millions of gold pieces promised to the kingdom of Solitude in the event of Princess Galana not marrying the king. She could bring it into her father, and perhaps as a reward he would not marry her to Mantiarco. Or perhaps not. She could blackmail her father and the Emperor with it, and make a tidy sum of money. Or she could produce it when she became Queen of Solitude to fill her coffers, and buy anything she wanted. More than a daedric katana, that was for certain.

So many possibilities, Potema thought. And she found herself not bored anymore.

Book Two

by Waughin Jarth

From the pen of the first century third era sage Montocai:

3E 82:

A year after the wedding of his 14-year-old granddaughter the Princess Potema to King Mantiarco of the Nordic kingdom of Solitude, the Emperor Uriel Septim II passed on. His son Pelagius Septim II was made emperor, and he faced a greatly depleted treasury, thanks to his father's poor management.

As the new Queen of Solitude, Potema faced opposition from the old Nordic houses, who viewed her as an outsider. Mantiarco had been widowed, and his former queen was loved. She had left him a son, Prince Bathorgh, who was two years older than his stepmother, and loved her not. But the king loved his queen, and suffered with her through miscarriage after miscarriage, until her 29th year, when she bore him a son.

3E 97:

"You must do something to help the pain!" Potema cried, baring her teeth. The healer Kelmeth immediately thought of a she-wolf in labor, but he put the image from his mind. Her enemies called her the Wolf Queen for certes, but not because of any physical resemblance.

"Your Majesty, there is no injury for me to heal. The pain you feel is natural and helpful for the birth," he was going to add more words of consolation, but he had to break off to duck the mirror she flung at him.

"I'm not a pignosed peasant girl!" She snarled, "I am the Queen of Solitude, daughter of the Emperor! Summon the daedra! I'll trade the soul of every last subject of mine for a little comfort!"

"My Lady," said the healer nervously, drawing the curtains and blotting out the cold morning sun. "It is not wise to make such offers even in jest. The eyes of Oblivion are forever watching for just such a rash interjection."

"What would you know of Oblivion, healer?" she growled, but her voice was calmer, quieter. The pain had relaxed. "Would you fetch me that mirror I hurled at you?"

"Are you going to throw it again, your Majesty?" said the healer with a taut smile, obeying her.

"Very likely," she said, looking at her reflection. "And next time I won't miss. But I do look a fright. Is Lord Vhokken still waiting for me in the hall?"

"Yes, your Majesty."

"Well, tell him I just need to fix my hair and I'll be with him. And leave us. I'll howl for you when the pain returns."

"Yes, your Majesty."

A few minutes later, Lord Vhokken was shown into the chamber. He was an enormous bald man whose friends and enemies called Mount Vhokken, and when he spoke it was with the low grumble of thunder. The Queen was one of the very few people Vhokken knew who was not the least bit intimidated by him, and he offered her a smile.

"My queen, how are you feeling?" he asked.

"Damned. But you're looking like Springtide has come to Mount Vhokken. I take it from your merry disposition that you've been made warchief."

"Only temporarily, while your husband the King investigates whether there is evidence behind the rumors of treason on the part of my predecessor Lord Thone."

"If you've planted it as I've instructed, he'll find it," Potema smiled, propping herself up in the bed. "Tell me, is Prince Bathorgh still in the city?"

"What a question, your highness," laughed the mountain. "It's the Tournament of Stamina today, you know the prince would never miss that. The fellow invents new strategies of self-defense every year to show off during the games. Don't you recall last year, where he entered the ring unarmored and after twenty minutes of fending off six bladesmen, left the games without a scratch? He dedicated that bout to his late mother, Queen Amodetha."

"Yes, I recall."

"He's no friend to me or you, your highness, but you must give the man his due respect. He moves like lightning. You wouldn't think it of him, but he always seems to use his awkwardness to his advantage, to throw his opponents off. Some say he learned the style from the orcs to the south. They say he learned from them how to anticipate a foe's attack by some sort of supernatural power."

"There's nothing supernatural about it," said the Queen, quietly. "He gets it from his father."

"Mantiarco never moved like that," Vhokken chuckled.

"I never said he did," said Potema. Her eyes closed and her teeth gritted together. "The pain's returning. You must fetch the healer, but first, I must ask you one other thing — has the new summer palace construction begun?"

"I think so, your Highness."

"Do not think!" she cried, gripping the sheets, biting her lips so a stream of blood dripped down her chin. "Do! Make certain that the construction begins at once, today! Your future, my future, and the future of this child depend on it! Go!"

Four hours later, King Mantiarco entered the room to see his son. His queen smiled weakly as he gave her a kiss on the forehead. When she handed him the child, a tear ran down his face. Another one quickly followed, and then another.

"My Lord," she said fondly. "I know you're sentimental, but really!"

"It's not only the child, though he is beautiful, with all the fair features of his mother," Mantiarco turned to his wife, sadly, his aged features twisted in agony. "My dear wife, there is trouble at the palace. In truth, this birth is the only thing that keeps this day from being the darkest in my reign."

"What is it? Something at the tournament?" Potema pulled herself up in bed. "Something with Bathorgh?"

"No, it's isn't the tournament, but it does relate to Bathorgh. I shouldn't worry you at a time like this. You need your rest."

"My husband, tell me!"

"I wanted to surprise you with a gift after the birth of our child, so I had the old summer palace completely renovated. It's a beautiful place, or at least it was. I thought you might like it. Truth to tell, it was Lord Vhokken idea. It used to be Amodetha's favorite place." Bitterness crept into the king's voice. "Now I've learned why."

"What have you learned?" asked Potema quietly.

"Amodetha deceived me there, with my trusted warchief, Lord Thone. There were letters between them, the most perverse things you've ever read. And that's not the worst of it."

"No?"

"The dates on the letters correspond with the time of Bathorgh's birth. The boy I raised and loved as a son," Mantiarco's voice choked up with emotion. "He was Thone's child, not mine."

"My darling," said Potema, almost feeling sorry for the old man. She wrapped her arms around his neck, as he heaved his sobs down on her and their child.

"Henceforth," he said quietly. "Bathorgh is no longer my heir. He will be banished from the kingdom. This child you have borne me today will grow to rule Solitude."

"And perhaps more," said Potema. "He is the Emperor's grandson as well."

"We will name him Mantiarco the Second."

"My darling, I would love that," said Potema, kissing the king's tear-streaked face. "But may I suggest Uriel, after my grandfather the Emperor, who brought us together in marriage?"

King Mantiarco smiled at his wife and nodded his head. There was a knock at the door.

"My liege," said Mount Vhokken. "His highness Prince Bathorgh has finished the tournament and awaits you to present his award. He has successfully withstood attacks by nine archers and the giant scorpion we brought in from Hammerfell. The crowd is roaring his name. They are calling him The Man Who Cannot Be Hit."

"I will see him," said King Mantiarco sadly, and left the chamber.

"Oh he can be hit, all right," said Potema wearily. "But it does take some doing."

Book Three
by Waughin Jarth

From the pen of the first century third era sage Montocai:

3E 98:

The Emperor Pelagius Septim II died a few weeks before the end of the year, on the 15th of Evening Star during the festival of North Wind's Prayer, which was considered a bad omen for the Empire. He had ruled over a difficult seventeen years. In order to fill the bankrupt treasury, Pelagius had dismissed the Elder Council, forcing them to buy back their positions. Several good but poor councilors had been lost. Many say the Emperor had died as a result of being poisoned by a vengeful former Council member.

His children came to attend his funeral and the coronation of the next Emperor. His youngest son Prince Magnus, 19 years of age, arrived from Almalexia, where he had been a councilor to the royal court. 21-year-old Prince Cephorus arrived from Gilane with his Redguard bride, Queen Bianki. Prince Antiochus at 43 years of age, the eldest child and heir presumptive, had been with his father in the Imperial City. The last to appear was his only daughter, Potema, the so-called Wolf Queen of Solitude. Thirty years old and radiantly beautiful, she arrived with a magnificent entourage, accompanied by her husband, the elderly King Mantiarco and her year-old son, Uriel.

All expected Antiochus to assume the throne of the Empire, but no one knew what to expect from the Wolf Queen.

3E 99:

"Lord Vhokken has been bringing several men to your sister's chambers late at night every night this week," offered the Spymaster. "Perhaps if her husband were made aware —"

"My sister is a devotee of the conqueror gods Reman and Talos, not the love goddess Dibella. She is plotting with those men, not having orgies with them. I'd wager I've slept with more men than she has," laughed Antiochus, and then grew serious. "She's behind the delay of the council offering me the crown, I know it. Six weeks now. They say they need to update records and prepare for the coronation. I'm the Emperor! Crown me, and to Oblivion with the formalities!"

"Your sister is surely no friend of yours, your majesty, but there are other factors at play. Do not forget how your father treated the Council. It is they who need following, and if need be, strong convincing," The Spymaster added, with a suggestive stab of his dagger.

"Do so, but keep your eye on the damnable Wolf Queen as well. You know where to find me."

"At which brothel, your highness?" inquired the Spymaster.

"Today being Fredas, I'll be at the Cat and Goblin."

The Spymaster noted in his report that night that Queen Potema had no visitors, for she was dining across the Imperial Garden at the Blue Palace with her mother, the Dowager Empress Quintilla. It was a warm night for wintertide and surprisingly cloudless though the day had been stormy. The saturated ground could not take any more, so the formal, structured gardens looked as if they had been glazed with water. The two women took their wine to the wide balcony to look over the grounds.

"I believe you are trying to sabotage your half-brother's coronation," said Quintilla, not looking at her daughter. Potema saw how the years had not so much wrinkled her mother as faded her, like the sun on a stone.

"It's not true," said Potema. "But would it bother you very much if it were true?"

"Antiochus is not my son. He was eleven years old when I married your father, and we've never been close. I think that being heir presumptive has stunted his growth. He is old enough to have a family with grown children, and yet he spends all his time at debauchery and fornication. He will not make a very good Emperor," Quintilla sighed and then turned to Potema. "But it is bad for the family for seeds of discontent to be sown. It is easy to divide up into factions, but very difficult to unite again. I fear for the future of the Empire."

"Those sound like the words — are you, by any chance, dying, mother?"

"I've read the omens," said Quintilla with a faint, ironic smile. "Don't forget — I was a renowned sorceress in Camlorn. I will dead in a few months time, and then, not a year later, your husband will die. I only regret that I will not live to see your child Uriel assume the throne of Solitude."

"Have you seen whether —" Potema stopped, not wanting to reveal too many of her plans, even to a dying woman.

"Whether he will be Emperor? Aye, I know the answer to that too, daughter. Don't fear: you'll live to see the answer, one way or the other. I have a gift for him when he is of age," The Dowager Empress removed a necklace with a single great yellow gem from around her neck. "It's a soul gem, infused with the spirit of a great werewolf your father and I defeated in battle thirty-six years ago. I've enchanted it with spells from the School of Illusion so its wearer may charm whoever he choses. An important skill for a king."

"And an emperor," said Potema, taking the necklace. "Thank you, mother."

An hour later, passing the black branches of the sculpted douad shrubs, Potema noticed a dark figure, which vanished into the shadows under the eaves at her approach. She had noticed people following her before: it was one of the hazards of life in the Imperial court. But this man was too close to her chambers. She slipped the necklace around her neck.

"Come out where I can see you," she commanded.

The man emerged from the shadows. A dark little fellow of middle-age dressed in black-dyed goatskin. His eyes were fixed, frozen, under her spell.

"Who do you work for?"

"Prince Antiochus is my master," he said in a dead voice. "I am his spy."

A plan formed. "Is the Prince in his study?"

"No, milady."

"And you have access?"

"Yes, milady."

Potema smiled widely. She had him. "Lead the way."

The next morning, the storm reappeared in all its fury. The pelting on the walls and ceiling was agony to Antiochus, who was discovering that he no longer had his youthful immunity to a late night of hard drinking. He shoved hard against the Argonian wench sharing his bed.

"Make yourself useful and close the window," he moaned.

No sooner had the window been bolted then there was a knock at the door. It was the Spymaster. He smiled at the Prince and handed him a sheet of paper.

"What is this?" said Antiochus, squinting his eyes. "I must still be drunk. It looks like orcish."

"I think you will find it useful, your majesty. Your sister is here to see you."

Antiochus considered getting dressed or sending his bedmate out, but thought better of it. "Show her in. Let her be scandalized."

If Potema was scandalized, she did not show it. Swathed in orange and silver silk, she entered the room with a triumphant smile, followed by the man-mountain Lord Vhokken.

"Dear brother, I spoke to my mother last night, and she advised me very wisely. She said I should not battle with you in public, for the good of our family and the Empire. Therefore," she said, producing from the folds of her robe a piece of paper. "I am offering you a choice."

"A choice?" said Antiochus, returning her smile. "That does sound friendly."

"Abdicate your rights to the Imperial throne voluntarily, and there is no need for me to show the Council this," Potema said, handing her brother the letter. "It is a letter with your seal on it, saying that you knew that your father was not Pelagius Septim II, but the royal steward Fondoukth. Now, before you deny writing the letter, you cannot deny the rumors, nor that the Imperial Council will believe that your father, the old fool, was quite capable of being cuckolded. Whether it's true or not, or whether the letter is a forgery or not, the scandal of it would ruin your chances of being the Emperor."

Antiochus's face had gone white with fury.

"Don't fear, brother," said Potema, taking back the letter from his shaking hands. "I will see to it that you have a very comfortable life, and all the whores your heart, or any other organ, desires."

Suddenly Antiochus laughed. He looked over at his Spymaster and winked. "I remember when you broke into my stash of Khajiiti erotica and blackmailed me. That was close to twenty years ago. We've got better locks now, you must have noticed. It must have killed you that you couldn't use your own skills to get what you wanted."

Potema merely smiled. It didn't matter. She had him.

"You must have charmed my servant here into getting you into my study to use my seal," Antiochus smirked. "A spell, perhaps, from your mother, the witch?"

Potema continued to smile. Her brother was cleverer than she thought.

"Did you know that Charm spells, even powerful ones, only last so long? Of course, you didn't. You never were one for magic. Let me tell you, a generous salary is a stronger motivation for keeping a servant in the long run, sister," Antiochus took out his own sheet of paper. "Now I have a choice for you."

"What is that?" said Potema, her smile faltering.

"It looks like nonsense, but if you know what you're looking for, it's very clear. It's a practice sheet — your handwriting attempting to look like my handwriting. It's a good gift you have. I wonder if you haven't done this before, imitating another person's handwriting. I understand a letter was found from your husband's dead wife saying that his first son was a bastard. I wonder if you wrote that letter. I wonder if I showed this evidence of your gift to your husband whether he would believe you wrote that letter. In the future, dear Wolf Queen, don't lay the same trap twice."

Potema shook her head, furious, unable to speak.

"Give me your forgery and go take a walk in the rain. And then, later today, unhatch whatever other plots you have to keep me from the throne." Antiochus fixed his eyes on Potema's. "I will be Emperor, Wolf Queen. Now go."

Potema handed her brother the letter and left the room. For a few moments, out in the hallway, she said nothing. She merely glared at the slivers of rainwater dripping down the marble wall from a tiny, unseen crack.

"Yes, you will, brother," she said. "But not for very long."

Book Four
by Waughin Jarth

From the pen of the first century third era sage Montocai:

3E 109:

Ten years after being crowned Emperor of Tamriel, Antiochus Septim had impressed his subjects with little but the enormity of his lust for carnal pleasures. By his second wife, Gysilla, he had a daughter in the year 104, who he named Kintyra, after his great-great-great grandaunt, the Empress. Enormously fat and marked by every venereal disease known to the Healers, Antiochus spent little time on politics. His siblings, by marked contrast, excelled in this field. Magnus had married Hellena, the Cyrodiil Queen of Lilmoth — the Argonian priest-king having been executed — and was representing the Imperial interests in Black Marsh admirably. Cephorus and his wife Bianki were ruling the Hammerfell kingdom of Gilane with a healthy brood of children. But no one was more politically active than Potema, the Wolf-Queen of the Skyrim kingdom of Solitude.

Nine years after the death of her husband, King Mantiarco, Potema still ruled as regent for her young son, Uriel. Their court had become very fashionable, particularly for rulers who had a grudge to bear against the Emperor. All the kings of Skyrim visited Castle Solitude regularly, and over the years, emissaries from the lands of Morrowind and High Rock did as well. Some guests came from even farther away.

3E 110:

Potema stood at the harbor and watched the boat from Pyandonea arrive. Against the gray, breaking waves where she had seen so many vessels of Tamrielic manufacture, it looked less than exotic. Insectoid, certainly, with its membranous sails and rugged chitin hull, but she had seen similar if not identical seacraft in Morrowind. No, if not for the flag which was markedly alien, she would not have picked out the ship from others in the harbor. As the salty mist ballooned around her, she held out her hand in welcome to the visitors from another island empire.

The men aboard were not merely pale, they were entirely colorless, as if their flesh were made of some white limpid jelly, but she had been forewarned. At the arrival of the King and his translator, she looked directly into their blank eyes and offered her hand. The King made noises.

"His Great Majesty, King Orgnum," said the translator, haltingly. "Expresses his delight at your beauty. He thanks you for giving him refuge from these dangerous seas."

"You speak Cyrodilic very well," said Potema.

"I am fluent in the languages of four continents," said the translator. "I can speak to the denizens of my own country Pyandonea, as well as those of Atmora, Akavir, and here, in Tamriel. Yours is the easiest, actually. I was looking forward to this voyage."

"Please tell his highness that he is welcome here, and that I am entirely at his disposal," said Potema, smiling. Then she added, "You understand the context? That I am just being polite?"

"Of course," said the translator, and then made several noises at the King, which the King reacted to with a smile. While they conversed, Potema looked up the dock and saw the now familiar gray cloaks watching her while they spoke with Levlet, Antiochus's man. The Psijic Order from the Summerset Isle. Very bothersome.

"My diplomatic emissary Lord Vhokken will show you to your rooms," said Potema. "Unfortunately, I have some other guests as well who require my attention. I hope your great majesty understands."

His Great Majesty King Orgnum did understand, and Potema made arrangements to dine with the Pyandoneans that evening. Meeting with the Psijic Order required all of her concentration. She dressed in her simplest black and gold robe and went to her stateroom to prepare. Her son, Uriel, was on the throne, playing with his pet joghat.

"Good morning, mom."

"Good morning, darling," said Potema, lifting her son in the air with feigned stain. "Talos, but you're heavy. I don't think I've ever carried such a heavy ten-year-old."

"That's probably because I'm eleven," said Uriel, perfectly aware of his mother's tricks. "And you're going to say that as an eleven-year-old, I should probably be with my tutor."

"I was fanatical about studying at your age," said Potema.

"I am king," said Uriel petulantly.

"But don't be satisfied with that," said Potema. "By all rights, you should be emperor already, you understand that, don't you?"

Uriel nodded his head. Potema took a moment to marvel at his likeness to the portraits of Tiber Septim. The same ruthless brow and powerful chin. When he was older and lost his baby fat, he'd be a splitting image of his great great great great great granduncle. Behind her, she heard the door opening and an usher bringing in several gray cloaks. She stiffened slightly, and Uriel, on cue, jumped down from the throne and left the stateroom, pausing to greet the most important of the Psijics.

"Good Morning, Master Iachesis," he said, enunciating each syllable with a regal accent that made Potema's heart soar. "I hope your accommodations at Castle Solitude meet with your approval."

"They do, King Uriel, thank you," said Iachesis, delighted and charmed.

Iachesis and his Psijics entered the chamber and the door was shut behind them. Potema sat only for a moment on the throne before stepping off the dais and greeting her guests.

"I am so sorry to have kept you waiting," said Potema. "To think that you sailed all the way from the Summerset Isles and I should keep you waiting any longer. You must forgive me."

"It's not all that long a voyage," said one of the gray cloaks, angrily. "It isn't as if we sailed all the way from Pyandonea."

"Ah. You've seen my most recent guests, King Orgnum and his retinue," said Potema breezily. "I suppose you think it unusual, me entertaining them, as we all know the Pyandoneans mean to invade Tamriel. You are, I take it, as neutral in this as you are in all political matters?"

"Of course," said Iachesis proudly. "We have nothing to gain or lose by the invasion. The Psijic Order preceded the organization of Tamriel under the Septim Dynasty and we shall survive under any political regime."

"Rather like a flea on whatever mongrel happens along, are you?" said Potema, narrowing her eyes. "Don't overestimate your importance, Iachesis. Your order's child, the Mages Guild, has twice the power you have, and they are entirely on my side. We are in the process of making an agreement with King Orgnum. When the Pyandoneans take over and I am in my proper place as Empress of this continent, then you shall know your proper place in the order of things."

With a majestic stride, Potema left the stateroom, leaving the grey cloaks to look from one to the other.

"We must speak to Lord Levlet," said one of the grey cloaks.

"Yes," said Iachesis. "Perhaps we should."

Levlet was quickly found at his usual place at the Moon and Nausea tavern. As the three grey cloaks entered, led by Iachesis, the smoke and the noise seemed to die in their path. Even the smell of tobacco and flin dissipated in their wake. He rose and then escorted them to a small room upstairs.

"You've reconsidered," said Levlet with a broad smile.

"Your Emperor," said Iachesis, and then corrected himself, "Our Emperor originally asked for our support in defending the west coast of Tamriel from the Pyandonean fleet in return for twelve million gold pieces. We offered our services at fifty. Upon reflection on the dangers that a Pyandonean invasion would have, we accept his earlier offer."

"The Mages Guild has generously — "

"Perhaps for as low ten million gold pieces," said Iachesis quickly.

Over the course of dinner, Potema promised King Orgnum through the interpreter, to lead an insurrection against her brother. She was delighted to discover that her capacity for lying worked in many different cultures. Potema shared her bed that night with King Orgnum, as it seemed the polite and diplomatic thing to do. As it turned out, he was one of the better lovers she had ever had. He gave her some herbs before beginning that made her feel as if she was floating on the surface of time, conscious only of the gestures of love after she had found herself making them. She felt herself like the cooling mist, quenching the fire of his lust over and over and over again. In the morning, when he kissed her on the cheek, and said with his bald white eyes that he was leaving her, she felt a stab of regret.

The ship left harbor that morning, en route to the Summerset Isles and the imminent invasions. She waved them off to sea as she footsteps behind her. It was Levlet.

"They will do it for eight million, your highness" he said.

"Thank Mara," said Potema. "I need more time for an insurrection. Pay them from my treasury, and then go to the Imperial City and get the twelve million from Antiochus. We should make a good profit from this game, and you, of course, will have your share."

Three months later, Potema heard that the fleet of the Pyandoneans had been utterly destroyed by a storm that had appeared suddenly off the Isle of Artaeum. The home port of the Psijic Order. King Orgnum and all of his ships had been utterly annihilated.

"Sometimes making people hate you," she said, holding her son Uriel close, "Is how you make a profit."

Book Five

by Waughin Jarth

From the pen of Inzolicus, Second Century Sage and Student of Montocai:

3E 119:

For twenty-one years, The Emperor Antiochus Septim ruled Tamriel, and proved an able leader despite his moral laxity. His greatest victory was in the War of the Isle in the year 110, when the Imperial fleet and the royal navies of Summerset Isle, together with the magical powers of the Psijic Order, succeeded in destroying the Pyandonean invading armada. His siblings, King Magnus of Lilmoth, King Cephorus of Gilane, and Potema, the Wolf Queen of Solitude, ruled well and relations between the Empire and the kingdoms of Tamriel were much improved. Still, centuries of neglect had not repaired all the scars that existed between the Empire and the kings of High Rock and Skyrim.

During a rare visitation from his sister and nephew Uriel, Antiochus, who had suffered from several illnesses over his reign, lapsed into a coma. For months, he lingered in between life and death while the Elder Council prepared for the ascension of his fifteen-year-old daughter Kintyra to the throne.

3E 120:

"Mother, I can't marry Kintyra," said Uriel, more amused by the suggestion than offended. "She's my first cousin. And besides, I believe she's engaged to one of the lords of council, Modellus."

"You're so squeamish. There's a time and a place for propriety," said Potema. "But you're correct at any rate about Modellus, and we shouldn't offend the Elder Council at this critical juncture. How do you feel about Princess Rakma? You spent a good deal of time in her company in Farrun."

"She's all right," said Uriel. "Don't tell me you want to hear all the dirty details."

"Please spare me your study of her anatomy," Potema grimaced. "But would you marry her?"

"I suppose so."

"Very good. I'll make the arrangements then," Potema made a note for herself before continuing. "King Lleromo has been a difficult ally to keep, and a political marriage should keep Farrun on our side. Should we need them. When is the funeral?"

"What funeral?" asked Uriel. "You mean for Uncle Antiochus?"

"Of course," sighed Potema. "Anyone else of note die recently?"

"There were a bunch of little Redguard children running through the halls, so I guess Cephorus has arrived. Magnus arrived at court yesterday, so it ought to be any day now."

"It's time to address the Council then," said Potema, smiling.

She dressed in black, not her usual colorful ensembles. It was important to look the part of the grieving sister. Regarding herself in the mirror, she felt that she looked all of her fifty-three years. A shock of silver wound its way through her auburn hair. The long, cold, dry winters in northern Skyrim had created a map of wrinkles, thin as a spiderweb, all across her face. Still, she knew that when she smiled, she could win hearts, and when she frowned, she could inspire fear. It was enough for her purposes.

Potema's speech to the Elder Council is perhaps helpful to students of public speaking.

She began with flattery and self-abasement: "My most august and wise friends, members of the Elder Council, I am but a provincial queen, and I can only assume to bring to issue what you yourselves must have already pondered."

She continued on to praise the late Emperor, who had been a popular ruler, despite his flaws: "He was a true Septim and a great warrior, destroying — with your counsel — the near invincible armada of Pyandonea."

But little time was wasted, before she came to her point: "The Empress Gysilla unfortunately did nothing to temper my brother's lustful spirits. In point of fact, no whore in the slums of the city spread out on more beds than she. Had she attended to her duties in the Imperial bedchamber more faithfully, we would have a true heir to the Empire, not the halfwit, milksop bastards who call themselves the Emperor's children. The girl called Kintyra is popularly believed to be the daughter of Gysilla and the Captain of the Guard. It may be that she is the daughter of Gysilla and the boy who cleans the cistern. We can never know for certain. Not as certainly as we can know the lineage of my son, Uriel. The eldest true son of the Septim Dynasty. My lords, the princes of the Empire will not stand for a bastard on the throne, that I can assure you."

She ended mildly, but with a call to action: "Posterity will judge you. You know what must be done."

That evening, Potema entertained her brothers and their wives in the Map Room, her favorite of the Imperial dining chambers. The walls were splashed with bright, if fading representations of the Empire and all the known lands beyond, Atmora, Yokunda, Akavir, Pyandonea, Thras. Overhead the great glass domed ceiling, wet with rain,

displayed distorted images of the stars overhead. Lightning flashed every other minute, casting strange phantom shadows on the walls.

"When will you speak to the Council?" asked Potema as dinner was served.

"I don't know if I will," said Magnus. "I don't believe I have anything to say."

"I'll speak to them when they announce the coronation of Kintyra," said Cephorus. "Merely as a formality to show my support and the support of Hammerfell."

"You can speak for all of Hammerfell?" asked Potema, with a teasing smile. "The Redguards must love you very much."

"We have a unique relationship with the Empire in Hammerfell," said Cephorus's wife, Bianki. "Since the treaty of Stros M'kai, it's been understood that we are part of the Empire, but not a subject."

"I understand you've already spoken to the Council," said Magnus's wife, Hellena, pointedly. She was a diplomat by nature, but as the Cyrodilic ruler of an Argonian kingdom, she knew how to recognize and confront adversity.

"Yes, I have," said Potema, pausing to savor a slice of braised jalfbird. "I gave them a short speech about the coronation this afternoon."

"Our sister is an excellent public speaker," said Cephorus.

"You're too kind," said Potema, laughing. "I do many things better than speaking."

"Such as?" asked Bianki, smiling.

"Might I ask what you said in your speech?" asked Magnus, suspiciously.

There was a knock on the chamber door. The head steward whispered something to Potema, who smiled in response and rose from the table.

"I told the Council that I would give my full support to the coronation, provided they proceed with wisdom. What could be sinister about that?" Potema said, and took her glass of wine with her to the door. "If you'll pardon me, my niece Kintyra wishes to have a word with me."

Kintyra stood in the hall with the Imperial Guard. She was but a child, but on reflection, Potema realized that at her age, she was already married two years to Mantiarco. There was a similarity, to be certain. Potema could see Kintyra as the young queen, with dark eyes and pallid skin smooth and resolute like marble. Anger flashed momentarily in Kintyra's eyes on seeing her aunt, but emotion left her, replaced with calm Imperial presence.

"Queen Potema," she said serenely. "I have been informed that my coronation will take place in two days time. Your presence at the ceremony will not be welcome. I have already given orders to your servants to have your belongings packed, and an escort will be accompanying you back to your kingdom tonight. That is all. Goodbye, aunt."

Potema began to reply, but Kintyra and her guard turned and moved back down the corridor to the stateroom. The Wolf Queen watched them go, and then reentered the Map Room.

"Sister-in-Law," said Potema, addressing Bianki with deep malevolence. "You asked what I do better than speaking? The answer is: war."

Book Six

From the pen of Inzolicus, Second Century Sage:

3E 120:

The fifteen-year-old Empress Kintyra Septim II, daughter of Antiochus, was coroneted on the 3rd day of First Seed. Her uncles Magnus, King of Lilmoth, and Cephorus, King of Gilane, were in attendance, but her aunt, Potema, the Wolf Queen of Solitude, had been banished from the court. Once back in her kingdom, Queen Potema began assembling the rebellion, which was to be known as the War of the Red Diamond. All the allies she had made over the years of disgruntled kings and nobles joined forces with her against the new Empress.

The first early strikes against the Empire were entirely successful. Throughout Skyrim and northern High Rock, the Imperial army found themselves under attack. Potema and her forces washed over Tamriel like a plague, inciting riots and insurrections everywhere they touched. In the autumn of the year, the loyal Duke of Glenpoint on the coast of High Rock sent an urgent request for reinforcements from the Imperial Army, and Kintyra, to inspire the resistance to the Wolf Queen, led the army herself.

3E 121:

"We don't know where they are," said the Duke, deeply embarrassed. "I've sent scouts out all over the countryside. I can only assume that they've retreated up north upon hearing of your army's arrival."

"I hate to say it, but I was hoping for a battle," said Kintyra. "I'd like to put my aunt's head on a spike and parade it around the Empire. Her son Uriel and his army are right on the border to the Imperial Province, mocking me. How are they able to be so successful? Are they just that good in battle or do my subjects truly hate me?"

She was tired after many months of struggling through the mud of autumn and winter. Crossing the Dragontail Mountains, her army nearly marched into an ambush. A blizzard snap in the normally temperate Barony of Dwynnen was so unexpected and severe that it must certainly have been cast by one of Potema's wizard allies. Everywhere she turned, she felt her aunt's touch. And now, her chance of facing the Wolf Queen at last had been thwarted. It was almost too much to bear.

"It is fear, pure and simple," said the Duke. "That is her greatest weapon."

"I need to ask," said Kintyra, hoping that by sheer will she could keep her voice from revealing any of the fear the Duke spoke of. "You've seen the army. Is it true that she has summoned a force of undead warriors to do her bidding?"

"No, as a matter of fact, it's not true, but she certainly fosters that rumor. Her army attacks at night, partly for strategic reasons, and partly to advance fears like that. She has, so far as I know, no supernatural aid other than the standard battlemages and nightblades of any modern army."

"Always at night," said Kintyra thoughtfully. "I suppose that's to disguise their numbers."

"And to move her troops into position before we're aware of them" added the Duke. "She's the master of the sneak attack. When you hear a march to the east, you can be certain she's already on top of you from the south. But listen, we'll discuss this all tomorrow morning. I've prepared the castle's best rooms for you and your men."

Kintyra sat in her tower suite and by the light of the moon and a single tallow candle, she penned a letter to her husband-to-be, Lord Modellus, back in the Imperial City. She hoped to be married to him in the summer at the Blue Palace her grandmother Quintilla had loved so much, but the war may not permit it. As she wrote, she gazed out the window at the courtyard below and the haunted, leafless trees of winter. Two of her guards stood on the battlements, several feet away from one another. Just like Modellus and Kintyra, she thought, and proceeded to expound on the metaphor in her letter.

A knock on the door interrupted her poetry.

"A letter, your majesty, from Lord Modellus," said the young courier, handing the note to her.

It was short, and she read it quickly before the courier had a chance to retire. "I'm confused by something. When did he write this?"

"One week ago," said the courier. "He said it was urgent that I make it here as quickly as possible while he mobilized the army. I imagine they've left the City already."

Kintyra dismissed the courier. Modellus said that he had received a letter from her, urgently calling for reinforcements to the battle at Glenpoint. But there was no battle at Glenpoint, and she had only just arrived today. Then who wrote the letter in her handwriting, and why would they want Modellus to bring a second army out of the Imperial City into High Rock?

Feeling a chill from the night air at the window, Kintyra went to shut the latch. The two guards on the battlements were gone. She leaned over at the sound of a muffled struggle behind one of the barren trees, and did not hear the door open.

When she turned, she saw Queen Potema and Mentin, Duke of Glenpoint, in the room with a host of guards.

"You move quietly, aunt," she said after a moment's pause. She turned to the Duke. "What turned you against your loyalty to the Empire? Fear?"

"And gold," said the Duke simply.

"What happened to my army?" asked Kintyra, trying to look Potema steadily in the face. "Is the battle over so soon?"

"All your men are dead," smiled Potema. "But there was no battle here. Merely quiet and efficient assassination. There will be battles ahead, against Modellus in the Dragontail Mountains and against the remnants of the Imperial Army in the City. I'll send you regular updates on the progress of the war."

"So I am to be kept here as your hostage?" asked Kintyra, flatly, suddenly aware of the solidity of the stones and the great height of her tower room. "Damn you, look at me! I am your Empress!"

"Think of it this way, I'm taking you from being a fifth rate ruler to a first rate martyr," said Potema with a wink. "But I understand if you don't want to thank me for that."

Book Seven

From the pen of Inzolicus, Second Century Sage:

3E 125:

The exact date of the Empress Kintyra Septim II's execution in the tower at Glenpoint Castle is open to some speculation. Some believe she was slain shortly after her imprisonment in the 121st year, while others maintain that she was likely kept alive as a hostage until shortly before her uncle Cephorus, King of Gilane, reconquered western High Rock in the summer of the 125th year. The certainty of Kintyra's demise rallied many against the Wolf Queen Potema and her son, who had been crowned Emperor Uriel Septim III four years previously when he invaded the under-guarded Imperial City.

Cephorus concentrated his army on the war in High Rock, while his brother Magnus, King of Lilmoth, brought his Argonian troops through loyal Morrowind and into Skyrim to fight in Potema's home province. The reptilian troops fought well in the summer months, but during the winter, they retired south to regroup and attack again when the

weather was warm. At this stalemate, the War lasted out two more years.

Also, in the 125th year, Magnus's wife Hellena gave birth to their first child, a boy who they named Pelagius, after the Emperor who fathered Magnus, Cephorus, the late Emperor Antiochus, and the dread Wolf Queen of Solitude.

3E 127:

Potema sat on soft silk cushions in the warm grass in front of her tent and watched the sun rise over the dark woods on the other side of the meadow. It was a peculiarly vibrant morning, typical of Skyrim summertide. The high chirrup of insects buzzed all around her and the sky surged with thousands of fallowing birds, rolling over one another and forming a multitude of patterns. Nature was unaware of the war coming to Falconstar, she surmised.

"Your highness, a message from the army in Hammerfell," said one of her maids, bringing in a courier. He was breathing hard, stained with sweat and mud. Evidence of a long, fast ride over many, many miles.

"My queen," said the courier, looking to the ground. "I bring grave news of your son, the Emperor. He met your brother King Cephorus's army in Hammerfell in the countryside

of Ichidag and there did battle. You would be proud, for he fought well, but in the end, the Imperial army was defeated and your son, our Emperor, was captured. King Cephorus is bringing him to Gilane."

Potema listened to the news, scowling. "That clumsy fool," she said at last.

Potema stood up and strolled into camp, where the men were arming themselves, preparing for battle. Long ago, the soldiers understood that their lady did not stand on ceremony, and she would prefer that they work rather than salute her. Lord Vhokken was ahead of her, already meeting with the commander of the battlemages, discussing last minute strategy.

"My queen," said the courier, who had been following her. "What are you going to do?"

"I'm going to win this battle with Magnus, despite his superior position holding the ruins of Kogmenthist Castle," said Potema. "And then when I know what Cephorus means to do with the Emperor, I'll respond accordingly. If there's a ransom to be paid, I'll pay it; if there's a prison exchange needed, so be it. Now, please, bath yourself and rest, and try not to get in the way of the war."

"It's not an ideal scenario," said Lord Vhokken when Potema had entered the commander's tent. "If we attack the castle from the west, we'll be running directly into the fire from their mages and archers. If we come from the east, we'll be going through swamps, and the Argonians do better in that type of environment than we do. A lot better."

"What about the north and south? Just hills, correct?"

"Very steep hills, your highness," said the commander. "We should post bowmen there, but we'll be too vulnerable putting out the majority of our force."

"So it's the swamp," said Potema, and added, pragmatically. "Unless we withdraw and wait for them to come out before fighting."

"If we wait, Cephorus will have his army here from High Rock, and we'll be trapped between the two of them," said Lord Vhokken. "Not a preferable situation."

"I'll talk to the troops," said the commander. "Try to prepare them for the swamp attack."

"No," said Potema. "I'll speak to them."

In full battlegear, the soldiers gathered in the center of camp. They were a motley collection of men and women, Cyrodiils, Nords, Bretons, and Dunmer, youngbloods and old veterans, the sons and daughters of nobles, shopkeepers, serfs, priests, prostitutes, farmers, academics, adventurers. All of them under the banner of the Red Diamond, the symbol of the Imperial Family of Tamriel.

"My children," Potema said, her voice ringing out, hanging in the still morning mist. "We have fought in many battles together, over mountaintops and beach heads, through forests and deserts. I have seen great acts of valor from each one of you, which does my heart proud. I have also seen dirty fighting, backstabbing, cruel and wanton feats of savagery, which pleases me equally well. For you are all warriors."

Warming to her theme, Potema walked the line from soldier to soldier, looking each one in the eye: "War is in your blood, in your brain, in your muscles, in everything you think and everything you do. When this war is over, when the forces are vanquished that seek to deny the throne to the true emperor, Uriel Septim III, you may cease to be warriors. You may choose to return to your lives before the war, to your farms and your cities, and show off your scars and tell tales of the deeds you did this day to your wondering neighbors. But on this day, make no mistake, you are warriors. You are war."

She could see her words were working. All around her, bloodshot eyes were focusing on the slaughter to come, arms tensing around weapons. She continued in her loudest cry, "And you will move through the swamplands, like an unstoppable power from the blackest part of Oblivion, and you will rip the scales from the reptilian things in Kogmenthist Castle. You are warriors, and you need not only fight, you must win. You must win!"

The soldiers roared in response, shocking the birds from the trees all around the camp.

From a vantage point on the hills to the south, Potema and Lord Vhokken had excellent views of the battle as it raged. It looked like two swarms of two colors of insect moving back and forth over a clump of dirt which was the castle ruins. Occasionally, a burst of flame or a cloud of acid from one of the mages would flicker over the battle arresting their attention, but hour after hour, the fighting seemed like nothing but chaos.

"A rider approaches," said Lord Vhokken, breaking the silence.

The young Redguard woman was wearing the crest of Gilane, but carried a white flag. Potema allowed her to approach. Like the courier from the morning, the rider was well travel-worn.

"Your Highness," she said, out of breath. "I have been sent from your brother, my lord King Cephorus, to bring you dire news. Your son Uriel was captured in Ichidag on the field in battle and from there transported to Gilane."

"I know all this," said Potema scornfully. "I have couriers of my own. You can tell your master that after I've won this battle, I'll pay whatever ransom or exchange —"

"Your Highness, an angry crowd met the caravan your son was in before it made it to Gilane," the rider said quickly, "Your son is dead. He had been burned to death within his carriage. He is dead."

Potema turned from the young woman and looked down at the battle. Her soldiers were going to win. Magnus's army was in retreat.

"One other item of news, your highness," said the rider. "King Cephorus is being proclaimed Emperor."

Potema did not look at the woman. Her army was celebrating their victory.

Book Eight

From the pen of Inzolicus, Second Century Sage:

3E 127:

Following the Battle of Ichidag, the Emperor Uriel Septim III was captured and, before he was able to be brought to his uncle's castle in the Hammerfell kingdom of Gilane, he met his death at the hands of an angry mob. This uncle, Cephorus, was thereafter proclaimed emperor and rode to the Imperial City. The troops formerly loyal to Emperor Uriel and his mother, the Wolf Queen Potema, pledged themselves to the new Emperor. In return for their support, the nobility of Skyrim, High Rock, Hammerfell, the Summerset Isle, Valenwood, Black Marsh, and Morrowind demanded and received a new level of autonomy and independence from the Empire. The War of the Red Diamond was at an end.

Potema continued to fight a losing battle, her area of influence dwindling and dwindling until only her kingdom of Solitude remained in her power. She summoned daedra to fight for her, had her necromancers resurrect her fallen enemies as undead warriors, and mounted attack after attack on the forces of her brothers, the Emperor Cephorus Septim I and King Magnus of Lilmoth. Her allies began leaving her as her madness grew, and her only companions were the zombies and skeletons she had amassed over the years. The kingdom of Solitude became a land of death. Stories of the ancient Wolf Queen being waited on by rotting skeletal chambermaids and holding war plans with vampiric generals terrified her subjects.

3E 137:

Magnus opened up the small window in his room. For the first time in weeks, he heard the sounds of a city: carts squeaking, horses clopping over the cobblestones, and somewhere a child laughing. He smiled as he returned to his bedside to wash his face and finish dressing. There was a distinctive knock on the door.

"Come in, Pel," he said.

Pelagius bounded into the room. It was obvious that he had been up for hours. Magnus marveled at his energy, and wondered how much longer battles would last if they were run by twelve-year-old boys.

"Did you see outside yet?" Pelagius asked. "All the townspeople have come back! There are shops, and a Mages Guild, and down by the harbor, I saw a hundred shops come in from all over the place!"

"They don't have to be afraid anymore. We've taken care of all the zombies and ghosts that used to be their neighbors, and they know it's safe to come back."

"Is Uncle Cephorus going to turn into a zombie when he dies?" asked Pelagius.

"I wouldn't put that past him," laughed Magnus. "Why do you ask?"

"I heard some people saying that he was old and sick," said Pelagius.

"He's not that old," said Magnus. "He's sixty years old. That's just two years older than I."

"And how old is Aunt Potema?" asked Pelagius.

"Seventy," said Magnus. "And yes, that is old. Any more questions will have to wait. I have to go meet with the commander now, but we can talk at supper. You can make yourself busy, and not get into any trouble?"

"Yes, sir," said Pelagius. He understood that his father had to continue to hold siege on aunt Potema's castle. After they took it over and locked her up, they would move out of the inn and into the castle. Pelagius was not looking forward to that. The whole town had a funny, sweet, dead smell, but he could not get even as close as the castle moat without gagging from the stench. They could dump a million flowers on the place and it wouldn't make any difference at all.

He walked through the city for hours, buying some food and then some ribbons for his sister and mother back in Lilmoth. He thought about who else he needed to buy gifts for and was stumped. All his cousins, the children of Uncle Cephorus, Uncle Antiochus, and Aunt Potema, had died during the war, some of them in battle and some of them during the famines because so many crops had been burned. Aunt Bianki had died last year. There was only he, his mother, his sister, his father, and his uncle the Emperor left. And Aunt Potema. But she didn't really count.

When he came upon the Mages Guild earlier that morning, he had decided not to go in. Those places always spooked him with their strange smoke and crystals and old books. This time, it occurred to Pelagius that he might buy a gift for Uncle Cephorus. A souvenir of Solitude's Mages Guild.

An old woman was having trouble with the front door, so Pelagius opened it for her. "Thank you," she said.

She was easily the oldest thing he had ever seen. Her face looked like an old rotted apple framed with a wild whirl of bright white hair. He instinctively moved away from her gnarled talon when she started to pat him on the head. But there was a gem around her neck that immediately fascinated him. It was a single bright yellow jewel, but it almost looked there was something trapped within. When the light hit it from the candles, it brought out the form of a four-legged beast, pacing.

"It's a soul gem," she said. "Infused with the spirit of a great demon werewolf. It was enchanted long, long ago with the power to charm people, but I've been thinking about giving it another spell. Perhaps something from the School of Alteration like Lock or Shield." She paused and looked at the boy carefully with yellowed, rheumy eyes. "You look familiar to me, boy. What's your name?"

"Pelagius," he said. He normally would have said "Prince Pelagius," but he was told not to draw attention to himself while in town.

"I used to know someone named Pelagius," the old woman said, and slowly smiled. "Are you here alone, Pelagius?"

"My father is... with the army, storming the castle. But he'll be back when the walls have been breached."

"Which I dare say won't take too much longer," sighed the old woman. "Nothing, no matter how well built, tends to last. Are you buying something in the Mages Guild?"

"I wanted to buy a gift for my uncle," said Pelagius. "But I don't know if I have enough gold."

The old woman left the boy to look over the wares while she went to the Guild enchanter. He was a young Nord, ambitious, and new to the kingdom of Solitude. It took little persuasion and a lot of gold to convince him to remove the charm spell from the soul gem and imbue it with a powerful curse, a slow poison that would drain wisdom from its wearer year by year until he or she lost all reason. She also purchased a cheap ring of fire resistance.

"For your kindness to an old woman, I've bought you these," she said, giving the boy the necklace and the ring. "You can give the ring to your uncle, and tell him it has been enchanted with a levitation spell, so if ever he needs to leap from high places, it will protect him. The soulgem is for you."

"Thank you," said the boy. "But this is too kind of you."

"Kindness has nothing to do with it," she answered, quite honestly. "You see, I was in the Hall of Records at the Imperial Palace once or twice, and I read about you in the foretellings of the Elder Scrolls. You will be Emperor one day, my boy, the Emperor Pelagius Septim III, and with this soul gem to guide you, posterity will always remember you and your deeds."

With those words, the old woman disappeared down an alley behind the Mages Guild. Pelagius looked after her, but he did not think to search behind a heap of stones. If he had, he would have found a tunnel under the city into the very heart of . And if he had found his way there, he would have found, past the shambling undead and the moldering remains of a once grand palace, the bedroom of the queen.

In that bedroom, he would find the Wolf Queen of Solitude in repose, listening to the sounds of her castle collapsing. And he would see a toothless grin growing on her face as she breathed her last.

3E 137:

Potema Septim died after a month long siege on her castle. While she lived, she had been the Wolf Queen of Solitude, Daughter of the Emperor Pelagius II, Wife of King Mantiarco, Aunt of the Empress Kintyra II, Mother of Emperor Uriel III, and Sister of the Emperors Antiochus and Cephorus. At her death, Magnus appointed his son, Pelagius, as the titular head of Solitude, under guidance from the royal council.

3E 140:

The Emperor Cephorus Septim died after falling from his horse. His brother was proclaimed the Emperor Magnus Septim.

3E 141:

Pelagius, King of Solitude, is recorded as "occasionally eccentric" in the Imperial Annals. He marries Katarish, Duchess of Vvardenfell.

3E 145:

The Emperor Magnus Septim dies. His son, who will be known as Pelagius the Mad, is coronated.

A Concise Account of the Great War Between the Empire and the Aldmeri Dominion

by Legate Justianus Quintius

Author's Note: Much of what is written in this book is pieced together from documents captured from the enemy during the war, interrogation of prisoners, and eyewitness accounts from surviving soldiers and Imperial officers. I myself commanded the Tenth Legion in Hammerfell and Cyrodiil until I was wounded in 175 during the assault on the Imperial City. That said, the full truth of some events may never be known. I have done my best to fill in the gaps with educated conjectures based on my experience as well as my hard-earned knowledge of the enemy.

The Rise of the Thalmor

Although it is not well known, Summerset Isle suffered from the Oblivion Crisis as much as Cyrodiil did. The elves made war upon the Oblivion invaders, occasionally even crossing over to close down Oblivion gates. As a nation they had more successes than Cyrodiil did, although the limitless daedric hordes made the outcome a foregone conclusion.

The Thalmor had always been a powerful faction within Summerset Isle, but had also always been a minority voice. During the crisis, the Crystal Tower was forced to give the Thalmor greater power and authority. Their efforts almost certainly saved Summerset Isle from being overrun. They capitalized on their success to seize total control in 4E 22. They renamed the nation Alinor, which hearkens back to an earlier age before the ascendency of man. Most people outside of the Aldmeri Dominion still call it Summerset Isle, either out of peevishness or ignorance.

In 4E 29, the government of Valenwood was overthrown by Thalmor collaborators and a union with Alinor proclaimed. It appears that Thalmor agents had formed close ties to certain Bosmeri factions even before the Oblivion Crisis. The Empire and its Bosmer allies, caught completely off guard, were quickly defeated by the much-better prepared Altmer forces that invaded Valenwood on the heels of the coup. Thus was the Aldmeri Dominion reborn.

Shortly afterward the Aldmeri Dominion severed all contact with the Empire. For seventy years they were silent. Most scholars believe there was some sort of internal strife in Alinor, but very little is known of the factional struggles that went on inside the Dominion while the Thalmor consolidated its power in Summerset and Valenwood.

In 4E 9s, the two moons, Masser and Secunda vanished. Within most of the Empire, this was viewed with trepidation and fear. In Elsweyr it was far worse. Culturally the

moons are much more influential to the Khajiit. After two years of the Void Nights, the moons returned. The Thalmor announced that they had restored the moons using previously unknown Dawn Magicks, but it is unclear if they truly restored the moons or just took advantage of foreknowledge that they would return.

Regardless of the truth of the matter, the Khajiit credited the Thalmor as their saviors. Within fifteen years, Imperial influence in Elsweyr had so diminished that the Empire was unable to respond effectively to the coup of 4E 115 which dissolved the Elsweyr Confederacy and recreated the ancient kingdoms of Anequina and Pelletine as client states of the Aldmeri Dominion. Once more the Empire failed to stop the advance of Thalmor power.

When Titus Mede II ascended the throne in 4E 168, he inherited a weakened empire. The glory days of the Septims were a distant memory. Valenwood and Elsweyr were gone, ceded to the Thalmor enemy. Black Marsh had been lost to Imperial rule since the aftermath of the Oblivion Crisis. Morrowind had never recovered fully from the eruption of Mount Vvardenfell. Hammerfell was plagued by infighting between Crowns and Forebears. Only High Rock, Cyrodiil and Skyrim remained prosperous and peaceful.

Emperor Titus Mede had only a few short years to consolidate his rule before his leadership was put to the ultimate test.

The War Begins

On the 30th of Frostfall, 4E 171, the Aldmeri Dominion sent an ambassador to the Imperial City with a gift in a covered cart and an ultimatum for the new Emperor. The long list of demands included staggering tributes, disbandment of the Blades, outlawing the worship of Talos, and ceding large sections of Hammerfell to the Dominion. Despite the warnings of his generals of the Empire's military weakness, Emperor Titus Mede II rejected the ultimatum. The Thalmor ambassador upended the cart, spilling over a hundred heads on the floor: every Blades agent in Summerset and Valenwood. And so began the Great War which would consume the Empire and the Aldmeri Dominion for the next five years.

Within days, Aldmeri armies invaded Hammerfell and Cyrodiil simultaneously. A strong force commanded by the Thalmor general Lord Naarifin attacked Cyrodiil from the south, marching out of hidden camps in northern Elsweyr and flanking the Imperial defenses along the Valenwood border. Leyawiin soon fell to the invaders, while Bravil was cut off and besieged.

At the same time, an Aldmeri army under Lady Arannelya crossed into western Cyrodiil from Valenwood, bypassing Anvil and Kvatch and crossing into Hammerfell. Smaller Aldmeri forces landed along the southern coastline of Hammerfell. The disunited Redguard forces offered only scattered resistance to the invaders, and much of the southern coastline was quickly overrun. The greatly outnumbered Imperial legions retreated across the Alik'r Desert in the now-famous March of Thirst.

4E 172–173: The Aldmeri Advance Into Cyrodiil

It appears now that the initial Aldmeri objective was in fact the conquest of Hammerfell, and that the invasion of Cyrodiil was intended only to pin down the Imperial legions while Hammerfell was overrun. However, the surprising initial success of Lord Naarifin's attack led the Thalmor to believe that the Empire was weaker than they had thought. The capture of the Imperial City itself and the complete overthrow of the Empire thus became their primary objective of the next two years. As we know, the Thalmor nearly achieved their objective. It was only because of our Emperor's determined leadership during the Empire's darkest hour that this disaster was averted.

During 4E 172, the Aldmeri advanced deeper into Cyrodiil. Bravil and Anvil both fell to the invaders. By the end of the year, Lord Naarifin had advanced to the very walls of the Imperial City. There were fierce naval clashes in Lake Rumare and along the Niben as the Imperial forces attempted to hold the eastern bank.

In Hammerfell, the Thalmor were content to consolidate their gains as they took control of the whole southern coastline, which was in fact their stated objective in the ultimatum delivered to the Emperor. Of the southern cities, only Hegathe still held out. The survivors of the March of Thirst regrouped in northern Hammerfell, joined by reinforcements from High Rock.

The year 4E 173 saw stiffening Imperial resistance in Cyrodiil, but the seemingly inexorable Aldmeri advance continued. Fresh legions from Skyrim bolstered the Emperor's main army in the Imperial City, but the Aldmeri forced the crossing of the Niben and began advancing in force up the eastern bank. By the end of the year, the Imperial City was surrounded on three sides – only the northern supply route to Bruma remained open.

In Hammerfell, Imperial fortunes took a turn for the better. In early 4E 173, a Forebear army from Sentinel broke the siege of Hegathe (a Crown city), leading to the reconciliation of the two factions. Despite this, Lady Arannelya's main army succeeded in crossing the Alik'r Desert. The Imperial Legions under General Decianus met them outside Skaven in a bloody and indecisive clash. Decianus withdrew and left Arannelya in possession of Skaven, but the Aldmeri were too weakened to continue their advance.

4E 174: The Sack of the Imperial City

In 4E 174, the Thalmor leadership committed all available forces to the campaign in Cyrodiil, gambling on a decisive victory to end the war once and for all. During the spring, Aldmeri reinforcements gathered in southern Cyrodiil, and on 12th of Second Seed, they launched a massive assault on the Imperial City itself. One army drove north to completely surround the city, while Lord Naarifin's main force attacked the walls from the south, east, and west. The Emperor's decision to fight his way out of the city rather than make a last stand was a bold one. No general dared advise him to abandon the capital, but Titus II was proven right in the end.

While the Eighth Legion fought a desperate (and doomed) rearguard action on the walls of the city, Titus II broke out of the city to the north with his main army, smashing through the surrounding the Aldmeri forces and linking up with reinforcements marching south from Skyrim under General Jonna. Meanwhile, however, the capital fell to the invaders and the infamous Sack of the Imperial City began. The Imperial Palace was burned, the White-Gold Tower itself looted, and all manner of atrocities carried out by the vengeful elves on the innocent populace.

In Hammerfell, General Decianus was preparing to drive the Aldmeri back from Skaven when he was ordered to march for Cyrodiil. Unwilling to abandon Hammerfell completely, he allowed a great number of "invalids" to be discharged from the Legions before they marched east. These veterans formed the core of the army that eventually drove Lady Arannelya's forces back across the Alik'r late in 174, taking heavy losses on their retreat from harassing attacks by the Alik'r warriors.

4E 175: The Battle of the Red Ring

During the winter of 4E 174-175, the Thalmor seem to have believed that the war in Cyrodiil was all but over. They made several attempts to negotiate with Titus II. The Emperor encouraged them in their belief that he was preparing to surrender; meanwhile, he gathered his forces to retake the Imperial City.

In what is now known as the Battle of the Red Ring, a battle that will serve as a model for Imperial strategists for generations to come, Titus II divided his forces into three. One army, with the legions from Hammerfell under General Decianus, was hidden in the Colovian Highlands near Chorrol. The Aldmeri were unaware that he was no longer in Hammerfell, possibly because the Imperial veterans Decianus had left behind led Lady Arannelya to believe that she still faced an Imperial army. The second army, largely of Nord legions under General Jonna, took up position near Cheydinhal. The main army was commanded by the Emperor himself, and would undertake the main assault of the Imperial City from the north.

On the 30th of Rain's Hand, the bloody Battle of the Red Ring began as General Decianus swept down on the city from the west, while General Jonna's legionnaires drove south along the Red Ring Road. In a two-day assault, Jonna's army crossed the Niben and advanced west, attempting to link up with Decianus's legions and thus surround the Imperial City. Lord Naarifin was taken by surprise by Decianus's assault, but Jonna's troops faced bitter resistance as the Aldmeri counterattacked from Bravil and Skingrad. The heroic Nord legionnaires held firm, however, beating off the piecemeal Aldmeri attacks. By the fifth day of the battle, the Aldmeri army in the Imperial City was surrounded.

Titus II led the assault from the north, personally capturing Lord Naarifin. It is rumored the Emperor wielded the famed sword Goldbrand, although this has never been officially confirmed by the Imperial government. An attempt by the Aldmeri to break out of the city to the south was blocked by the unbreakable shieldwall of General Jonna's battered legions.

In the end, the main Aldmeri army in Cyrodiil was completely destroyed. The Emperor's decision to withdraw from the Imperial City in 4E 174 was bloodily vindicated.

Lord Naarifin was kept alive for thirty-three days, hanging from the White-Gold tower. It is not recorded where his body was buried, if it was buried at all. Once source claims he was carried off by a winged daedra on the thirty-fourth day.

The White-Gold Concordat and the End of the War

Although victorious, the Imperial armies were in no shape to continue the war. The entire remaining Imperial force was gathered in Cyrodiil, exhausted and decimated by the Battle of the Red Ring. Not a single legion had more than half its soldiers fit for duty. Two legions had been effectively annihilated, not counting the loss of the Eighth during the retreat from the Imperial City the previous year. Titus II knew that there would be no better time to negotiate peace, and late in 4E 175 the Empire and the Aldmeri Dominion signed the White-Gold Concordat, ending the Great War.

The terms were harsh, but Titus II believed that it was necessary to secure peace and give the Empire a chance to regain its strength. The two most controversial terms of the Concordat were the banning of the worship of Talos and the cession of a large section of southern Hammerfell (most of what was already occupied by Aldmeri forces). Critics have pointed out that the Concordat is almost identical to the ultimatum the Emperor rejected five years earlier. However, there is a great difference between agreeing to such terms under the mere threat of war, and agreeing to them at the end of a long and destructive war. No part of the Empire would have accepted these terms in 4E 171, dictated by the Thalmor at swords-point. Titus II would have faced civil war. By 4E 175, most of the Empire welcomed peace at almost any price.

Epilogue: Hammerfell Fights On Alone

Hammerfell, however, refused to accept the White-Gold Concordat, being unwilling to concede defeat and the loss of so much of their territory. Titus II was forced to officially renounce Hammerfell as an Imperial province in order to preserve the hard-won peace treaty. The Redguards, understandably, looked on this as a betrayal. In this, the Thalmor certainly achieved one of their long-term goals by sowing lasting bitterness between Hammerfell and the Empire.

In the end, the heroic Redguards fought the Aldmeri Dominion to a standstill, although the war lasted for five more years and left southern Hammerfell devastated. The Redguards say that this proves that the White-Gold Concordat was unnecessary, and that if Titus II had kept his nerve, the Aldmeri could have been truly defeated by the combined forces of Hammerfell and the rest of the Empire. The truth of that assertion can, of course, never be known. But the Redguards should not forget the great sacrifice of Imperial blood – Breton, Nord, and Cyrodilic – at the Battle of the Red Ring that weakened the Dominion enough to allow the eventual Second Treaty of Stros M'kai in 4E 180 and the withdrawal of Aldmeri forces from Hammerfell.

There can be no doubt that the current peace cannot last forever. The Thalmor take the long view, as is proved by the sequence of events leading up to the Great War. All those who value freedom over tyranny can only hope that before it is too late, Hammerfell and the Empire will be reconciled and stand united against the Thalmor threat. Otherwise, any hope to stem the tide of Thalmor rule over all of Tamriel is dimmed.

Biography of Barenziah

Volume One

by Stern Gamboge
Imperial Scribe

ate in the Second Era, a girl-child, Barenziah, was born to the rulers of the kingdom of Mournhold in what is now the Imperial Province of Morrowind. She was reared in all the luxury and security befitting a royal Dark Elven child until she reached five years of age. At that time, His Excellency Tiber Septim I, the first Emperor of Tamriel, demanded that the decadent rulers of Morrowind yield to him and institute imperial reforms. Trusting to their vaunted magic, the Dark Elves impudently refused until Tiber Septim's army was on the borders. An Armistice was hastily signed by the now-eager Dunmer, but not before there were several battles, one of which laid waste to Mournhold, now called Almalexia.

Little Princess Barenziah and her nurse were found among the wreckage. The Imperial General Symmachus, himself a Dark Elf, suggested to Tiber Septim that the child might someday be valuable, and she was therefore placed with a loyal supporter who had recently retired from the Imperial Army.

Sven Advensen had been granted the title of Count upon his retirement; his fiefdom, Darkmoor, was a small town in central Skyrim. Count Sven and his wife reared the princess as their own daughter, seeing to it that she was educated appropriately—and more importantly, that the imperial virtues of obedience, discretion, loyalty, and piety were instilled in the child. In short, she was made fit to take her place as a member of the new ruling class of Morrowind.

The girl Barenziah grew in beauty, grace, and intelligence. She was sweet-tempered, a joy to her adoptive parents and their five young sons, who loved her as their elder sister. Other than her appearance, she differed from young girls of her class only in that she had a strong empathy for the woods and fields, and was wont to escape her household duties to wander there at times.

Barenziah was happy and content until her sixteenth year, when a wicked orphan stable-boy, whom she had befriended out of pity, told her he had overheard a conspiracy between her guardian, Count Sven, and a Redguard visitor to sell her as a concubine in Rihad, as no Nord or Breton would marry her on account of her black skin, and no Dark Elf would have her because of her foreign upbringing.

"Whatever shall I do?" the poor girl said, weeping and trembling, for she had been brought up in innocence and trust, and it never occurred to her that her friend the stable–boy would lie to her.

The wicked boy, who was called Straw, said that she must run away if she valued her virtue, but that he would come with her as her protector. Sorrowfully, Barenziah agreed to this plan; and that very night, she disguised herself as a boy and the pair escaped to the nearby city of Whiterun. After a few days there, they managed to get jobs as guards for a disreputable merchant caravan. The caravan was heading east by side roads in a mendacious attempt to elude the lawful tolls charged on the imperial highways. Thus the pair eluded pursuit until they reached the city of Rifton, where they ceased their travels for a time. They felt safe in Rifton, close as it was to the Morrowind border so that Dark Elves were enough of a common sight.

Volume Two

The first volume of this series told the story of Barenziah's origin–heiress to the throne of Mournhold until her father rebelled against His Excellency Tiber Septim I and brought ruin to the province of Morrowind. Thanks largely to the benevolence of the Emperor, the child Barenziah was not destroyed with her parents, but reared by Count Sven of Darkmoor, a loyal Imperial trustee. She grew up into a beautiful and pious child, trustful of her guardian's care. This trust, however, was exploited by a wicked orphan stable boy at Count Sven's estate, who with lies and fabrications tricked her into fleeing Darkmoor with him when she turned sixteen. After many adventures on the road, they settled in Riften, a Skyrim city near the Morrowind borders.

The stable boy, Straw, was not altogether evil. He loved Barenziah in his own selfish fashion, and deception was the only way he could think of that would cement possession of her. She, of course, felt only friendship toward him, but he was hopeful that she would gradually change her mind. He wanted to buy a small farm and settle down into a comfortable marriage, but at the time his earnings were barely enough to feed and shelter them.

After only a short time in Riften, Straw fell in with a bold, villainous Khajiit thief named Therris, who proposed that they rob the Imperial Commandant's house in the central part of the city. Therris said that he had a client, a traitor to the Empire, who would pay well for any information they could gather there. Barenziah happened to overhear this plan and was appalled. She stole away from their rooms and walked the streets of Riften in desperation, torn between her loyalty to the Empire and her love for her friends.

In the end, loyalty to the Empire prevailed over personal friendship, and she approached the Commandant's house, revealed her true identity, and warned him of her friends' plan. The Commandant listened to her tale, praised her courage, and assured her that no harm would come to her. He was none other than General Symmachus, who had been scouring the countryside in search of her since her disappearance, and had just arrived in Riften, hot in pursuit. He took her into his custody, and informed her that, far

from being sent away to be sold, she was to be reinstated as the Queen of Mournhold as soon as she turned eighteen. Until that time, she was to live with the Septim family in the newly built Imperial City, where she would learn something of government and be presented at the Imperial Court.

At the Imperial City, Barenziah befriended the Emperor Tiber Septim during the middle years of his reign. Tiber's children, particularly his eldest son and heir Pelagius, came to love her as a sister. The ballads of the day praised her beauty, chastity, wit, and learning. On her eighteenth birthday, the entire Imperial City turned out to watch her farewell procession preliminary to her return to her native land. Sorrowful as they were at her departure, all knew that she was ready for her glorious destiny as sovereign of the kingdom of Mournhold.

Volume Three

In the second volume of this series, it was told how Barenziah was kindly welcomed to the newly constructed Imperial City by the Emperor Tiber Septim and his family, who treated her like a long-lost daughter during her almost one-year stay. After several happy months there learning her duties as vassal queen under the Empire, the Imperial General Symmachus escorted her to Mournhold where she took up her duties as Queen of her people under his wise guidance. Gradually they came to love one another and were married and crowned in a splendid ceremony at which the Emperor himself officiated.

After several hundred years of marriage, a son, Helseth, was born to the royal couple amid celebration and joyous prayer. Although it was not publicly known at the time, it was shortly before this blessed event that the Staff of Chaos had been stolen from its hiding place deep in the Mournhold mines by a clever, enigmatic bard known only as the Nightingale.

Eight years after Helseth's birth, Barenziah bore a daughter, Morgiah, named after Symmachus' mother, and the royal couple's joy seemed complete. Alas, shortly after that, relations with the Empire mysteriously deteriorated, leading to much civil unrest in Mournhold. After fruitless investigations and attempts at reconciliation, in despair Barenziah took her young children and travelled to the Imperial City herself to seek the ear of then Emperor Uriel Septim VII. Symmachus remained in Mournhold to deal with the grumbling peasants and annoyed nobility, and do what he could to stave off an impending insurrection.

During her audience with the Emperor, Barenziah, through her magical arts, came to realize to her horror and dismay that the so-called Emperor was an impostor, none other than the bard Nightingale who had stolen the Staff of Chaos. Exercising great self-control she concealed this realization from him. That evening, news came that Symmachus had fallen in battle with the revolting peasants of Mournhold, and that the kingdom had been taken over by the rebels. Barenziah, at this point, did not know where to seek help, or from whom.

The gods, that fateful night, were evidently looking out for her as if in redress of her loss. King Eadwyre of High Rock, an old friend of Uriel Septim and Symmachus, came by on a social call. He comforted her, pledged his friendship–and furthermore, confirmed her suspicions that the Emperor was indeed a fraud, and none other than Jagar Tharn, the Imperial Battlemage, and one of the Nightingale's many alter egos. Tharn had supposedly retired into seclusion from public work and installed his assistant, Ria Silmane, in his stead. The hapless assistant was later put to death under mysterious circumstances–supposedly a plot implicating her had been uncovered, and she had been summarily executed. However, her ghost had appeared to Eadwyre in a dream and revealed to him that the true Emperor had been kidnapped by Tharn and imprisoned in an alternate dimension. Tharn had then used the Staff of Chaos to kill her when she attempted to warn the Elder Council of his nefarious plot.

Together, Eadwyre and Barenziah plotted to gain the false Emperor's confidence. Meanwhile, another friend of Ria's, known only as the Champion, who apparently possessed great, albeit then untapped, potential, was incarcerated at the Imperial Dungeons. However, she had access to his dreams, and she told him to bide his time until she could devise a plan that would effect his escape. Then he could begin on his mission to unmask the impostor.

Barenziah continued to charm, and eventually befriended, the ersatz Emperor. By contriving to read his secret diary, she learned that he had broken the Staff of Chaos into eight pieces and hidden them in far-flung locations scattered across Tamriel. She managed to obtain a copy of the key to Ria's friend's cell and bribed a guard to leave it there as if by accident. Their Champion, whose name was unknown even to Barenziah and Eadwyre, made his escape through a shift gate Ria had opened in an obscure corner of the Imperial Dungeons using her already failing powers. The Champion was free at last, and almost immediately went to work.

It took Barenziah several more months to learn the hiding places of all eight Staff pieces through snatches of overheard conversation and rare glances at Tharn's diary. Once she had the vital information, however — which she communicated to Ria forthwith, who in turn passed it on to the Champion—she and Eadwyre lost no time. They fled to Wayrest, his ancestral kingdom in the province of High Rock, where they managed to fend off the sporadic efforts of Tharn's henchmen to haul them back to the Imperial City, or at the very least obtain revenge. Tharn, whatever else might be said of him, was no one's fool–save perhaps Barenziah's — and he concentrated most of his efforts toward tracking down and destroying the Champion.

As all now know, the courageous, indefatigable, and forever nameless Champion was successful in reuniting the eight sundered pieces of the Staff of Chaos. With it, he destroyed Tharn and rescued the true Emperor, Uriel Septim VII. Following what has come to be known as the Restoration, a grand state memorial service was held for Symmachus at the Imperial City, befitting the man who had served the Septim Dynasty for so long and so well.

Barenziah and good King Eadwyre had come to care deeply for one another during their trials and adventures, and were married in the same year shortly after their flight from the Imperial City. Her two children from her previous marriage with Symmachus remained with her, and a regent was appointed to rule Mournhold in her absence.

Up to the present time, Queen Barenziah has been in Wayrest with Prince Helseth and Princess Morgiah. She plans to return to Mournhold after Eadwyre's death. Since he was already elderly when they wed, she knows that that event, alas, could not be far off as the Elves reckon time. Until then, she shares in the government of the kingdom of Wayrest with her husband, and seems glad and content with her finally quiet, and happily unremarkable, life.

The Firsthold Revolt

by Maveus Cie

ou told me that if her brother won, she would be sister to the King of Wayrest, and Reman would want to keep her for the alliance. But her brother Helseth lost and has fled with his mother back to Morrowind, and still Reman has not left her to marry me." Lady Gialene took a long, slow drag of the hookah and blew out dragon's breath, so the scent of blossoms perfumed her gilded chamber. "You make a very poor advisor, Kael. I might have spent my time romancing the king of Cloudrest or Alinor instead of the wretched royal husband of Queen Morgiah."

Kael knew better than to hurt his lady's vanity by the mere suggestion that the King of Firsthold might have come to love his Dunmer Queen. Instead he gave her a few minutes to pause and look from her balcony out over the high cliff palaces of the ancient capitol. The moons shone like crystal on the deep sapphire waters of the Abecean Sea. It was ever springtide here, and he could well understand why she would prefer a throne in this land than in Cloudrest or Alinor.

Finally, he spoke: "The people are with you, my lady. They do not relish the idea of Reman's dark elf heirs ruling the kingdom when he is gone."

"I wonder," she said calmly. "I wonder if as the King would not give up his Queen for want of alliances, whether she would give herself up out of fear. Of all the people of Firsthold, who most dislikes the Dunmer influence on the court?"

"Is this a trick question, my lady?" asked Kael. "The Trebbite Monks, of course. Their credo has ever been for pure Altmer bloodlines on Summurset, and among the royal families most of all. But, my lady, they make very weak allies."

"I know," said Gialene, taking up her hookah again thoughtfully, a smile creeping across her face. "Morgiah has seen to it that they have no power. She would have exterminated them altogether had Reman not stopped her for all the good they do for the country folk. What if they found themselves with a very powerful benefactress? One with intimate knowledge of the court of Firsthold, the chief concubine of the King, and all the gold to buy weapons with that her father, the King of Skywatch, could supply?"

"Well-armed and with the support of the country people, they would be formidable," nodded Kael. "But as your advisor, I must warn you: if you make yourself an active foe of Queen Morgiah, you must play to win. She has inherited much of her mother Queen Barenziah's intelligence and spirit of vengeance."

"She will not know I am her foe until it is too late," shrugged Gialene. "Go to the Trebbite monastery and bring me Friar Lylim. We must strategize our plan of attack."

For two weeks, Reman was advised about growing resentment in the countryside from peasants who called Morgiah the "Black Queen," but it was nothing that he had not heard before. His attention was on the pirates on a small island off the coast called

Calluis Lar. They had been more brazen as late, attacking royal barges in organized raids. To deliver a crushing blow, he ordered the greatest part of his militia to invade the island — an incursion he himself would lead.

A few days after Reman left the capitol, the revolt of the Trebbite Monks exploded. The attacks were well-coordinated and without warning. The Chief of the Guards did not wait to be announced, bursting into Morgiah's bedchamber ahead of a flurry of maidservants.

"My Queen," he said. "It is a revolution."

By contrast, Gialene was not asleep when Kael came to deliver the news. She was seated by the window, smoking her hookah and looking at the fires far off in the hills.

"Morgiah is with council," he explained. "I am certain they are telling her that the Trebbite Monks are behind the uprising, and that the revolution will be at the city gates by morning."

"How large is the revolutionary army in contrast to the remaining royal militia?" asked Gialene.

"The odds are well in our favor," said Kael. "Though not perhaps as much as we hoped. The country folk, it seems, like to complain about their queen, but stop short of insurrection. Primarily, the army is composed of the Monks themselves and a horde of mercenaries your father's gold bought. In a way of thinking, it is preferable this way — they are more professional and organized that a common mob. Really, they are a true army, complete with a horn section."

"If that doesn't frighten the Black Queen into abdication, nothing will," smiled Gialene, rising from her chair. "The poor dear must be beside herself with worry. I must fly to her side and enjoy it."

Gialene was disappointed when she saw Morgiah come out of the Council Chambers. Considering that she had been woken from a deep sleep with cries of revolution and had spent the last several hours in consultation with her meager general force, she looked beautiful. There was a sparkle of proud defiance in her bright red eyes.

"My Queen," Gialene cried, forcing real tears. "I came as soon as I heard! Will we all be slaughtered?"

"A distinct possibility," replied Morgiah simply. Gialene tried to read her, but the expressions of women, especially alien women, were a far greater challenge than those of Altmer men.

"I hate myself for even thinking to propose this," said Gialene. "But since the cause of their fury is you, perhaps if you were to give up the throne, they might disperse. Please understand, my queen, I am thinking only of the good of the kingdom and our own lives."

"I understand the spirit of your suggestion," smiled Morgiah. "And I will take it under advisement. Believe me, I've thought of it myself. But I don't think it will come to that."

"Have you a plan for defending us?" asked Gialene, contorting her features to an expression she knew bespoke girlish hope.

"The king left us several dozen of his royal battlemages," said Morgiah. "I think the mob believes we have nothing but palace guards and a few soldiers to protect us. When they get to the gates are greeted with a wave of fireballs, I find it highly likely that they will lose heart and retreat."

"But isn't there some protection they could be using against such an assault?" asked Gialene in her best worried voice.

"If they knew about it, naturally there is. But an unruly mob is unlikely to have mages skilled in the arts of Restoration, by which they could shield themselves from the spells, or Mysticism, by which they could reflect the spells back on my battlemages. That would be the worst scenario, but even if they were well-organized enough to have Mystics in their ranks — and enough of them to reflect so many spells — it just isn't done. No battlefield commander would advise such a defense during a siege unless he knew precisely what he was going to be meeting. And then, of course, once the trap is sprung" Morgiah winked. "It's too late for a countering spell."

"A most cunning solution, your highness," said Gialene, honestly impressed.

Morgiah excused herself to meet with her battlemages, and Gialene gave her an embrace. Kael was waiting in the palace garden for his lady.

"Are there Mystics among the mercenaries?" she asked quickly.

"Several, in fact," replied Kael, bewildered by her query. "Largely rejects from the Psijic Order, but they know enough to cast the regular spells of the school."

"You must sneak out the city gates and tell Friar Lylim to have them cast reflection spells on all the front line before they attack," said Gialene.

"That's most irregular battlefield strategy," frowned Kael.

"I know it is, fool, that's what Morgiah is counting on. There's a gang of battlemages who are going to be waiting on the battlements to greet our army with a barrage of fire balls."

"Battlemages? I would have thought that King Reman would have brought them with him to fight the pirates."

"You would have thought that," laughed Gialene. "But then we would be defeated. Now go!"

Friar Lylim agreed with Kael that it was a bizarre, unheard-of way to begin a battle, casting reflection spells on all one's troops. It went against every tradition, and as a Trebbite Monk, he valued tradition above every other virtue. There was little other choice, though, given the intelligence. He had few enough healers in the army as it were, and their energies could not be wasted casting resistance spells.

At dawn's light, the rebel army was in sight of the gleaming spires of Firsthold. Friar Lylim gathered together every soldier who knew even the rudimentary secrets of Mysticism, who knew how to tap in to the elementary conundrums and knots of the energies of magicka. Though few were masters of the art, their combined force was powerful to behold. A great surge of entangling power washed over the army, crackling, hissing, and infusing all with their ghostly force. When they arrived at the gates, every soldier, even the least imaginative, knew that no spell would touch him for a long time.

Friar Lylim watched his army batter into the gate with the great satisfaction of a commander who has counteracted an unthinkable attack with an outrageous defense. The smile quickly faded from his face.

They were met at the battlements not by mages but by common archers of the palace guard. As the flaming arrows fell upon the siegers like a red rain, the healers ran in to help the wounded. Their healing spells reflected off the dying men, one after the other. Chaos ruled as the attackers suddenly found themselves defenseless and began a panicked, unorganized retreat. Friar Lylim himself considered briefly holding his ground before fleeing himself.

Later, he would send furious notes to Lady Gialene and Kael, but they were returned. Even his best secret agents within the palace were unable to find their whereabouts.

Neither had, as it turns out, much previous experience with torture, and they soon confessed their treachery to the King's satisfaction. Kael was executed, and Gialene was sent back with escort to her father's court of Skywatch. He has still to find a husband for her. Reman, by contrast, has elected not to take a new royal concubine. The common folk of Firsthold consider this break in palace protocol to be more of the sinister alien influence of the Black Queen, and grumble to all who will listen.

An Explorer's Guide to Skyrim

by Marcius Carvain,
Viscount Bruma

Far too often, noble visitors from Cyrodiil see little more of Skyrim than the view from their carriage. To be sure, this coarse, uncivilized province is far from hospitable, but it is also a place of fierce, wild beauty, with grand vistas and inspiring natural wonders awaiting those with the will to seek them out and the refinement to truly appreciate them. If you are of a mind to see Skyrim for yourself, I recommend beginning your adventure as I did, by seeking out Stones of Fate.

No doubt you are taken aback by the name, as I once was. The provincials and village folk have all manner of dark tales about these ancient monuments. Stories of necromantic rituals and fell spirits, of great and terrible powers conferred on any who dare to touch them.

The stories are, as Jarl Igrof once told me, "A load of mammoth dung." A bit uncouth, but you get the point.

To be sure, keep your guards with you at all times – brigands and wild animals are never to be taken lightly. But the stones themselves are nothing to fear. Quite the contrary, their proximity to cities and roads makes them ideal destinations for the novice explorer, and many boast spectacular views that make the journey well worth the effort.

To whet your appetite, here are four such locations:

Most travelers enter Skyrim by way of Helgen, "Gateway to the North." If you find yourself in this backwater hovel, consider taking an afternoon's ride to the north, keeping to the road as it winds down the cliffs at the eastern end of Lake Ilinalta. Just off the path, on a small bluff, lie the three Guardian Stones, the greatest concentration of standing stones in all Skyrim. The view of the lake here at sunset is simply sublime.

Visitors from Cheydinhal will pass through Riften, city of intrigue and larceny since Tiber Septim's day. If you seek adventure in the Rift, leave the city by the southern gate and cast your gaze upon the bluff that rises to the south. Atop it sits the Shadow Stone, a fitting symbol for the city of thieves.

Whiterun is the heart of Skyrim, its towering palace rivaling even the great castles of Cyrodiil. But should you tire of the Jarl's hospitality, another adventure awaits a few hours to the east of the city, along the road that rises above White River Gorge. The Ritual Stone can be found atop the lone hill that rises on the north side of the road, set into an ancient monument. Take time to soak in the incredible view of Whiterun, the tundra, and the gorge from this unique spot.

More seasoned explorers may wish to visit Markarth, the ancient city of stone far to the west. The recent Forsworn Rebellion has made travel in the Reach perilous, but for those determined to seek adventure no matter the cost, another stone can be found to the east of the city, perched on the mountain above Kolskeggr Mine. Though the climb is difficult, reaching the summit is a milestone any explorer could be proud of.

There are other Stones of Fate to be found in Skyrim – I myself have seen several more, perched on the most remote mountain peaks, or wreathed in fog amid the northern marshes. But the true joy of exploration is in the discovery, and so I leave the rest to you. May the Eight guide your steps.

Songs Of Skyrim
Revised Edition
Compiled by Giraud Gemaine
Historian of the Bards College Solitude

'Ragnar the Red' is a traditional song of Whiterun. Despite the grim final image the song is generally regarded as light and rollicking and a favorite in inns across Skyrim.

Ragnar The Red

There once was a hero named Ragnar the Red,
who came riding to Whiterun from ole Rorikstead!
And the braggart did swagger and brandish his blade,
as he told of bold battles and gold he had made!
But then he went quiet, did Ragnar the Red,
when he met the shieldmaiden Matilda who said...
Oh, you talk and you lie and you drink all our mead!
Now I think it's high time that you lie down and bleed!
And so then came the clashing and slashing of steel,
as the brave lass Matilda charged in full of zeal!
And the braggart named Ragnar was boastful no moooooree...
when his ugly red head rolled around on the floor!

'The Dragonborn Comes' has been handed down from generation to generation of bards. The Dragonborn in Nord culture is the archetype of what a Nord should be. The song itself has been used to rally soldiers and to bring hope.

The Dragonborn Comes

Our hero, our hero, claims a warrior's heart.
I tell you, I tell you, the Dragonborn comes.
With a Voice wielding power of the ancient Nord art.
Believe, believe, the Dragonborn comes.
It's an end to the evil, of all Skyrim's foes.
Beware, beware, the Dragonborn comes.
For the darkness has passed, and the legend yet grows.
You'll know, You'll know the Dragonborn's come.

'The Age of Oppression' and 'The Age of Aggression' are variants of one song. It isn't known which of the two was written first but the tune, with loyalty appropriate lyrics, is quite popular on both sides of the war.

The Age of Oppression

We drink to our youth, and to days come and gone.
For the age of oppression is now nearly done.
We'll drive out the Empire from this land that we own.
With our blood and our steel we will take back our home.
All hail to Ulfric! You are the High King!
In your great honor we drink and we sing.
We're the children of Skyrim, and we fight all our lives.
And when Sovngarde beckons, every one of us dies!
But this land is ours and we'll see it wiped clean.
Of the scourge that has sullied our hopes and our dreams.

The Age of Aggression

We drink to our youth, to days come and gone.
For the age of aggression is just about done.
We'll drive out the Stormcloaks and restore what we own.
With our blood and our steel we'll take back our home.
Down with Ulfric the killer of kings.
On the day of your death we'll drink and we'll sing.
We're the children of Skyrim, and we fight all our lives.
And when Sovngarde beckons, every one of us dies!
But this land is ours and we'll see it wiped clean.
Of the scourge that has sullied our hopes and our dreams.

The following is an ancient song we've only recently been able to translate. Without a tune or a sure pronunciation the song is lost to time. It's included here to show the deep history of song here in Skyrim.

The original version...

Dovahkiin, Dovahkiin, naal ok zin los vahriin,
wah dein vokul mahfaeraak ahst vaal!
Ahrk fin norok paal graan fod nust hon zindro zaan,
Dovahkiin, fah hin kogaan mu draal!
Huzrah nu, kul do od, wah aan bok lingrah vod,
Aahrk fin tey, boziik fun, do fin gein!
Wo lost fron wah ney dov, ahrk fin reyliik do jul,
voth aan suleyk wah ronit faal krein!
Ahrk fin zul, rok drey kod, nau tol morokei frod,

rul lot Taazokaan motaad voth kein!
Sahrot Thu'um, med aan tuz, vey zeim hokoron pah,
ol fin Dovahkiin komeyt ok rein!
Ahrk fin Kel lost prodah, do ved viing ko fin krah,
tol fod zeymah win kein meyz fundein!
Alduin, feyn do jun, kruziik vokun staadnau,
voth aan bahlok wah diivon fin lein!
Nuz aan sul, fent alok, fod fin vul dovah nok,
fen kos nahlot mahfaeraak ahrk ruz!
Paaz Keizaal fen kos stin nol bein Alduin jot,
Dovahkiin kos fin saviik do muz!

And the translation...

Dragonborn, Dragonborn, by his honor is sworn,
To keep evil forever at bay!
And the fiercest foes rout when they hear triumph's shout,
Dragonborn, for your blessing we pray!
Hearken now, sons of snow, to an age, long ago,
and the tale, boldly told, of the one!
Who was kin to both wyrm, and the races of man,
with a power to rival the sun!
And the Voice, he did wield, on that glorious field,
when great Tamriel shuddered with war!
Mighty Thu'um, like a blade, cut through enemies all,
as the Dragonborn issued his roar!
And the Scrolls have foretold, of black wings in the cold,
that when brothers wage war come unfurled!
Alduin, Bane of Kings, ancient shadow unbound,
with a hunger to swallow the world!
But a day, shall arise, when the dark dragon's lies,
will be silenced forever and then!
Fair Skyrim will be free from foul Alduin's maw,
Dragonborn be the savior of men!

'Tale of the Tongues' is a newer song. One that has come in to favor since the Dragonborn put down Alduin. It actually describes the events of the first battle against the dragons.

Tale of the Tongues

Alduin's wings, they did darken the sky.
His roar fury's fire, and his scales sharpened scythes.
Men ran and they cowered, and they fought and they died.
They burned and they bled as they issued their cries.
We need saviors to free us from Alduin's rage.
Heroes on the field of this new war to wage.
And if Alduin wins, man is gone from this world.
Lost in the shadow of the black wings unfurled.
But then came the Tongues on that terrible day.
Steadfast as winter, they entered the fray.
And all heard the music of Alduin's doom.
The sweet song of Skyrim, sky-shattering Thu'um.
And so the Tongues freed us from Alduin's rage.
Gave the gift of the Voice, ushered in a new Age.
If Alduin is eternal, then eternity's done.
For his story is over and the dragons are... gone.

Skyrim's Rule: An Outsider's View

by Abdul-Mujib Ababneh

In my travels, and they have been many, I have encountered many strange peoples and cultures, in many different provinces of the Empire. And in each, I have found a method of governing and customs of leadership unique to that particular province.

In Black Marsh, for example, the Argonian King relies upon his Shadowscale Assassins to eliminate threats secretly, without the common knowledge of his people. In the Imperial Province of Cyrodiil, the Emperor may rule directly, but the power granted to his Elder Council cannot be understated.

During a recent journey to Skyrim, that harsh, frozen realm of the Nords, I was able for the first time to witness the unique manner of rule of this strong, proud people.

It would appear that the entire province of Skyrim is separated into territories known as "holds," and each hold finds its seat of power in one of the great, ancient cities. And in each of those cities, there rules that hold's king, known as a Jarl.

The Jarls of Skyrim are, as a whole, a fierce sight indeed. Sitting on their thrones, ready to administer justice, or send their forces out to quell some local threat, be it a pack of feral wolves or a terrifying giant that has wandered too close to a settlement.

In observing these Jarls, I found each to of course have his or her own unique personality and leadership style. But what I perhaps did not expect – especially considering the Nord leaders' unfair reputation as barbarians or uncivilized chieftains – was the formal structure of each Jarl's court. For while that hold's leader may be the one to sit on the throne, there is also a collection of functionaries who serve very specific and important roles.

The court wizard counsels the Jarl in all matters magical, and may even sell services or spells to the keep's visitors. The Steward is the Jarl's primary advisor, and generally takes care of the more mundane aspects of running the keep, the city, or even the hold, depending on the situation. And woe is the fool who defies the Housecarl – a personal bodyguard who rarely leaves the Jarl's side, and has pledged to sacrifice his or her own life to save that of their honored leader, if ever the need should arrive.

But as mighty and influential as each individual Jarl is, Skyrim's true power comes from the strength of its High King. The High King is ruler above all, and is always one of the Jarls, selected by a body called the "Moot" – a specially convened council of all the Jarls, who meet with the express purpose of choosing Skyrim's High King. Or so it is, in theory.

The reality, however, is that the High King swears fealty to the Emperor, and as Solitude is the city most directly influenced by Imperial culture and politics, the Jarl of Solitude has served as High King for generations. The Moot, therefore, is more formality and theater than anything else.

But as I prepared to leave Skyrim, I could feel a change in the air, sense the trepidation of some of the good Nord people. Many seemed unhappy with the Empire's continued presence in their land. And the outlawing of the worship of Talos as the Ninth Divine – a stipulation of the White-Gold Concordat, the peace treaty between the Empire and Aldmeri Dominion – has only strengthened that division.

So while the Jarls of Skyrim still control their holds, and those Jarls are ruled over by their Imperial-sanctioned High King, will there come a day when the Moot convenes to select a new High King – one that is not, as many would say, the Emperor's "Solitude puppet"?

If that day comes, I will be thankful to be far away from Skyrim, in my own home of Hammerfell. For such a decision could well mean civil war, and I fear that such a conflict would tear the fierce and beautiful Nord people asunder.

The Holds of Skyrim: A Field Officer's Guide

For Use by Officers of the Imperial Legion

Welcome, loyal officer of the Empire. You have been given this guide to help you, and those men under your command, better understand the geography of Skyrim. Since you will be serving in Skyrim for a lengthy period of time, this information should prove invaluable.

Skyrim is organized into nine holds. A hold is a large area of land roughly equivalent to a county in Cyrodiil. Each hold is governed by a Jarl who maintains his court in the hold's capital city.

Four of these holds are fairly small and sparsely populated. As a result, the capitals are little more than towns. The five major cities of Skyrim act as capitals for the larger holds.

Following is a detailed review of each hold.

EASTMARCH

Located in the eastern reaches of Skyrim, Eastmarch shares a common border with Morrowind. Jarl Ulfric Stormcloak rules from the ancient city of Windhelm, and he and his followers should be considered your most serious threat.

Do not tread lightly in Eastmarch, for the Stormcloaks are at their strongest and most organized in these lands. As an Imperial soldier, you will find few friends here.

HAAFINGAR

Solitude, the seat of High King of Skyrim and the capital of Haafingar hold, has always welcomed the Empire with open arms. Much commerce flows along the rivers here, and you will find the folk of this hold to be among the most hospitable in Skyrim.

As you venture forth in your campaigns, be sure to maintain a secure supply line back to Solitude. The Empire maintains ample provisions in Castle Dour, from which General Tullius commands all the legions stationed in Skyrim.

HJAALMARCH

This hold is divided evenly between wind-swept tundra dotted with farms and a huge, stinking salt marsh. There is little of interest here, save perhaps for the hold's capital, Morthal.

Jarl Idgrod Ravencrone has been cooperative enough with the Empire in the past, but will ultimately look out for her own iterests if put in a difficult position.

While the hold offers minimal strategic value to the Empire, it would make an ideal staging ground for a Stormcloak siege of Solitude, and so must be held against the enemy.

THE PALE

The Pale is a barren realm covered by vast fields of ice and snow. Its boundaries stretch from the center of Skyrim all the way to its northern coast. Here, at the capital city of Dawnstar, can be found one of the busiest ports in the province.

With access to the coastal waterways of Skyrim, Dawnstar could prove vital in the war effort. Should the Stormcloaks choose to attack Solitude from the river, this port would make a tempting target due to its close proximity.

THE REACH

Dominating the western border of Skyrim, the Reach is made up almost entirely of steep, craggy mountains. Little grows in this forbidding realm, but the capital city of Markarth is a nigh-impregnable stone fortress that would make an excellent defensive position for either side in the war.

Be aware that this dangerous region of Skyrim is home to the Forsworn, the rebellious natives of the Reach. They know the terrain, can strike without warning, and count the Empire as an enemy. If they attack, you must neither give nor expect any mercy.

THE RIFT

This hold occupies the southeast corner of Skyrim, and much like the Reach in the west, is dominated by tall mountain peaks. The climate in the Reach is milder than in the northern holds, and there is more vegetation to be found here. Farming thrives as a result.

A word of warning about Riften, the hold's capital city. Our agents have reason to suspect that the Thieves' Guild makes it home here, though it is now much diminished from its strength of previous years.

Nevertheless, mind that your men keep an eye on their coin purses should they have reason to spend any length of time in the city.

WHITERUN

This central hold is characterized by wide, grassy plains that are home to numerous farms. Many roads pass through Whiterun, joining the more distant holds together.

The hold's capital city, also called Whiterun, sits high on a rocky promontory amid a large, flat swath of scrubland. Among the wealthiest cities of Skyrim, Whiterun has usually proven friendly to the Emperor's soldiers.

WINTERHOLD

This bleak, snow-blown hold in the northeast corner of Skyrim is utterly inhospitable. Perhaps the mages at the College of Winterhold chose to make their home there because they knew they would be left largely alone.

As with Whiterun, the name Winterhold describes both the hold and its capital city, though the word "city" hardly applies. The hold capital is a meager village built near the mages' college.

Few other noteworthy settlements exist in this frozen waste, and it is unlikely to play any significant part in the war.

A Gentleman's Guide to Whiterun

by Mikael the Bard

elcome, good sir, to this indispensible guide. Within these pages, I, your humble author and guide, will describe to you the great city of Whiterun, the Jewel of the North.

Whiterun offers numerous diversions for the man in search of adventure, fortune and companionship, whether for a night or for a lifetime. The city is graced with not one, but two worthy taverns and there are maids and wenches aplenty.

The city is located rather centrally in Skyrim, and this is well, for it is not far from anywhere. Perched high upon a rocky hill, Whiterun dominates the grassy plains that surround it. High wooden walls protect its denizens from the wolves, mammoths, bandits and other dangers lurking beyond.

When you first enter through the city's main gate, you will find yourself in the Plains District. This is so named because it is the lowest of the city's three neighborhoods.

Ah, but here can be found the Bannered Mare, which I count among the finest taverns in all Skyrim. The scenery within is quite compelling, if you have an eye for the fairer sex.

A stout lass named Hulda tends the bar. Don't let that stony Nord exterior fool you, for she is possessed of that same fiery passion that all Nord

women try so hard to conceal. Saadia, the barmaid, is an exotic Redguard beauty. She is quite mysterious, and your humble author is determined to learn her secrets.

Outside the Bannered Mare is a modest marketplace, and here is where I found true love. Though I would never deter a fellow hunting hound from the chase – for indeed, why should I author these tomes, if not to provide guidance in this very matter? – I must ask that you do me this one kindness.

Her name is Carlotta Valentia, and she is a magnificent beauty who makes a modest living selling bread and produce in the daylight hours. By the gods, I will make that feisty beauty mine someday!

And of course, there are other services to be found in the Plains district. Belethor's General Goods offers various and sundry wears for the adventurous traveler, and Arcadia's Cauldron offers what tonics and herbs one would expect from an apothecary's shop.

Arcadia herself is an amiable sort. I often visit her to make conversation, as she is a fellow Imperial far from home. She is, however, a bit old for my taste. A gentleman of advanced years might find in her a worthy companion.

Should you need your blade sharpened or your armor hammered, Warmaiden's offers smithing services very near the main gate. The smith is a pretty Nord named Adrianne Avenicci, but she is married to a great hulking brute named Ulfberth War-Bear.

Adrianne is quite fair, but I should not want to find myself being introduced to the keen edge of that husband's war-axe. If married ladies are your preferred sport, then have at, but don't say that you weren't warned!

Near to the smith is the Drunken Huntsman. Here, some of the wealthier gentlemen gather to share both drink and rumors of the wide world. If you prefer a more distinguished class of company while you sip fine wine, you'll be well at home here.

Of the Wind district I have little to say. Most of the buildings in this second tier of the city are residences, though there is also a Temple of Kynareth and Jorrvaskr, the mead hall of the Companions.

There are some intriguing prospects to be found in the mead hall should you favor a strong and fearless warrior-woman. You will find little game at the temple, however. The priestess, Danica Pure-Spring, is interested almost exclusively in spiritual matters.

At last we come to the Cloud District, exclusive domain of the Jarl's castle. I have had some merry adventures within the stone walls of Dragonsreach, let me tell you. The serving girls are most easily impressed by a well-spoken Imperial. After all, the nights in Skyrim do grow quite cold, if you take my meaning.

And I will not deny that I have visited the town's jail once or twice, which can be found in the lower levels of the palace.

As for the Jarl and his court, take pains to avoid them. I find that they lack any sense of humor or appreciation for the Imperial culture. Besides which, they are all wealthy men and so must be viewed as your most serious competition. These Nords are simple folk, after all, and too easily swayed by the sight of fine clothes and a purse full of septims.

Now I will conclude this work by wishing you great success in your pursuits of women and wine. Spare a moment in your revels to think of me, your humble author, and the risks I have taken to bring you this most thorough report on all thing of interest to the discerning gentleman in the grand city of Whiterun.

Ah, but I will not lie and say that it was all a hardship. After all, who could want to sleep alone in such a cold and hard land as this? Not I!

Walking the World Volume XI: Solitude

by Spatior Munius

Welcome, friend. In our latest volume, we cover Solitude. Spatior could not be more pleased to be at the very seat of Imperial power in Skyrim. In the course of our tour, you'll see that Solitude's riches extend from her people to the history and architecture that make up the city itself.

As ever, we begin our journey outside the city walls, this time at the bottom of the hill that ascends all the way to Solitude's massive gates.

Solitude's Surroundings

Before scaling the hill to the city, you should be sure to take in the sights. Wander the track that leads down to the docks, and you can stop to enjoy one of the best views of the Great Arch.

Originally serving as both a landmark and windbreak for Solitude's port, the easily-defended Great Arch also provided an ideal building site for the ancient Nords.

The city gradually grew to extend across the entire length of the arch. This growth culminated in the building of the Blue Palace, home of the High Kings and Queens of Skyrim. We will visit the palace later.

The Gates of Solitude

Entrance to Solitude is guarded by two gates and three towers. The first of these towers, situated at the crossroads, is Sky Tower. It's mostly a lookout, although in times of war, barricades are erected across the nearby road to act as a first line of defense.

The second tower and first, smaller gate are collectively known as the Squall Gate. Here, attacking armies meet their first real resistance. Last and certainly most impressive is the Storm Gate.

While Castle Dour, found just within the city's main gate, has always been a massive walled structure, Solitude's outer walls and gates were not added until shortly after the coronation of High King Erling.

Looking up and to the left of the main gate, you can see a small hint of Erling's preference for a more rounded style of architecture that we will see later in the Castle Dour extension, as well as the interior arch and the windmill.

Now we pass through the gates and enter the main shopping district of Solitude.

The Well District

Stepping inside Solitude's gates, you get your first view of the city itself. Rising tall and proud before you, banners waving from its crown, is the Emperor's Tower. Home to the Kings of Haafingar before the consolidation of Skyrim and the creation of the Blue Palace, the Emperor's Tower is now used exclusively as guest quarters for Emperors who come to visit the city.

To your left and right are Solitude's inn and shops. Here can be found some of the finest imported goods in Skyrim. After all, Solitude is a wealthy city with ready access to the major shipping lanes of Tamriel.

Continuing ahead, you'll come to the ramp that takes you up to Castle Dour. From here, you can truly feel the weight of this stone bastion's looming presence. The left-most tower, topped by the pointed roof of Erling's extension, was once the castle barracks and jail. Today, the tower is the center of military power here in Solitude.

Looking right past the looming Emperor's tower, you can glimpse Solitude's natural bridge arcing gracefully over to the windmill. Built during High King Erling's day, the bridge was said to be used used to discretely allow Captain Jytte, the famous privateer, to enter Castle Dour. Some historians claim that she and the High King were simply attempting to keep their business dealings quiet. Others believe the Jytte and Erling were involved on a more personal level.

At the end of the bridge is the windmill. The tower and the windmill serve as one of Solitude's most recognizable man-made landmarks. The Windmill's power was once used to open the gates to what is now the East Empire Company Warehouse, but today that task falls to the strong backs of the dock workers.

In the shadow of the windmill you'll find the outdoor market and the well. Here, you can buy a number of local delicacies including the famous spiced wine made exclusively in Solitude.

From here we'll travel up the ramp and into Castle Dour Courtyard.

Castle Dour

As you enter the courtyard of Castle Dour, you are confronted with the banner of Solitude hanging over the door to what is now Castle Dour proper.

At the far end of the courtyard stands the impressive Temple of the Divines. The founders of Solitude were deeply devout and Solitude is the only place in Skyrim where all of the divines are worshiped in a single temple. All three of the buildings here are well worth taking a look inside, but only the Temple and Castle Dour's military wing are open.

If you do venture inside the temple, take special note of the alcoves at the front. You can see the empty alcove that once held the shrine of Talos before Talos worship was outlawed.

From the courtyard, travel out the exit between Castle Dour and the Temple and you'll get your first sight of the Blue Palace. Along the way, be sure to stop outside the Bards College, a large building on your left marked by the Flame of Callisos burning beside the steps.

Named for a famous bard, it is said that as long as the flame burns, the college will stand.

The Bards College

Looking up from the Bards College steps, you can see that the college stands taller than the Blue Palace itself. The bards who train here can be heard throughout Skyrim, singing songs that capture the history of the ages. If you get a chance you should be sure to catch the Burning of King Olaf, an ancient festival where "King Olaf" is burned in effigy.

Continue up the road from the college and you'll reach the courtyard of the Blue Palace, our final destination.

The Blue Palace

The Blue Palace is home to the Jarls of Solitude, who for centuries have also served as the High Kings and High Queens of Skyrim. The northeast wing, on your left as you enter, holds the living quarters of the Jarl and her court on the top level and various servants below.

The southwest wing, known as the Pelagius Wing, has fallen into a state of disrepair. Named for the famous High King, Pelagius the Mad, the wing is rumored to be haunted by the king's ghost. The wing has been locked and left alone since shortly after Pelagius's death.

You should be sure to venture inside the Blue Palace. The grand atrium and court chambers are a sight not to be missed.

Other Points of Interest

Spatior has shown you Solitude in all its grandeur, but there are a few places more to see. The walls of the city are easily accessible and well worth climbing for the remarkable view. The Solitude Docks are also worth a visit, as they are the largest in Skyrim.

That's all for Walking the World Volume XI. Spatior does not know his next destination yet, but you can be sure that where he does go he will leave you a record of the best things to see.

The City of Stone:
A Sellsword's Guide to Markarth

by Amanda Alleia
Mercenary

f you're cutting your coins across Skyrim, you'll want to point your blade towards Markarth, the capital city of the Reach. There's no end of trouble in the City of Stone, and that means plenty of ways for you to earn your supper. Your sellsword instincts should point you towards the wealthiest patrons with the fattest purses to work for, but you need to mind yourself during your resting hours.

Markarth isn't like your Whiterun, where mercenary companies like the Companions make a sellsword an honored professional. No, Markarth has its own rules, rules the natives aren't going to just tell you. Lucky for you, old Ms. Alleia is here to shine the torchlight over your thick skulls.

First thing you'll notice in the City of Stone is... the stone. They say dwarves cut out the city from the mountain, and maybe they did by the look of it. But what it really means is that the whole place is vertical, and the streets are really cliffs. Long story short, be careful when you've got a bellyful of mead.

When you enter the city proper, you'll immediately hit the market. The merchants usually sell food and jewelry on the streets. Meat is the preferred ration, the craggy rocks in the area make for poor farming land, and silver is what's used to make most all the rings and necklaces you might by, thanks to the large silver mine in the city (we'll get to that in a bit).

Whatever you do, don't ask the Markarth city guard about anything. They're about as helpful as an angry Frostbite Spider while you're caught in its web, and if you mention anything about the Forsworn to them they might spit in your eye. Speaking of the Forsworn, these wildmen and women will be your main source of income while you're in Markarth. The Jarl almost always has a bounty on some Forsworn leader or another, and if you don't mind going blade-to-axe with someone two septims short of a pint of ale, it's steady work.

The Silver-Blood Inn is where you want to head into after seeing the market. The drinks are, as usual, watered down (and judging by the metallic taste, with water from the rivers that run through the city's smelter district). What's important here is getting a room to stay in. You won't find any friendly faces to con your way into a cheap place to stay in Markarth. The natives don't trust strangers, so save yourself the trouble and put down your coin to rent a real room.

After you've spent a day recovering from travel, you'll see that Markarth is divided in two sides by the big crag in the center. The part with the big river running through it is called the Riverside, and the other is called the Dryside. The Riverside is where the smelter and native workers live, so don't bother going there. Instead, head directly to Dryside and talk to the local Nord nobles and see what problems you can start solving (at the highest rate).

Two major places to see are the Temple of Dibella and Cidhna Mine. The temple rests on the top of the central crag. A good place to go if you're on good terms with the Divines, but be warned, the Priestesses of Dibella don't allow men into their Inner Sanctums, so

don't go crashing down in there uninvited unless you want a short trip to a long fall.

Cidhna Mine is the place where all the silver comes from that I mentioned before. But it's also the jail. Markarth uses prisoners to mine the ore, and there's a lot of it, so don't get caught doing something illegal in the city or you'll be hauled down there to dig. Apparently, the whole place is owned by one of the big families in the city, the Silver-Bloods (notice the inn is named after them? Always keep your sellsword eye open for hints like that). I tried meeting with the head of the Silver-Blood family to see if they had any work, but guarding their mines isn't the blood-rush I become a mercenary for. Something to keep in mind for yourself if you're thinking of staying a few months.

The final place I'll talk about here is Understone Keep, the home of the Jarl in Markarth. It's a fancy palace like any other (assuming your palace is built underground), but what you need to know is the city underneath the keep. That's right, there's another city below Markarth. One of those old dwarven ruins. They sometimes have expeditions in the ruins that makes for a good job, guarding the scholars and maybe lifting a few stones here and there. If you're lucky, you might come across one of those old dwarven machines, and you can bring back a souvenir after you're done breaking it apart.

All right, Ms. Alleia's hand is getting tired and that means this guide is done. Last piece of advice, don't cause trouble in Markarth. Don't start fights. Don't stop fights. Don't stick your head anywhere without someone from the city paying you for it, because believe me, no one in Markarth wants you there. Make your gold, drink your mead, see what's there to see, and move on. Nothing changes in the City of Stone, and that's just fine.

Of Crossed Daggers: The History of Riften

by Dwennon Wyndell

ituated on the eastern banks of Lake Honrich, the city of Riften serves as a reminder of a bygone era. The once-proud streets and buildings have vanished and been replaced with a collection of wooden structures and rough stonework shrouded in a permanent fog-like mist. In order to understand how such a large city became nothing more than a glorified fortress, one need only look to the history books for answers.

Riften was a major hub of activity for trade caravans and travellers to and from Morrowind. Fishing skiffs could be seen dotting the lake at all hours of the day and the bustling city was alive with activity at night. The city guard was formiddable and maintained a tight grasp on its populace, keeping them safe from harm. The marketplace in Riften was also quite a draw, containing numerous stands offering wares from across Tamriel.

In 4E 98, amidst the confusion of the Void Nights, Hosgunn Crossed-Daggers was installed as Jarl when the previous Jarl had been assassinated. Although many believe that Hosgunn was responisble, and cries of protest filled the streets of Riften, the Jarl took the throne and immediately took action to protect his station. Using the city guard, he had the streets cleared of protesters and initiated a curfew. Any caught breaking the curfew was immediately jailed without process or executed if it was a repeat offence.

For over 40 years, Hosgunn ruled Riften with a black heart and an iron fist. He imposed ridiculous taxes upon his subjects and any merchants that wished to sell their wares within the city walls. Hosgunn kept most of the coin for himself, using it to construct a massive wooden castle with unecessarily lavish quartering within. The castle took seven years to build, and became a visual reminder of the people's oppression which earned it the nickname "Hosgunn's Folly." Towards the end of his reign, the streets of Riften became littered with refuse and it's people plagued by disease and hunger.

Then, in 4E 129, the people had finally had enough. With their numbers, they were able to temporarily overhwelm the city guard long enough to set Hosgunn's Folly on fire with the greedy Jarl still within. As the fighting recommensed, the fire spread through the city unchecked. By the morning, the people had emerged victorious, but not without great cost. Most of the city was now in ruins and many had died.

It took five years to rebuild Riften into the smaller city that it is today. And even though over fifty years had passed since then, it still has yet to fully recover. Some believe it will never achieve the level of affluence it saw at the beginning of the Fourth Era, but there are a few who still hold on to the hope that Riften can return from the ashes and become a center of commerce once again.

Scourge of the Gray Quarter

by Frilgeth Horse-Breaker

he tragedies befalling Morrowind do bring forth pity from even the stoutest Nordic heart. The dark elves deserve our condolences, but thus far they do not show themselves deserving of the simplest acts of charity. There are very different approaches to how to deal with the imminent problem of Morrowind, and I offer two options as seen in practice in Skyrim. One should serve as an exemplar, the other a cautionary tale.

Consider Riften, which shares a border with the ruined province. A number of the dark elves have made their homes there, but they are expected to earn their livelihoods as is any other citizen of the great city. They ply trades as merchants, work in the temple, and serve in the keep. Honest labor, to be admired from a race that was so recently in such dire straits as to even warrant this discussion. Today the city still has its share of problems, but they are not traceable to any influx of outsiders in their presence. In short, the dark elves have properly assimilated themselves into the Skyrim way of life, to be expected from any newcomer to these lands.

For an alternative approach, we only have to look at the once-proud city of Windhelm

to see what can happen when our arms are cast too wide open in welcome. To think that the city of Ysgramor, whose very name was made in driving out the elves from our sacred home, would open itself as a welcome destination for any refugee from the smoking sulphur, is a disgrace to the very idea of being a Nord.

And what has become of this? Predictably, the lazy, discontented rabble has descended into squalor in an area now delicately referred to as "the Gray Quarter" of the city. They were not expected to contribute and so have not. That they attempt to make over a proud Nord city into a little pocket of Morrowind is insulting enough, but the amount of unrest they have provoked even within the proper city walls should give any other Jarl reason to fear.

The Nords I talk to in the city speak of constant strife and crime coming from the Gray Quarter, with no respite in sight. The city guard barely patrol there, leaving the dark elves to mete out whatever passes for justice in their native customs. The respectable families of the city, the Cruel-Seas and Shatter-Shields, speak with an almost parental affection of the Argonians in their employ, but the dark elves have made no effort to ingratiate or assimilate themselves to the proper city-dwellers.

There is cause for optimism, though, as Jarl Ulfric is not nearly so tolerant of these substandard beings as his fathers were. Indeed, the soft hand of Hoag can be seen in the cities Argonian population as well; the fish-men, at least, have learned how to best contribute to their new home. They have proven themselves as models, toiling at the docks with utmost efficiency and bright smiles. It would do the dark elves well to pay heed to their scaly cousins. I would expect in due course that they will find themselves either contributing more directly or once again wandering the land in search of roof and warmth.

The Windhelm Letters

The following transcribed letters were recovered from a strongbox found after a fire consumed a house in Solitude in the early part of the 3rd Era. Nobody by the addressed name lived at the home, and it is unknown how long the family had owned the strongbox. The letters are believed to have been written during the reign of Jarl Elgryr the Unminded, who ruled Windhelm in the Second Era and about whom few other records are extant.

My dearest Thessalonius,

I hope this letter reaches you, and finds you well. It is getting more difficult to find paper within the city, but I still save the scraps sent by the city's tax agents. I hope you don't mind a household reckoning on the reverse of this.

    Windhelm remains as cold as ever, but nothing compared to the heart of her king. Smoke and revelry rise from the palace daily, while we have little wood or coal to keep the chill off. I fear for the little ones, but they're so brave, having never known any other kind of life. We all speak of you daily, and hope that we may come to see you soon.

Yours,
Reylia

Dear Thessalonius,

Your last message arrived safely, but the promised gold mentioned within did not. When I mentioned this to the courier, she shrugged and turned to the door with no other word. While hearing from you brings joy to us all, I would caution you to not trust that particular woman again.

    The minds of the city grow numb with cold and silence. We starve, and the unminded one makes no appearance, no speech, nothing to succor his people. His wizard has been seen walking the streets of the city at odd hours, visiting homes. I saw him paint some horrid symbol on one door — it dripped like blood before vanishing like sand in the wind. The next dawn, nobody who lived there still drew breath. I am a friend to one of the scullery maids who was sent to clean out the house. She described the most horrible things to me and the children, but I will spare you the details.

    The worst of it is, that was a house that supported the king. If that's what happens to his friends, what will be the fate of the rest of us?

    But don't let this shift your mind from its important tasks. We all know you work to free us, and pray for your success and swift return.

Love,
Reylia

This next letter was scribbled onto a piece of cloth with what appears to be charcoal.

Thess.,

I hope you didn't actually ... [illegible] ... efforts are important, but our sufferings must remain ... [illegible] ... retaliation can be swift and terrible. If you no longer care for me, at least think of your ... [illegible] .... Love always, R

Dear Thessalonius,

Weeks go by and we have no word from Solitude. I tell the children that you're simply very busy, but it's getting harder to make excuses for you. If you can no longer send money (and I understand, smuggling anything of value into the city has become a fool's errand), at least send word that you still live and work for the freedom of Windhelm.

As regards your issue that I mentioned previously, worry not. With food shortages being what they are, I have removed it from my concerns.

Always yours,
Reylia

My dearest Thessalonius,

It was good to hear from you at last. Please forgive the rantings of a starving mind. We have at last depleted the basement stores of food, even with the strictest rationing. I see the little ones' faces growing thin and my heart weeps for them. They are, in some ways, brave. I think they're looking after me moreso than I them.

Please come home. I strongly desire to look upon your face.

— R

Papa,

Ma said to write you, so we love and miss you. Ma is tired a lot, but has lots of visitors, so we are being good and helpping.

Love,
Stessl and Shapl

Thessalonius,

I don't have much time. The city has finally broken. The gates of the palace will not keep us out. The storming begins soon. I have gathered those who still have a spirit to live, and we are taking our own fortunes to hand. I hope to see you on the other side of this. Pray for us as we once prayed for you.

Your Reylia

On Stepping Lightly: The Nordic Ruins of Skyrim

by Sigilis Justus

otting the landscape of Skyrim, the ancient Nordic Ruins are a testament to the ingenuity of the Nordic people of the past. When constructing the final resting places of their noble class, these supposedly "barbaric" people proved quite the opposite; developing some of the most sophisticated and clever defenses ever encountered. Coupled with the presence of the fearsome draugr, these tombs have become quite a challenge for the would-be treasure hunter.

The most often-overlooked obstacles are the abundance of traps spread throughout the tombs. Ranging from simple tripwire-activated rock falls to complex pressure plate-triggered dart traps, the Nords utilize these devices abundantly. Most of the traps can be avoided by simply looking for the trigger mechanism and avoiding them. Since they are most often placed in areas where distractions abound, remember to keep your eyes to the floor.

One of the keys to survival in a Nordic Ruin is through the clever use of these traps to gain an upper hand against its denizens. In many cases, it's trivial to lure them across the triggering mechanism in hopes that they'll fall victim to the trap's effect. This

advantage can come heavily into play when encountering an oil trap. Using a ranged attack, lure your victim onto the oil and then loose an arrow at the fire pot hanging above. The moment the fire pot shatters, the entire pool of oil will ignite and engulf the enemy. Just be certain that you're standing clear of the oil yourself, or else this trick could end your expedition in an untimely manner.

Perhaps one of the most amazing engineering marvels of all to be found in the ruins has little to do with the traps designed to kill. Utilizing all manner of pull chains, levers, switches and pressure plates, some of the most frustrating obstacles can occur in the form of puzzles that could threaten to block your progress. Watch for the telltale signs of these barriers: groups of levers in a single place, rotating pillars with carvings on all faces and even large arrays of pressure plates covering the floor of a room. In most cases, the puzzle might take experimentation, in others the solution could actually be present elsewhere in the complex. It's recommended to keep a writing implement and a journal handy in the latter case.

Although Nordic Ruins are commonly infested with vermin such as skeever and spiders, these creatures pale in comparison to the mighty draugr. These horrific, animated dead beings are commonly found as guardians in most of the tombs and will defend them mercilessly. Since the draugr tends to lay dormant until someone happens upon their resting place, it's advisable to keep an eye on any niches or sarcophaguses that you encounter. These undead beings animate rather rapidly and silently, so always watch your back – any remains you may have passed could suddenly animate and set upon you without warning.

The perils of the Nordic Ruin are not without reward. The burial chambers in some of the larger complexes have been known to contain all manners of riches, from gold coins to even the occasional enchanted weapon or armor. Never dismiss the small ceremonial urns that dot the ruins, they are commonly filled with ancient offerings of great value. There are rumors that most, if not all of these ruins contain large walls with magical inscriptions upon them, but these have yet to be confirmed.

While this might seem like comprehensive guide to the ruins, there are certain to be dangers lurking within that remain undiscovered. Just be sure to always enter these tombs with plenty of equipment and a good, solid weapon by your side. With a bit of patience, a keen eye and a light step, the Nordic Ruin can bring you great wealth – do without these simple safety measures and you risk becoming a permanent resident like many before you.

The Death of a Wanderer

Anonymous

The last time I saw the old Argonian, I was taken by how alive he seemed, even though he was in the throes of death.

"The secret," he said, "of staying alive... is not in running away, but swimming directly at danger. Catches it off-guard."

"Is that how you managed to find this claw?" I asked, brandishing the small carving as if it were a weapon. I had found it among his possessions, which I was helping him to divvy amongst his beneficiaries. "Should it also go to your cousin? Dives-From-Below?"

At this, his mouth widened, exposing his fangs. If I hadn't known him as long as I had I would think he was snarling, but I knew that to be a smile. He croaked a few times to attempt laughter, but ended up wheezing and coughing, his rancid blood spraying across the bedsheets.

"Do you know what that is?" he asked between coughing fits.

"I've heard stories," I answered, "the same as you. Looks like one of the claws, for opening the sealing-doors in the ancient crypts. I've never seen one myself, before."

"Then you know I would only wish that thing upon a mortal enemy. Giving it to my cousin would just be encouraging him to run into one of those barrows and get split by a Draugr blade."

"So you want me to have it, then?" I joked. "Where did you even get this?"

"My kind can find things that your people assumed were gone. Drop something to the bottom of a lake, and a Nord will never see it again. Amazing what you can find along the bottoms."

He was staring at the ceiling now, and but the way his fogged eyes darted around, I could tell he was seeing his memories instead of the cracked stone above us.

"Did you ever try to use it?" I whispered to him, hoping he could hear me through his fog.

"Of course!" he snapped, suddenly lucid. His eyes widened and fixed on me. "Where do you think I got this?" he barked, tearing his tunic open to show a white scar forming a large star-shaped knot in the scales beneath his right shoulder. "Blasted Draugr got the drop on me. Just too many of them."

I felt awful, since I knew how much he hated talking about the battles he had been in. To him, it was enough that he had survived, and any stories would amount to boasting. We both sat quietly for several minutes, his labored breathing the only sound.

He was the one to break the silence. "You know what always bothered me?" he asked. "Why they even bothered with the symbols."

"The what?"

"The symbols, you fool, look at the claw."

I turned it over in my hand. Sure enough, etched into the face were three animals. A bear, an owl, and some kind of insect.

"What do the symbols mean, Deerkaza?"

"The sealing-doors. It's not enough to just have the claw. They're made of massive stone wheels that must align with the claw's symbols before they'll open. It's a sort of lock, I suppose. But I didn't know why they bothered with them. If you had the claw, you also had the symbols to open the door. So why..."

He was broken up by a coughing fit. It was the most I had heard him speak in months, but I could tell how much of a struggle it was. I knew his mind, though, and helped the thought along.

"Why even have a combination if you're going to write it on the key?"

"Exactly. But as I lay bleeding on that floor, I figured it out. The Draugr are relentless, but far from clever. Once I was downed, they continued shuffling about. To no aim. No direction. Bumping against one another, the walls."

"So?"

"So the symbols on the doors weren't meant to be another lock. Just a way of ensuring

the person entering was actually alive and had a functioning mind."

"Then the doors..."

"Were never meant to keep people out. They were meant to keep the Draugr in."

And with that, he fell back asleep. When he awoke several days later, he refused to talk about the Draugr at all, and would only wince and clutch his shoulder if I tried to bring them up.

The Fall of Saarthal

by Heseph Chirirnis, Mages Guild Scholar

Assigned to Imperial Archaeologist Sentius Floronius

et it be known that the esteemed archaeologist has chosen to focus his boundless talents on the cooking and baking habits of early First Era Nords. While this work will no doubt bring great glory and benefit to the Empire, it is clear that my limited expertise is of no use to this effort.

I have instead been using my considerable free time to investigate a particular avenue of study, namely that of the Fall of Saarthal. Every child of the Empire knows what happened here; that the first city of Man on Tamriel was sacked by the elves, jealous and fearful of the threat men posed to them. Relations have obviously improved considerably since then, but to be able to see the results of the destruction first-hand, it is quite striking to note the degree of effort that went into the venture.

The first task before me was differentiating between areas of original architecture and those that were rebuilt after Ysgramor retook the city with his five hundred companions. Initially relying heavily on the expertise of archaeologist Floronius, my ability to discern the difference for myself improved over time. Indeed, I was surprised to find that many areas of the city, far more than I would have believed, retained much of the original stonework. Work was clearly done to remedy the effects of the city being burned after the elves' assault, but I suspect they underestimated the durability of Nordic craftsmanship.

Or rather, that is what I initially thought. Perhaps it was a mistaken sense of pride in the accomplishments of these early men, or perhaps it was just my inexperience that led me to this conclusion. Something was amiss, though. Repeated attempts to consult the exceedingly perceptive archaeologist were unfruitful, often digressing into lectures on the bathing habits of Saarthal residents, or the average number of potted plants in homes. I was again forced to rely on my limited powers of observation and deduction.

And so I have no conclusive results to report at this time. I can say with certainty that the initial attack on Saarthal seems to have been very focused, and does not appear to correlate to any locations that have been established as points of defense or importance. While the eminent scholar Sentius has yet to examine my findings, or indeed show any interest in them, my inclination is to suggest that not only did the elves know the apparent layout of the city, but that their assault was based on a specific directive and perhaps a singular goal.

My humble investigations shall continue as time permits.

A Minor Maze: Shalidor and Labyrinthian

Labyrinthian's modern notoriety was gained in the early part of the Third Era. Part of the Staff of Chaos was recovered from the Labyrinthian, which became instrumental in the overthrow of Jagar Tharn, ending the Imperial Simulacrum. The site has since become embedded in the minds of all subjects of the Empire, and the ruins are occasionally visited by Loyalist pilgrims, re-tracing the steps of the Eternal Champion.

The namesake of Labyrinthian is somewhat less commonly known, however.

The foreboding ruins were originally built as a temple to the Dragons. This grew into Bromjunaar, a great city of that era. Bromjunaar is believed by some to have been the capital of Skyrim at the height of the Dragon Cult's influence there. Little historical record exists to verify or refute this, but it is known that the highest ranking Priests of the Cult met at Labyrinthian to discuss matters of ruling.

Bromjunaar crumbled, however, along with the rest of the Dragon Cult, and the site lay abandoned for many years, a deteriorating reminder of those benighted days for the Nords. Not until the days of Shalidor would the ruins come into use again.

Shalidor the Archmage was famous for his exploits in the First Era. Various tales tell of him battling Dwemer legions single-handedly, building the city of Winterhold with a whispered spell, stealing the secret of life from Akatosh, or constructing Labyrinthian himself.

While many Shalidor legends are hyperbole or outright fabrication, we can discover some truth behind his involvement with Labyrinthian.

Shalidor stood at the forefront of a movement to enact higher standards among mages, and to discourage spell-use among the common castes. This effort is dubiously credited with the original organization and formation of the schools of magic and the foundation of the College at Winterhold.

Consistent with this mentality, Shalidor constructed his Labyrinth deep within the ruins of Bromjunaar to test new Archmages. While navigating the destroyed city itself was not explicitly a part of the test, many candidates did not survive the journey. Shalidor valued both academic knowledge as well as practical skill, and simply getting to the Labyrinth required the latter.

Shalidor's Labyrinthian is actually two intersecting mazes, in an hourglass pattern. One maze could not be completed without exiting the other first, which makes the only existing instruction for the test especially mysterious:

ENTER TWICE – EXIT ONLY ONCE
ALTERATION WILL LEAD
YOU TO DESTRUCTION
ONLY ILLUSION SHOWS THE
WAY TO RESTORATION
CONJURE NOT, BUT
BE CONJURED INSTEAD

We can only guess at what the solution to the test may have been, as Labyrinthian became notorious not only for the number of potential archmages who died there, but for the intense secrecy of those who succeeded.

Labyrinthian eventually ceased to be used, and is regarded as a symbol of a more brutal age by modern institutions for magical studies. The ruins lay empty again, overrun with wild animals and avoided by travelers. The long history and legacy of this place, however, seems as likely to be erased from our minds as the ruins themselves are likely to sink into the sea.

The Guardian and the Traitor

by Lucius Gallus
Fellow of the Imperial Library

Year 376 of the Third Era

ne of the more intriguing legends found on the island of Solstheim is the story of a mythical figure whose name is long forgotten, but whom time remembers as "the Traitor."

Certain that this myth is rooted in history I set out to learn what I could and perhaps piece together a presumptive account of the events that gave rise to the legend.

The tale is remembered best by the shamans of the Skaal, that unique tribe of Nords whose culture evolved along an entirely divergent path than that of their brethren in Skyrim.

I spoke at length to the shaman of Skaal Village, a wise and hospitable man named Breigr Winter-Moon. He described an age long ago when dragons ruled over the whole world and were worshipped as gods by men. Presiding over this cult of dragon-worshippers were the Dragon Priests, powerful mages who could speak the dragon language and call upon the power of the thu'um, or Voice.

According to the legend, one such Dragon Priest was seduced by a dark spirit named Herma-Mora, an unmistakable analogue for the Daedric prince Hermaeus Mora. Lured by promises of power, this treacherous priest secretly plotted against his dragon master.

The Traitor's plot was discovered by one of his contemporaries, another Dragon Priest whom legend named The Guardian. The two fought a mighty battle that lasted for days, each hurling terrible arcane energies and thu'um shouts at the other.

So great and terrible were the forces unleashed in this contest that Solstheim was torn apart from the mainland of Skyrim. Here, the myth clearly descends into the realm of pure fantasy.

The Guardian, whom the legend presents as a paragon of loyalty and nobility, finally defeats the despicable Traitor, who seems to represent all that is corrupt and evil in men. Their epic duel is clearly representative of a greater struggle between good and evil. Perhaps it is this timeless quality that has kept the tale alive for so long.

Unlike many similar myths, the tale of the Guardian and the Traitor does not feature a suitably heroic ending. Herma-Mora snatches the Traitor away just as the Guardian is about to strike the killing blow.

The dragons appoint the Guardian ruler of Solstheim, but not before he is compelled to swear an oath of vigilance to watch for the Traitor's return. His reign is, by all accounts, a time of peace and prosperity for the people of the island, and he is remembered as a wise and just leader.

No further mention is made of the Traitor, but neither is he thought to be dead. The legend ends on a cautionary note that the people of Solstheim, the heirs of the Guardian, must remain wary, lest the dark influence of Herma-Mora, or even the Traitor himself, return someday.

Although no physical clues exist now on Solstheim to suggest the presence of the dragon cult, is it hardly difficult to believe that it might once have flourished here. Perhaps some hidden tomb still waits to be discovered that will tell the truth of the tale.

There are other tantalizing clues, though perhaps these connections strain the bonds of credibility. For example, is it possible that the Skaal deity, the All-Maker, is some distant echo of mighty Alduin, the World-Eater of the ancient Nord pantheon?

Perhaps not, but one thing is certain: Solstheim's history is riddled with unanswered questions. Perhaps future generations will pull aside the veils of mystery and reveal the truth about the origins of the Skaal and the identities of the Guardian and the Traitor.

A Short History of Morrowind

by Jeanette Sitte

From the Introduction

Led by the legendary prophet Veloth, the ancestors of the Dunmer, exiles from Altmer cultures in present-day Summerset Isle, came to the region of Morrowind. In earliest times the Dunmer were harassed or dominated by Nord sea raiders. When the scattered Dunmer tribes consolidated into the predecessors of the modern Great House clans, they threw out the Nord oppressors and successfully resisted further incursions.

The ancient ancestor worship of the tribes was in time superseded by the monolithic Tribunal Temple theocracy, and the Dunmer grew into a great nation called Resdayn. Resdayn was the last of the provinces to submit to Tiber Septim; like Black Marsh, it was never successfully invaded, and was peacefully incorporated by treaty into the Empire as the Province of Morrowind.

Almost four centuries after the coming of the Imperial Legions, Morrowind is still occupied by Imperial legions, with a figurehead Imperial King, though the Empire has reserved most functions of the traditional local government to the Ruling Councils of the Five Great Houses....

On Vvardenfell District

In 3E 414, Vvardenfell Territory, previously a Temple preserve under Imperial protection, was reorganized as an Imperial Provincial District. Vvardenfell had been maintained as a preserve administrated by the Temple since the Treaty of the Armistice, and except for a few Great House settlements sanctioned by the Temple, Vvardenfell was previously uninhabited and undeveloped. But when the centuries-old Temple ban on trade and settlement of Vvardenfell was revoked by King of Morrowind, a flood of Imperial colonists and Great House Dunmer came to Vvardenfell, expanding old settlements and building new ones.

The new District was divided into Redoran, Hlaalu, Telvanni, and Temple Districts, each separately administered by local House Councils or Temple Priesthoods, and all under the advice and consent of Duke Dren and the District Council in Ebonheart. Local law became a mixture of House Law and Imperial Law in House Districts, jointly enforced by House guards and Legion guards, with Temple law and Imperial law enforced in the Temple district by Ordinators. The Temple was still recognized as the majority religion, but worship of the Nine Divines was protected by the legions and encouraged by Imperial cult missions.

The Temple District included the city of Vivec, the fortress of Ghostgate, and all sacred and profane sites (including those Blighted areas inside the Ghostfence) and all unsettled and wilderness areas on Vvardenfell. In practice, this district included all parts of Vvardenfell not claimed for Redoran, Hlaalu, or Telvanni Districts. The Temple stubbornly fought all development in their district, and were largely successful.

House Hlaalu in combination with Imperial colonists embarked on a vigorous campaign of settlement and development. In the decades after reorganization, Balmora and the Ascadian Isles regions have grown steadily. Caldera and Pelagiad are completely new settlements, and all legion forts were expanded to accommodate larger garrisons.

House Telvanni, normally conservative and isolationist, has been surprisingly aggressive in expanding beyond their traditional tower villages. Disregarding the protests of the other Houses, the Temple, the Duke, and the District council, Telvanni pioneers have been encroaching on the wild lands reserved to the Temple. The Telvanni council officially disavows responsibility for these rogue Telvanni settlements, but it is an open secret that they are encouraged and supported by ambitious Telvanni mage-lords.

Under pressure from the Temple, conservative House Redoran has steadfastly resisted expansion in their district. As a result, House Redoran and the Temple are in danger of being politically and economically marginalized by the more aggressive and expansionist Hlaalu and Telvanni interests.

The Imperial administration faces many challenges in the Vvardenfell district, but the most serious are the Great House rivalries, animosity from the Ashlander nomads, internal conflicts within the Temple itself, and the Red Mountain blight. Struggles between Great House, Temple, and Imperial interests to control Vvardenfell's resource could at any time erupt into full-scale war. Ashlanders raid settlements, plunder caravans, and kill foreigners on their wild lands. The Temple has unsuccessfully attempted to silence criticism and calls for reform within its ranks.

But most serious are the plagues and diseased hosts produced by the blight storms sweeping out from Red Mountain. Vvardenfell and all Morrowind have long been menaced by the legendary evils of Dagoth Ur and his ash vampire kin dwelling beneath Red Mountain. For centuries the Temple has contained this threat within the Ghostfence. But recently the Temple's resources and will have faltered, and the threat from Red Mountain has grown in scale and intensity. If the Ghostfence should fail, and hosts of blighted monsters were to spill out across Vvardenfell's towns and villages, the Empire might have no choice but to evacuate Vvardenfell district and abandon it to disease and corruption.

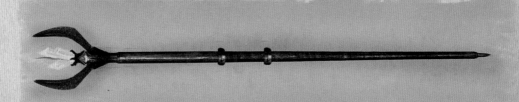

The Red Year

Volume I

by Melis Ravel

hen I originally decided to write this accounting of the Red Year, I elected to travel across Morrowind and speak to the Dunmer people themselves. I sought first-hand accounts and personal views about the cataclysmic event. I felt that if I simply did the research in the library stacks at the College of Winterhold, I wasn't really telling the tale that needed to be told. What struck me as I moved from city to city, town to town, camp to camp is that all of the Dunmer I met shared an incredible bond of sheer courage and unshakable faith. So what began as a chronicle of one of the worst events in the history of Morrowind became something altogether different, the celebration of a people who can never be defeated.

Drallin Vess
Tear

"The ground... it just turned into mush. There was almost no warning. I mean, we were what... perhaps a mile from the nearest swamps? It was like the swamp suddenly swallowed up half of the city."

I asked him to describe what happened from the beginning.

"I owned a farm just outside of Tear at the time. We were planting the next season's crops and getting ready to store what we had harvested. Everything was going well until the Red Mountain exploded. Almost immediately, the ground rumbled and shook. Cracks started forming everywhere and then the water just started seeping through. It was awful. In a matter of hours, I was knee-deep in swamp water running for my life. Where I was running, I had no idea. At first I ran towards the city itself, but it looked like the walls were cracking. All around me, people were desperately trying to save their livestock and their families from the rising water. Just when the ground shaking finally died down, and I had a moment to think, there was a horrible cracking noise. I'll never forget it, because I knew what it was before I looked. The entire southern wall of Tear collapsed sending guards tumbling into the swamp. I heard people screaming as they were covered by the rubble and forced down into the water. Forgetting my own problems, I looked over at my fellow farmers who were all staring at the carnage unfolding before us. Suddenly, we all just forgot our own problems and ran to help.

There must have been hundreds of the poorer folks who lived outside the walls helping the richer ones who lived in the city. Never saw anything like that. I think we must have saved hundreds more that day."

Neria Relethyl
Gnisis

Neria was badly burned by the eruption, and had trouble speaking to me. She is currently convalescing at the Temple of Azura in Blacklight even after all these years. I've tried to record her story to the best of my ability.

"It was such a terrible thing... the fire. It burned everything in its path. It flattened trees, turned our huts into splinters and knocked over towers like they were made from parchment. It all happened in an instant. A rumbling sound, then a massive wall of flame... it was so high it blocked out the sun. I thought that the world itself had split apart. It passed over the water and turned it to steam... vaporized everything it touched. When it finally hit us, I was blown off of my feet... didn't even have time to run away or seek shelter. I ended up in the riverbed next to town, which kept some of the flames off of me. All around... could smell the charred stench of death. There were Dunmer that were burned alive and some never even saw it coming. I lay in that riverbed for two days before the healers found me. When I could finally stand, Gnisis was gone. There wasn't a thing left... it's as though it was wiped from the face of Tamriel."

Volume II
Foreword

When I originally decided to write this accounting of the Red Year, I elected to travel across Morrowind and speak to the Dunmer people themselves. I sought first-hand accounts and personal views about the cataclysmic event. I felt that if I simply did the research in the library stacks at the College of Winterhold, I wasn't really telling the tale that needed to be told. What struck me as I moved from city to city, town to town, camp to camp is that all of the Dunmer I met shared an incredible bond of sheer courage and unshakable faith. So what began as a chronicle of one of the worst events in the history of Morrowind became something altogether different, the celebration of a people who can never be defeated.

Saldus Llervu
Vivec City

"I was a trader back then. Ran a pack guar from Vivec City clear down to Narsis. I was walking along the south road when the strangest thing happened. All of the noise around me stopped... the normal things one hears as they travel like the sound of the wind blowing through the treetops. It was just deathly quiet. I felt a tingling sensation all over my body and my guar began to stomp around. Whatever it was, it was driving him crazy. As I tried to get him under control, there was a massive explosion from the center of the city. I saw the cantons fall apart before I was knocked off my feet. Then I remember the ground starting to rumble. It lasted for a long time and it receded into the distance as if directed towards the center of Vvardenfell. A few minutes later, the Red Mountain erupted, sending a huge cloud of fire into the sky. My pack guar had long since fled, and I decided I should do the same. I never stopped running until I reached Narsis."

I asked him if he knew what had happened Vivec City.

"I didn't hear until much later that the Ministry of Truth had struck the heart of the city. What I do know for certain is that many Dunmer lost their lives that day and that Vivec City is no more."

Deros Dran
Mournhold

The Red Year didn't heavily affect Mournhold itself, but it touched many of the people who lived there. A lot of us had relatives somewhere on Vvardenfell, and after the first day that the eruption occurred we started receiving reports of widespread devastation in Vivec City, Sadrith Mora, Balmora and Ald'ruhn. I don't think a single night went by for months where you wouldn't hear someone openly weeping. It was a sad time for all of us."

I asked if Mournhold had sustained any damage during the Red Year.

"I don't know why, but the destruction seemed to pass us by. A few Dunmer claimed that it was the Tribunal watching over us, but others claimed that the Tribunal was to blame for everything. I actually saw a few of those disagreements come to blows. It was a strange time."

I got an interesting response from Deros regarding Mournhold's role during the Red Year.

"Relief efforts began almost a month after the mountain erupted. It was actually a directive that came from the House Redoran councilor that was living in Mournhold at the time. I can't remember his name, but he took charge of the situation and sent soldiers, supplies and able-bodied Dunmer to the outlying settlements that had been hit the hardest. I was sent to Balmora. The place was a mess; hardly anything left in town was still standing. I spent maybe two months there, helping to rebuild the town and getting my fellow Dunmer back on their feet. It started out as a burden, but it ended up being the most rewarding thing I'd ever done in my life. I started some friendships there that still last to this day, including my beloved wife."

The History of Raven Rock

Volume I

by Lyrin Telleno

Raven Rock is one of the more interesting colonies of Morrowind of the last two centuries. So much has happened to this tiny town in such a short amount of time, and so many lives have been affected by it, I felt it necessary to describe its rich history within these volumes. During my research, I lived in Raven Rock for almost three years, and I got to know many of my fellow Dunmer who call Raven Rock their home. I hope that my readers will appreciate the amount of fortitude and perseverance that it must take to endure life in such an inhospitable and untamed land.

Raven Rock was founded in 3E 427 by the East Empire Company in response to the discovery of a rich ebony mine on the southern edge of the island of Solstheim. The construction of the town took several months, and the mine immediately started yielding ebony ore that the miner's shipped to Windhelm in Skyrim. By 3E 432, the town was home to over thirty people, all of whom depended on the mine for their livelihood. At this time, Raven Rock was almost exclusively inhabited by Imperials and a few Nords who were drawn to the mine's wealth.

When the Oblivion Crisis arose in 3E 433, Raven Rock remained largely untouched by Mehrunes Dagon's forces and work continued as usual. The bulk of the Imperial Guard that was stationed in Raven Rock was recalled to Cyrodiil to fight the invading forces, but a few soldiers remained behind in order to protect the ebony mine from bandits. It's uncertain whether any Oblivion Gates ever opened on Solstheim, as there appears to be no record of such an event ever occurring there.

In the first year of the Fourth Era, after the destruction of Ald'ruhn, many of the Dunmer Great Houses sent out small groups of their own to seek places to reestablish themselves. House Redoran's group was led by Brara Morvayn who immediately struck out for Solstheim. After some quick negotiations with the East Empire Company (and some speculate quite a bit of coin changing hands), Brara's group was allowed to settle in Raven Rock where they quickly became a part of the mining colony's way of life. The Dunmer proved to be both hard-working and reliable when it came to working in the mines, impressing the East Empire Company and solidifying their relationship.

All was going quite well until that fateful day in 4E 5 when the Red Mountain suddenly erupted, sending a massive blast across the Sea of Ghosts that struck Solstheim with its full fury. Raven Rock was heavily damaged by this wave of force, which toppled several of its stone structures and obliterated many of the wooden ones. Ironically, the mine once again proved to be the town's saving grace, as most of the population of Raven Rock was working underground at the time, and was completely shielded from the blast. This event wasn't without cost, however. Raven Rock was heavily dependent on nearby Fort Frostmoth for its defense, but the eruption had almost completely wiped it from the face of Solstheim. The few soldiers that survived took residence in Raven Rock itself and attempted to set up a makeshift garrison there, but these scant few were hardly a match for potential threats to their town. With the East Empire Company's permission, Brara brought in some of House Redoran's elite "Redoran Guard" to fill the void. The guard proved to be an ideal replacement for the fallen Imperial soldiers and have been guarding the town ever since.

Volume II

After a few years, the relentless ash storms from the ever-erupting Red Mountain had transformed Solstheim's southern reaches into pure ash wastes reminiscent of those present on Vvardenfell itself. The storms would leave behind deep dunes of ash that made life exceedingly difficult in Raven Rock. In order to protect the town from these drifts, Brara Morvayn proposed that the East Empire Company construct a large wall of her own design to protect the east end of town. The company quickly agreed and provided the necessary funds. After almost a year, the construction was complete and the huge edifice was named "The Bulwark." The wall proved to be extremely effective and allowed work to continue unabated in the mines.

In 4E 16, when Solstheim was passed into the hands of the Dunmer people, the East Empire Company was forced to relinquish Raven Rock's control to House Redoran. The Council quickly named Brara Morvayn as councilor of their new town, and allowed her

to rule Solstheim as she saw fit. As a result of this changing of the guard, almost the entire Imperial population left Raven Rock and returned to Cyrodiil. Brara continued to welcome the Dunmer that elected to settle on Solstheim. Some chose to stay in Raven Rock to work in the mines, and other took to more familiar territory and began a nomadic lifestyle in the ash wastes.

The next few decades were the golden years for Raven Rock. Brara Morvayn was keeping the peace, the mines were still producing large quantities of ebony and the Dunmer that lived on the island were happy. After almost fifty years of prosperity, in 4E 65, Brara Morvayn finally succumbed to old age and passed away. She was interred in the family's ancestral tomb and her son, Lleril Morvayn, took her place. The people who had lived in Raven Rock during Brara's time as councilor were pleased to discover that Lleril shared his mother's notions of rulership. He was fair and compassionate, which kept the people on the island quite happy for many decades.

Volume III

All was going well in Raven Rock until 4E 95, when an attempt on Lleril's life was made without warning. Fortunately, the attack was unsuccessful thanks to the prowess of the Redoran Guard. Under questioning by Captain Modyn Veleth, the assassin was revealed to be Vilur Ulen of House Hlaalu. House Hlaalu had been at odds with House Redoran for years following their removal from the Council of Great Houses. The Hlaalu believe that House Redoran was instrumental in this reorganization, and have held a grudge ever since. Their attempt on Lleril's life was meant to send a message to the Council that House Redoran was not as mighty as they purported to be and that they were truly vulnerable and weak. The Redoran Guard investigated futhur and discovered that Vilur had been organizing a coup in Raven Rock in an attempt to fully wrest control of the island from Lleril's grasp. Vilur and his conspirators were executed and the coup was quelled.

Several recent events have served to solidify the Dunmer people's respect for Lleril Morvayn. In 4E 130, the Bulwark began to show its age and threatened to crumble. The councilor elected to use the bulk of his personal fortune to have it repaired. In 4E 150, a small force of Argonians landed on Solstheim with the intent of wreaking havoc on the island, and Councillor Morvayn led the charge against them personally. And in 4E 170, when the ebony mine finally began to dry up, he drained the remainder of his coffers keeping the people fed.

By 4E 181, the mine's ebony veins were completely exhausted. Lleril ordered the mine to be shut down, and Raven Rock turned to hunting and fishing for its trade. A few Dunmer families departed Solstheim and returned to the mainland, but most stayed behind.

At present, Lleril Morvayn is still the ruler of Raven Rock. The Redoran Guard continues to maintain order within the town and the surrounding area, keeping Raven

Rock's residents safe, and in line. If even so much as a rumor of dissent reaches Lleril's ears, he has it quashed immediately. He's well aware that there may be a few Hlaalu loyalists still present among her population that would like to see him dead. The future may appear bleak for Raven Rock, but the spirit of its inhabitants will never be broken.

Mysterious Akavir

Akavir means "Dragon Land". Tamriel means "Dawn's Beauty." Atmora means "Elder Wood". Only the Redguards know what Yokuda ever meant.

Akavir is the kingdom of the beasts. No Men or Mer live in Akavir, though Men once did. These Men, however, were eaten long ago by the vampiric Serpent Folk of Tsaesci. Had they not been eaten, these Men would have eventually migrated to Tamriel. The Nords left Atmora for Tamriel. Before them, the Elves had abandoned Aldmeris for Tamriel. The Redguards destroyed Yokuda so they could make their journey. All Men and Mer know Tamriel is the nexus of creation, where the Last War will happen, where the Gods unmade Lorkhan and left their Adamantine Tower of secrets. Who knows what the Akaviri think of Tamriel, but ask yourself: why have they tried to invade it three times or more?

There are four major nations of Akavir: Kamal, Tsaesci, Tang Mo, and Ka Po' Tun. When they are not busy trying to invade Tamriel, they are fighting with each other.

Kamal is "Snow Hell". Demons live there, armies of them. Every summer they thaw out and invade Tang Mo, but the brave monkey-folk always drive them away. Once Ada'Soom Dir-Kamal, a king among demons, attempted to conquer Morrowind, but Almalexia and the Underking destroyed him at Red Mountain.

Tsaesci is "Snake Palace", once the strongest power in Akavir (before the Tiger-Dragon came). The serpent-folk ate all the Men of Akavir a long time ago, but still kind of look like them. They are tall, beautiful (if frightening), covered in golden scales, and immortal. They enslave the goblins of the surrounding isles, who provide labor and fresh blood. The holdings of Tsaesci are widespread. When natives of Tamriel think of the Akaviri they think of the Serpent-Folk, because one ruled the Cyrodilic Empire for four hundred years in the previous era. He was Potentate Versidue-Shaie, assassinated by the Morag Tong.

Tang Mo is the "Thousand Monkey Isles". There are many breeds of monkey-folk, and they are all kind, brave, and simple (and many are also very crazy). They can raise armies when they must, for all of the other Akaviri nations have, at one time or another, tried to enslave them. They cannot decide who they hate more, the Snakes or the Demons, but ask one, and he will probably say, "Snakes". Though once bitter enemies, the monkey-folk are now allies with the tiger-folk of Ka Po' Tun.

Ka Po' Tun is the "Tiger-Dragon's Empire". The cat-folk here are ruled by the divine Tosh Raka, the Tiger-Dragon. They are now a very great empire, stronger than Tsaesci (though not at sea). After the Serpent-Folk ate all the Men, they tried to eat all the

Dragons. They managed to enslave the Red Dragons, but the black ones had fled to (then) Po Tun. A great war was raged, which left both the cats and the snakes weak, and the Dragons all dead. Since that time the cat-folk have tried to become the Dragons. Tosh Raka is the first to succeed. He is the largest Dragon in the world, orange and black, and he has very many new ideas.

"First," Tosh Raka says, "is that we kill all the vampire snakes." Then the Tiger-Dragon Emperor wants to invade Tamriel.

The Book of the Dragonborn

by Prior Emelene Madrine

Order of Talos, Weynon Priory

Year 360 of the Third Era,
Twenty-First of the Reign of His Majesty Pelagius IV

Many people have heard the term "Dragonborn" – we are of course ruled by the "Dragonborn Emperors" – but the true meaning of the term is not commonly understood. For those of us in the Order of Talos, this is a subject near and dear to our hearts, and in this book I will attempt to illuminate the history and significance of those known as Dragonborn down through the ages.

Most scholars agree that the term was first used in connection with the Covenant of Akatosh, when the blessed St. Alessia was given the Amulet of Kings and the Dragonfires in the Temple of the One were first lit. "Akatosh, looking with pity upon the plight of men, drew precious blood from his own heart, and blessed St. Alessia with this blood of Dragons, and made a Covenant that so long as Alessia's generations were true to the dragon blood, Akatosh would endeavor to seal tight the Gates of Oblivion, and to deny the armies of daedra and undead to their enemies, the Daedra-loving Ayleids." Those blessed by Akatosh with "the dragon blood" became known more simply as Dragonborn.

The connection with the rulers of the Empire was thus there from the beginning – only those of the dragon blood were able to wear the Amulet of Kings and light the Dragonfires. All the legitimate rulers of the Empire have been Dragonborn – the Emperors and Empresses of the first Cyrodilic Empire founded by Alessia; Reman Cyrodiil and his heirs; and of course Tiber Septim and his heirs, down to our current Emperor, His Majesty Pelagius Septim IV.

Because of this connection with the Emperors, however, the other significance of the Dragonborn has been obscured and largely forgotten by all but scholars and those of us dedicated to the service of the blessed Talos, Who Was Tiber Septim. Very few realize that being Dragonborn is not a simple matter of heredity – being the blessing of Akatosh Himself, it is beyond our understanding exactly how and why it is bestowed. Those who become Emperor and light the Dragonfires are surely Dragonborn – the proof is in the wearing of the Amulet and the lighting of the Fires. But were they Dragonborn and thus able to do these things – or was the doing the sign of the blessing of Akatosh descending upon them? All that we can say is that it is both, and neither – a divine mystery.

The line of Septims have all been Dragonborn, of course, which is one reason the simplistic notion of it being hereditary has become so commonplace. But we know for certain that the early Cyrodilic rulers were not all related. There is also no evidence

that Reman Cyrodiil was descended from Alessia, although there are many legends that would make it so, most of them dating from the time of Reman and likely attempts to legitimize his rule. We know that the Blades, usually thought of as the Emperor's bodyguards, originated in Akaviri crusaders who invaded Tamriel for obscure reasons in the late First Era. They appear to have been searching for a Dragonborn – the events at Pale Pass bear this out – and the Akaviri were the first to proclaim Reman Cyrodiil as Dragonborn. In fact it was the Akaviri who did the most to promote his standing as Emperor (although Reman himself never took that title in his lifetime). And of course there is no known hereditary connection between Tiber Septim and any of the previous Dragonborn rulers of Tamriel.

Whether there can be more than one Dragonborn at any time is another mystery. The Emperors have done their best to dismiss this notion, but of course the Imperial succession itself means that at the very least there are two or more potential Dragonborn at any time: the current ruler and his or her heirs. The history of the Blades also hints at this – although little is known of their activities during the Interregnum between Reman's Empire and the rise of Tiber Septim, many believe that the Blades continued to search out and guard those they believed were (or might be) Dragonborn during this time.

Lastly, we come to the question of the true meaning of being Dragonborn. The connection with dragons is so obvious that it has almost been forgotten – in these days when dragons are a distant memory, we forget that in the early days being Dragonborn meant having "the dragon blood". Some scholars believe that was meant quite literally, although the exact significance is not known. The Nords tell tales of Dragonborn heroes who were great dragonslayers, able to steal the power of the dragons they killed. Indeed, it is well known that the Akaviri sought out and killed many dragons during their invasion, and there is some evidence that this continued after they became Reman Cyrodiil's Dragonguard (again, the connection to dragons) – the direct predecessor to the Blades of today.

I leave you with what is known as "The Prophecy of the Dragonborn". It often said to originate in an Elder Scroll, although it is sometimes also attributed to the ancient Akaviri. Many have attempted to decipher it, and many have also believed that its omens had been fulfilled and that the advent of the "Last Dragonborn" was at hand. I make no claims as an interpreter of prophecy, but it does suggest that the true significance of Akatosh's gift to mortalkind has yet to be fully understood.

When misrule takes its place at the eight corners of the world
When the Brass Tower walks and Time is reshaped
When the thrice-blessed fail and the Red Tower trembles
When the Dragonborn Ruler loses his throne, and the White Tower falls
When the Snow Tower lies sundered, kingless, bleeding
The World-Eater wakes, and the Wheel turns upon the Last Dragonborn.

The Dragon War

by Torhal Bjorik

In the Merethic Era, when Ysgramor first set foot on Tamriel, his people brought with them a faith that worshipped animal gods. Certain scholars believe these primitive people actually worshipped the divines as we know them, just in the form of these totem animals. They deified the hawk, wolf, snake, moth, owl, whale, bear, fox, and the dragon. Every now and then you can stumble across the broken stone totems in the farther reaches of Skyrim.

Foremost among all animals was the dragon. In the ancient nordic tongue it was drah-gkon. Occasionally the term dov-rha is used, but the language or derivation of that is not known. Using either name was forbidden to all except the dragon priests. Grand temples were built to honor the dragons and appease them. Many of them survive today as ancient ruins haunted by draugr and undead dragon priests.

Dragons, being dragons, embraced their role as god-kings over men. After all, were they not fashioned in Akatosh's own image? Were they not superior in every way to the hordes of small, soft creatures that worshipped them? For dragons, power equals truth. They had the power, so therefore it must be truth. Dragons granted small amounts of power to the dragon priests in exchange for absolute obedience. In turn, the dragon priests ruled men as equals to the kings. Dragons, of course, could not be bothered with actually ruling.

In Atmora, where Ysgramor and his people came from, the dragon priests demanded tribute and set down laws and codes of living that kept peace between dragons and men. In Tamriel, they were not nearly as benevolent. It's unclear if this was due to an ambitious dragon priest, or a particular dragon, or a series of weak kings. Whatever the cause, the dragon priests began to rule with an iron fist, making virtual slaves of the rest of the population.

When the populace rebelled, the dragon priests retaliated. When the dragon priests could not collect the tribute or control the masses, the dragons' response was swift and brutal. So it was the Dragon War began.

At first, men died by the thousands. The ancient texts reveal that a few dragons took the side of men. Why they did this is not known. The priests of the Nine Divines claim it was Akatosh himself that intervened. From these dragons men learned magics to use against dragons. The tide began to turn and dragons began to die too.

The war was long and bloody. The dragon priests were overthrown and dragons were slaughtered in large numbers. The surviving dragons scattered, choosing to live in remote places away from men. The dragon cult itself adapted and survived. They built the dragon mounds, entombing the remains of dragons that fell in the war. They believed that one day the dragons would rise again and reward the faithful.

Olaf and the Dragon

by Adonato Leotelli

ne of the more colorful legends in Nord folklore is the tale of Olaf One–Eye and Numinex.

Long ago in the First Age, a fearsome dragon named Numinex ravaged the whole of Skyrim. The dreadful drake wiped out entire villages, burned cities and killed countless Nords. It seemed that no power in Tamriel could stop the monster.

This was a troubled time in Skyrim's history, for a bitter war of succession raged between the holds. The Jarls might have been able to conquesr the beast if they had worked together, but trust was in desperately short supply.

A skillful warrior named Olaf came forward and promised to defeat the beast. In some accounts, he is the Jarl of Whiterun. In other versions of the legend, Olaf promises the people of Whiterun that he will capture the monster if they will name him Jarl.

At any rate, Olaf ventures forth with a handful of his most trusted warriors and seeks the beast out, eventually finding Numinex in his lair atop Mount Athor. Needless to say, it's an epic battle.

First, Olaf comes at the dragon with his axe and his shield. Some variants of the legend say that Olaf and the beast battled with blade and claw for days, but were too evenly matched for either to gain an advantage.

Most accounts hold that Olaf, perhaps frustrated that his weapons are completely ineffectual against the dragon, finally casts them aside. Giving voice to the rage that has been building within him, Olaf unleashes a terrible shout.

Here again, the stories diverge. Many accounts hold that Olaf did not realize he possessed the power of Dragon-speech, while others suggest that he had long possessed this gift, but wished to test himself against the dragon in martial combat first.

Virtually all variations of the legend, however, agree on what happened next.

Using the awesome powers of the Dragon language, Numinex and Olaf engage in an epic shouting duel atop Mount Athor. So forceful are their words, they are said to shatter the stone and split the sky.

Finally, Numinex collapses from a combination of injury and sheer exhaustion. Somehow – and this detail is conspicuously absent in virtually every account – Olaf manages to convey the dragon all the way back to the capital city of Whiterun.

The people of Whiterun are suitably impressed with Olaf's hostage. They build a huge stone holding cell at the rear of the palace, which they rename "Dragonsreach". This enormous cell serves as Numinex's prison until his death.

Olaf himself eventually becomes the High King of Skyrim, putting an end to the war of succession. Presumably, his great deed made him the only leader upon whom all the people could agree, and so the land once again has peace.

As a visitor to Skyrim, I find this tale both fascinating and highly entertaining. It is one the most celebrated legends of the Nords, and one can easily understand why. It's a story of surpassing heroism, in which a resourceful and worthy Nord does battle with a truly terrifying adversary and emerges victorious by yelling him into submission. The only way in which this could have been even more of a Nordic tale would be if Olaf beat Numinex in a drinking contest.

The legend is not without its doubters, however. The bard Svaknir, who lived during Olaf's reign, wrote and performed an alliterative verse that challenged Olaf's version of events. Enraged, the High King threw the rebellious bard in prison and destroyed all written copies of the verse.

How I would love to lay hands on a copy of that verse! I admit, I am immensely curious to know what assertions Svaknir made about how Olaf really defeated Numinex.

There are a few ancient bard texts that provide one possible answer. These tomes suggest that Numinex was particularly foul-tempered because he was extremely old. In these accounts, the dragon spends his final years terrorizing the country side before flying off to the top of Mount Athor to die in peace.

When Olaf finds Numinex, the dragon is too weak to defend himself. Olaf and his men capture the beast without effort, but decide to take advantage of the situation by fabricating a heroic tale. It is worth noting that all of Olaf's warriors who were said to witness the shout duel went on to become wealthy leaders during Olaf's reign as High King.

However, it is equally likely that Svaknir had some grudge against Olaf, and his scandalous verse was an attempt to damage the High King's reputation. Alas, we will never know.

I leave you now, good reader, with this gentle reminder: A good historian must remain impartial, and consider all points of view. Time has a way of distorting our record of events, so the closer you can get to the original sources, the better!

There Be Dragons

by Torhal Bjorik

The last known sighting of a dragon in Tamriel was in the time of Tiber Septim. He made a pact with the few remaining dragons, swearing to protect them if they would serve him. Despite his promise, dragons were still hunted and slain. It's not clear if the last ones fled Tamriel or if they were exterminated.

There is no credible story of how dragons came to be. According to dremora that the College of Whispers have "questioned," they just were, and are. Eternal, immortal, unchanging, and unyielding. They are not born or hatched. They do not mate or breed. There are no known examples of dragon eggs or dragonlings. The Iliac Bay area has stories of such things, but so far all have proven false. The eggs turned out to be eggs of other reptiles. The small dragons were merely oversized lizards and no relation to true dragons.

Although they are not born, dragons can die. During the Dragon War of the Merethic Era, their numbers were decimated. The Akaviri invaders of the late First Era are said to have hunted and killed scores of them, before and after their defeat by Emperor Reman. Some sources say the Akaviri brought over dragon-killing spells. Others claim they built cunning traps. One tale even speaks of a rare poison.

It is well accepted that a dragon's most fearsome weapon is its fiery breath. Because they could fly overhead and rain down flaming death, archers and wizards were necessary when hunting them. It is less well known that some dragons could breathe a freezing spray of frost. The reports indicate that dragon might do one or the other, but not both.

Most people think of dragons as mere beasts. However, logically they must have had language in order for Tiber Septim to have negotiated with them. Indeed, the historical record is quite clear that dragons were highly intelligent. They had their own language, but could also speak the languages of men and elves.

The records of Reman's hunts contain reports of dragons that breathe or spit fire. Recently some were unearthed that described dragons blowing freezing blasts of cold. The more fanciful tales have them summoning storms and even stopping time. These should be discounted as myths and faery tales. Even without this most fearsome weapon, their nearly impenetrable hide and granite-like teeth and claws made them terrifying opponents.

There is some confusion over when the last dragon was killed. It seems the last few vanished all at once. Some tales speak of a dragon king who devoured all of them rather than let mankind kill them. One of the more far-fetched stories has Tiber Septim absorbing their essences when he ascended to godhood. Although the exact cause is unknown, they are all gone. No dragon has been seen for centuries. There are a few known examples of dragon bones fused with the stone and rocks of cliffs and caves. Just enough proof to make the stories undeniable.

Ahzidal's Descent

by Halund Greycloak

In the days beyond memory, when men first walked the lands of Skyrim, there arose in the city of Saarthal a great enchanter. As a boy, his gift for magic and artifice had been evident to his tutors. As a man, his skill surpassed them all. And finding nothing more to learn among his kin, he left wife and child, and set out to train under the elven masters.

A year became two, then three. And when finally his path led him back to Saarthal, he found only ruins: for the elves had sacked the city, and all that lived there were dead or gone. Amid the ashes, in the smoldering ruins of his home, he swore a terrible oath of vengeance. And from that comes the name the legends give him: Ahzidal, the embittered destroyer.

Alone, he could do nothing. And so, he bided his time, delving deeper into his art than any before him. From the Dwemer, he learned the seven natures of metal and how to harmonize them. From the Ayleids, the ancient runes and dawn-magic even the elves had begun to forget. Among Falmer and Chimer and Altmer he traveled, taking what he could from each, and all the while plotting how he might turn that knowledge against them.

Finally, word reached him of Ysgramor and his Companions, newly-arrived from Atmora. For three days and nights, he rode north, and met them as they made landfall on the icy coast near the ruins of Saarthal, which the elves had fortified against them. He offered the Companions his service, and all he had produced in his years of labor. And with Atmoran steel imbued with his enchantments, the elves fell before them, and at last he had his revenge.

But he was not content. His craft had become his life, and his hunger for knowledge still gnawed at him, driving him to delve ever deeper. At long last, he exhausted the lore of the elves, but it was not enough. He sought the secrets of Dragon-runes, and won for himself a seat among their high priests, but it was not enough. And at length, he turned his gaze to the planes of Oblivion, and found there both power and madness.

Some say he ventured there, never to return. Others, that he was betrayed by his fellow Dragon Priests, and killed, or driven into hiding in the ruins beneath his beloved Saarthal. Among the Skaal of Solstheim, it is said he fled to their island, and was sealed in the depths of Kolbjorn Barrow, together with the last of his relics.

But that is the tale, as it was told among the bards of Winterhold. Whatever the truth, the legend of Ahzidal was intended as a warning: in pursuit of perfection, one must take care that the pursuit itself does not become all-consuming.

The Alduin/Akatosh Dichotomy

By Alexandre Simon

High Priest of the Akatosh Chantry, Wayrest

As High Priest of the Akatosh Chantry, I have dedicated my life to the service of the Great Dragon. He who was first at the Beginning. He who is greatest and most powerful of all the Divines. He who is the very embodiment of infinity.

I am, quite obviously, a man of deep and unwavering faith. But not blind faith, for I am also a man of scholarly endeavors, and have always valued education and the pursuit of truth, in all its forms. And so, I have had the honor and privilege of making it my life's work to discover the truth about Akatosh, in all of our beloved Divine's incarnations.

Throughout the civilized world (and I refer not only to the Empire, but to every nation on great Nirn that has embraced the virtues of learning and letters), the Great Dragon is worshipped. Usually, the highest of Divines is referred to as Akatosh. But what some may not be aware of is that he is occasionally referred to by two other names as well.

The Aldmer refer to Akatosh as Auri-El. The Nords call him Alduin. These names come up repeatedly in certain ancient texts, and in each one, it is clear that the deity in question is none other than he whom we call Akatosh.

Yet there are those who believe, even in this enlightened age, that this is not so. That the regional interpretations of Akatosh are not interpretations of Akatosh at all. Rather, they are references to altogether different deities, deities who may or may not share the same aspects or be the Great Dragon at all.

Many Altmer of Summerset Isle worship Auri-El, who is the soul of Anui-El, who in turn is the soul of Anu the Everything. But if you ask the high elves themselves (as I did, when I traveled to Summerset Isle to continue my research), the majority will concede that Auri-El is but Akatosh with a different name, colored by their own cultural beliefs.

So maybe it comes as no surprise that the real theological dissention lies in Skyrim, among the Nord people – renowned as much for their stubbornness as they are their hardiness and prowess on the fields of valor. When I journeyed to the stark white province, I was surprised to find a people whose views on Akatosh are almost diametrically opposed to those of the Altmer. The majority of Nord people seem to believe that their Alduin of legend is not Akatosh, but another deity entirely. A great dragon, yes, but not the Great Dragon.

Determined to get to the heart of this matter, I consulted with several Nords, chief among them an old and respected clan chief by the name of Bjorn Much-Bloodied. And what surprised me most about those I talked to was not that they believed in Alduin instead of Akatosh, but that they recognized Alduin in addition to Akatosh. In fact, most children of Skyrim seem to view Akatosh in much the same way I do – he is, in fact,

the Great Dragon. First among the Divines, perseverance personified and, more than anything, a force of supreme good in the world.

Alduin, they claim, is something altogether different.

Whether or not he is actually a deity remains in question, but the Alduin of Nord folklore is in fact a dragon, but one so ancient, and so powerful, he was dubbed the "World Eater," and some accounts even have him devouring the souls of the dead to maintain his own power. Other stories revolve around Alduin acting as some sort of dragon king, uniting the other dragons in a war against mankind, until he was eventually defeated at the hands of one or more brave heroes.

It is hard to deny that such legends are compelling. But as both High Priest and scholar, I am forced to ask that most important of questions – where is the evidence?

The Nords of Skyrim place a high value on their oral traditions, but such is the core of their unreliability. A rumor passed around the Wayrest market square can change so dramatically in the course of a few simple hours, that by the end of the day, one might believe half the city's residents were involved in any number of scandalous activities. How then is an educated, enlightened person possibly supposed to believe a legend that has been passed down, by word of mouth only, for hundreds, or even thousands of years?

The answer to such a question is simple – he cannot.

And so, it is my conclusion that the Alduin of Nord legend is in fact mighty Akatosh, whose story grew twisted and deformed through centuries of retelling and embellishment. Through no real fault of their own, the primitive peoples of Skyrim failed to understand the goodness and greatness of the Great Dragon, and it was this lack of understanding that formed the basis of what became, ironically, their most impressive creative achievement – "Alduin," the World Eater, phantom of bedtime stories and justification for ancient (if imagined deeds).

Alduin is Real, and He Ent Akatosh

by Thromgar Iron-Head, prowd Nord

s my da used to say – Imperials are *idiutts*!

That is why I am riting this book. I ent never rote a book before, and I do not reckon to rite one agenn, but sometimes a man must do what a man must do. And what I must do is set the recerd strate about the god called Akatosh and the dragon called Alduin. They ent the same thing, no matter what them Imperials mite say, or how thay mite wish it to be so.

My da was never one for the gods, but my ma was. She wershipped all the Divines, and tot me lots of things. So I noe a thing or two about Akatosh. Just as much as any Imperial. I noe he was the first of all the gods to take shape in the Beginning Place. And I noe he has the shape of a dragon.

My da even told me the story of Martyn Septim, and the things what happened when the gates to Oblivion opened. Septim turned into the spirit of Akatosh and killed Mehrunes Dagon. Now I dont noe about you, but any dragon that fites the Prince of Destruction is okay by me.

Now I hope you understand the problim. Akatosh is good. Everyone, from Nord to Imperial, noes that. But Alduin? He ent good! He's the oposit of good! That Alduin is evil thrue and thrue. So you see, Akatosh and Alduin cant be one and the same.

Growing up as a lad in Skyrim, I herd all the stories. Told to me by my da, who was told by his da, who was told by his da, and so on. And one of those stories was about Alduin. But see, he was not Akatosh. He was another dragon and a real wun at that.

Akatosh is some kind of spirit dragon I think, wen he bothers to be a dragon at all (and not a god livin in sum kind of god plac like Obliviun). But Alduin is a real dragon, with flesh and teeth and a mean streak

longer than the White River. And there was a time when Alduin tried to rool over all of Skyrim with his other dragons. In the end, it took sum mitey strong heroes to finally kill Alduin and be dun with his hole sorry story.

So I got to ask – does that sound like Akatosh to you? No, frend. No it do not.

And so I, Thromgar Iron-Head do firmly say, with the utmost connvicshun, that Alduin is real, and he ent Akatosh!

Dragon Language: Myth no More

by Hela Thrice-Versed

Dragon. The very word conjures nightmare images of shadowed skies, hideous roaring, and endless fire. Indeed, the dragons were terrifying beasts that were once as numerous as they were deadly.

But what most Nords don't realize is that the dragons were in fact not simple, mindless beasts. Indeed, they were a thriving, intelligent culture, one bent on the elimination or enslavement of any non-dragon civilization in the entire world.

It therefore stands to reason that the dragons would require a way to communicate with one another. That they would need to speak. And through much research, scholars have determined that this is exactly what the dragons did. For the mighty roars of the beasts, even when those roars contained fire, or ice, or some other deadly magic, were actually much more – they were words. Words in an ancient, though decipherable, tongue.

Nonsense, you say? Sheer folly on the part of some overeager academics? I thought precisely the same thing. But then I started hearing rumors. The odd snippet of a conversation from some brave explorer or gold-coveting crypt diver. And always, always, it was the same word repeated:

Wall.

So I listened more. I began to arrange the pieces of the puzzle, and slowly unravel the mystery.

Spread throughout Skyrim, in ancient dungeons, burial grounds, and other secluded places, there are walls. Black, ominous walls on which is written a script so old, so unknown, none who had encountered it could even begin its translation.

In my heart, I came to know the truth: this was proof of the ancient dragon language! For what else could it possibly be? It only made sense that these walls were constructed by the ancient Nords, Nords who had lived in the time of the dragons, and out of fear or respect, had somehow learned and used the language of the ancient beasts.

But at that point, all I had was my own gut instinct. What I needed was proof. Thus began the adventure of my life. One spanning 17 months and the deaths of three courageous guides and two sellsword protectors. But I choose not to dwell on those grim details, for the end result was so glorious, it made any hardship worth it.

In my travels, I found many of the ancient walls, and every suspicion proved true. It did in fact appear as if the ancient Nords had copied the language of the dragons of old, for the characters of that language very much resemble claw marks, or scratches. One can almost envision a majestic dragon using his great, sharp talons to carve the symbols into the stone itself. And a human witness – possibly even a thrall or servant – learning, observering, so that he too could use the language for his own ends.

For as I observed the walls I found, I noticed something peculiar about some of the words. It was as if they pulsed with a kind of power, an unknown energy that, if unlocked, might be harnessed by the reader. That sounds like nonsense, I know, but if you had stood by these walls – seen their blackness, felt their power – you would understand that of which I speak.

Thankfully, although entranced, I was able to retain enough sense to actual transcribe the characters I saw. And, in doing so, I began to see patterns in the language – patterns that allowed me to decipher what it was I was reading.

For example, I transcribed the following passage:

ᛁᛏᚷᛂ ᚽᛄᚲᛖ ᚹᛄᛃᛄᛂᛄᛎ ᛃᛄᛁᛟ ᛒᛄᛂᛂᚽ ᚽᛃ ᛁᛟᛂᛁ ᚹᛁᛟ ᛖᛃᛖᛁᛃᚽ ᛃᛏᚽ ᛁᛖᛃᛂᛁᛟ ᛁᚽ ᛒᛂᚲᛄᛁᛃᛖ ᚽᛄᛁᛂᚷ ᛁᛃᛁᛂᚷᛏᚽ ᛁᛃᛏᛂ ᛁᛃᛁᛄᛂ ᛒᛃᛖ ᛁᛃᛁᛒᛂᚷ

Assigning those scratchings to actual Tamrielic langauge characters, I further translated what I saw into this:

Het nok Yngnavar Gaaf-Kodaav, wo drey Yah moron au Frod do Krosis, nuz sinon siiv dinok ahrk dukaan.

Which translates into the Tamrielic as follows:

Here lies Yngnavar Ghost-Bear, who did Seek glory on the Battlefield of Sorrows, but instead found death and dishonor.

Then, in another crypt, I encountered a wall with this transcription:

ᛁᛏᚷᛂ ᚽᛄᚲᛖ ᛒᛄᛂᛁᛂᚷ ᛁᛃ ᛁᛃᛂᛃᛟ ᚷᛁᛁ ᛁᛒᚽ ᚽᛃ ᛃᛁᛂᛁ ᚷᛖ ᛃᛂᚽᛂᚷ ᚽᛁ ᛖᛃ ᛒᛄᛂᛃᛖᛂ ᛂᛁᛃᛖᚷ ᚷᛏᚽ ᛁᛏᛂ ᛒᛄᛂᛄᛃᚷᛂ ᛁᛃᛄᚽᛂᛃᛂ ᛁᛃ ᛂᚽᛂ ᛒᛄᛂᛃᛖᛃᛖ

Which translates into:

Het nok kopraan do Iglif Iiz-Sos, wo grind ok oblaan ni ko morokei vukein, nuz ahst munax haalvut do liiv krasaar.

Which ultimately translates into the Tamrielic as:

Here lies the body of Iglif Ice-Blood, who met his end not in glorious combat, but at the cruel touch of the withering sickness.

And there you see the pattern. The repeated words "Here lies" – which could only mean one thing: those walls marked actual ancient Nord burial grounds.

You can imagine my nearly uncontainable excitement. It all started to make sense. The anicent Nords used the dragon langauge for these walls for very specific reasons. One of them was obviously to mark the grave of some important figure. But what else? Were they all graves, or did they serve other purposes as well?

I set off to find out, and was well rewarded for my efforts. Here is what I discovered. This passage:

ᚾᛚᚷᚢ ᛞᛗᚾ ᚳᛟᛗᛀᛋᚾᚷᛑᛞ ᚳᛟᛋᚾᛑᛋ ᛁᛐᛋᛑᛀᛑᛑᚾᛋ ᛟᚢᛟᚾᛀ
ᛁᚾᚾᛑᛀᛋᛋ ᛋᛟᚷᛀ ᛑᛟᚷᛋᛋ, ᛋᚷᛋ, ᛀᛋᛟ ᛐᚾᛀᛀᛑ ᚾᚾᚷᚾᛀ
ᛐᛋ ᚳᛟᛋᛋᚾ ᛋᚾ ᛋᚾᚾᛋᚷᚾ

Translates into this:

Het mah tahrodiis tafiir Skorji Lun-Sinak, wen klov govey naal rinik hahkun rok togaat wah gahrot.

Which in Tamrielic translates into this:

Here fell the treacherous thief Skorji Leech-Fingers, whose head was removed by the very axe he was attempting to steal.

So here we see a wall that marks the spot where some significant ancient Nord died.

This passage:

ᛋᛋᚷᚾᛁᚾᚳᛋᛀᛋᛟ ᛋᚾᛐᛀᚾᛑᛋᛋ ᛐᛋᛋᛁᛋᛑ ᚾᚾᛟᛋᛟ ᛑᛋᚾᛐ
ᛐᛋᛋ ᛋᛐᛋᛋᛋᛋᛁ ᚾᚾᛋᛋ ᛋᛋ ᛋᛋᛋᛀᛟ ᛑᛟ ᛁᛋᚾᛐ ᛀᛋᛋᛟ
ᛑᛋᛀᛋᛋᛋᛋ ᚾᚾᛑᛋᛋᛋ ᛐᛋᛋ ᛑᛐᛋᚾᚾᛋᛑ ᛀᛑᛑᛋᛋᛀ

Translates into this:

Qethsegol vahrukiv daanik Fahliil kiir do Gravuun Frod, wo bovul ko Maar nol kinzon zahkrii do kruziik hokoron.

Which in Tamrielic translates into this:

This stone commemorates the doomed elf children of the Autumn Field, who fled in Terror from the sharp swords of the ancient enemy.

This wall seems to commemorate some ancient, long-forgotten event in Tamrielic history. Whether that event occurred on or near the place where the wall was erected, we will probably never know.

And finally, this passage:

ᛋᛋᚾᛀᛋ ᛋᚾᛟᛋᛀᛋᛋᚷᚢᛁᚾᚳᛋᛀᛋᛟᛋᛐᛀᛀᛀᚾᛑ ᛋᚾᛐᛀᚾᛑᛋᚢ
ᚷᛟᛋᛑᛀᛑᛋᛋᛟᛐᛐ ᚾᚾᛀᛀ ᛀᛟᚾ ᛋᛋᛀ ᚾᚾᛋᛟᛑᛀᛀᛋᛑ ᚾᚾᛀᛀᛀᛟᛟ
ᚾᚾᛑᛋᛋ ᛀᛀᛑ

Which translates into this:

Aesa wahlaan qethsegol briinahii vahrukt, Thohild fin Toor, wen smoliin ag frin ol Sahqo Heim.

Which in Tamrielic translates into this:

Aesa raised this stone for her sister, Thohild the Inferno, whose passion burned hot as the Red Forge.

This wall (and I encountered quite a few like this) was obviously commissioned or built by a specific person, to honor someone important to them. What was the significance of the location? Was it important to the person who died? Or is it the actual location of that person's death? Again, those answers are probably lost to time, and will never be know.

And so you see, the ancient dragon language is, indeed, myth no more. It existed. But better yet, it still exists, and probably will until the end of time, thanks to the ancient Nords and their construction of these many "word walls."

But don't take my word for it. For the walls are there for the discovering, in Skyrim's dangerous, secret places. They serve as a bridge between the realm of the ancient Nords, and our own. The dragons may never return to our world, but now we can return to theirs.

And someday, someday, we may even unlock the strange, unknown power hidden in their words.

Province of Skyrim

©4E 182 Nataly Dravarol, Cartographer